W9-BXL-412

# In League with Sherlock Holmes

# In League with Sherlock Holmes

## Stories Inspired by the Sherlock Holmes Canon

Edited by **Laurie R. King**
and **Leslie S. Klinger**

PEGASUS CRIME
NEW YORK LONDON

IN LEAGUE WITH SHERLOCK HOLMES

Pegasus Crime is an imprint of
Pegasus Books, Ltd.
148 West 37th Street, 13th Floor
New York, NY 10018



First Pegasus Books cloth edition December 2020

Interior design by Maria Fernandez



Library of Congress Cataloging-in-Publication Data is available.

ISBN: 978-1-64313-582-3

10 9 8 7 6 5 4 3 2 1

Printed in the United States of America
Distributed by Simon & Schuster
www.pegasusbooks.com

*To Sir Arthur Conan Doyle:*
*Steel true, blade straight*

# CONTENTS

# INTRODUCTION

## *by Laurie R. King and Leslie S. Klinger*

When Dr. Watson suggests to Sherlock Holmes in "The Five Orange Pips" that the identity of a late-night caller ringing their bell might be "some friend" of Holmes, Holmes famously answers, "Except yourself I have none." We know that this is an exaggeration, for Holmes must admit to at least a few close acquaintances: Wilson Hargreave of the New York police; old Sherman, the taxidermist and owner of the dog Toby; young Stamford, who introduced Dr. Watson to him; the French detective Francois Le Villard; and of course, Mrs. Hudson, who was so fond of him. Perhaps the truest measure of a man's friends is the roster of those who attend his funeral. As can be seen by the contemporary newspaper report discovered by Leslie Klinger in 2012, * Holmes's

* The article, which appeared in the May 27, 1891, issue of the *Yorkshire Evening Press*, is reprinted in Leslie S. Klinger, "In Memoriam Sherlock Holmes," *Baker Street Journal* 62, no. 2 (Summer 2012): 22–28, and a collection of Klinger's writing, *Baker Street Reveries* (Indianapolis: Gasogene Books, 2018). The memorial service in question, held in St. Monica's Church in May 1891, was, of course, a sham, perpetrated by his brother Mycroft, for unbeknownst to Dr. Watson and virtually everyone else in the world, Holmes was alive and well in 1891.

mourners included dozens of professional colleagues, former clients, and others whose lives he had touched (as well as, it must be admitted, some who wanted to be sure that he was dead).

The circle of Holmes's friends continued to expand long after his active years, as Dr. Watson's accounts of their years together grew more and more popular. Films of Holmes's cases made him the most popular subject in the history of cinema. Thousands of radio broadcasts and stage plays further spread his fame and won him new friends. Today, there are over three hundred members of the Baker Street Irregulars, hundreds of members of Holmes societies in numerous countries, and thousands who belong to local Sherlockian groups, every one of whom would name Holmes as their friend.

The origin of this series of anthologies has been told before. We were asked to appear on a panel on the subject of Holmes at a mystery convention and requested the addition of Lee Child, Michael Connelly, and Jan Burke. When the organizer protested that those were the guests of honor of the convention, we mentioned that they were also secret admirers of Holmes and would be fine panelists. After a splendid panel discussion, we thought, "Why don't we ask them to write stories inspired by Holmes?" The panelists agreed, and the rest, as they say, is history: This series now extends to more than ninety distinguished writers—drawn from the genres of crime fiction, thrillers, fantasy, science fiction, horror, and other fields, including artists, novelists, screenwriters, and short story specialists—all happy to count themselves "in league with Sherlock Holmes."

We've been approached by agents asking if their clients could submit stories. We've been asked by well-known writers of Holmesian tales if they could join the company. We've turned these down, not because the materials we would have received would fall below our standards but because we've tried to keep to a simple and consistent approach. Firstly, we have limited the contributors to our friends. This is, after all, a project for our own enjoyment—not "work"—and the pay is far below what these fine writers usually command. Secondly, we have strictly—well, pretty strictly*—required that the contributors must be persons not previously known to be friends of Holmes. There are dozens of fine anthologies consisting of pastiches of the Holmes tales written by dozens of well-known pasticheurs. Ours are intended to be different, because—thirdly—we have emphasized that we are not asking for stories about Sherlock Holmes; rather, we seek stories *inspired* by Dr. Watson's tales of Holmes.

The responses to our invitations have been delightful, astonishing, amusing, and even breathtaking (which should be no surprise, considering the credentials of those we've invited to contribute). Here you'll find tales of persons who think like Holmes or admire Holmes or set out to emulate Holmes. There's even stories featuring Holmes. You'll discover secrets about some of Holmes's acquaintances and his foes. You will journey to Victorian England, the modern New Jersey shore, the teeming metropolises of London and New York, and many points in between. Some of what follows are detective stories, some are not. We hope that you will be as delighted, astonished, and amused as we were—and henceforth boldly proclaim yourselves to be "in league with Sherlock Holmes"!

Laurie R. King and
Leslie S. Klinger

---

* Neil Gaiman, John Lescroart, and Jonathan Maberry were exceptions in two of the previous anthologies, each having previously written a single story about Holmes, but we really, really wanted them to participate.

# THE STRANGE JUJU AFFAIR AT THE GACY MANSION

*by Kwei Quartey*

During the months of June to August, the weather in my hometown Liati Wote, which lies at the base of Ghana's Mount Afadja, can be quite cold—at least for a Ghanaian. It was there one evening, during a weekend off from my detective work, that I joined my dear friend Prosper around a crackling wood stove, simmering upon which was a large pot of palm soup, emitting the most heavenly aroma. As we awaited the readiness of the meal, I told him the tale of the murder at the Gacy mansion.

As I told Prosper, I would almost certainly never have solved the crime had I not consulted one Superintendent Mensah Blay. The legendary detective, known for his formidable powers of observation and deduction, had retired after a rumored nervous breakdown during his final days in the Ghana Police

Service (GPS). What had caused his abrupt decline was unclear. Some suggested that it was the death of his beloved wife, while others claimed that Blay's own genius had "overpowered him" and inflicted irreparable harm to his psyche.

At the time I went to see the superintendent, I was a young, inexperienced homicide detective at least half Blay's age. My colleagues at the Criminal Investigation Department had decried my idea of seeking his help, even though the case had us all completely at sea.

"Superintendent Blay doesn't like to see anyone," a colleague warned me.

Another, "He is not taking on any new cases."

"He will kick you out," said yet another.

From what I knew, Mensah Blay now spent much of his retirement time engaged in the hobby that had become his livelihood—making wooden toys for children. When Blay had been much younger, he had made them for his own children and then, with the passage of time, his grandchildren. Blay's delightful yet robust replicas of cars, planes, and trains had functional moving parts, as did his dollhouses, with doors and windows that opened up to reveal perfect tiny furniture and staircases within. As a matter of fact, I had bought one of his miniature cars for my own little boy.

After asking around, I found out that the superintendent lived in Kasoa, a bustling suburb in the Central Region. It would mean a somewhat prolonged journey from my home in Accra, and without any way to contact him in advance, I had no assurances he would be there.

The morning I set out to Kasoa, the weather was miserable. An intense monsoon-like downpour had caused flash floods in several Accra neighborhoods. To get to my humble little Toyota, I rolled up the hem of my trousers and took a splashing run across a street along which water was rushing like a muddy stream. People in Accra are famously unprepared for the rain.

Traffic to Kasoa is always dense. The fifteen-mile journey took me all of two hours, by which time the rain had ceased and the sun was attempting to sneak around the clouds blocking its way. I followed some vague directions given to me by an old policeman who claimed he knew where Superintendent Blay lived. The difficulty was that his directions lacked clarity, containing such descriptions as, "near the Barclays Bank" and "opposite the MaxMart store." What I did know, however, was that the superintendent lived atop a hill in a house he had built himself. Along the way, I came across a vendor roasting plantain on a grill at the side of the road and asked her if she knew the whereabouts of the retired police superintendent.

"You mean Mr. Blay?" she said, expertly flipping the slices of plantain. She nodded and pointed up the road behind her. "Go straight."

I followed this terse direction and went up a rutted laterite road that ended in a thicket of neem trees, at which point I could proceed no farther on wheels. I ditched the car and continued on foot. The sun was now fully out again, and as the climb was rather steep, I perspired quite a bit despite my relative youth and vigor. On the crest of the hill, I came to a house painted a lurid green. A dog with a sandy coat came out barking and wagging its tail. It wasn't too serious about defending its property and didn't object to my patting its head. It followed me amiably as I approached the house but stopped at its guard post under the shade of a mango tree.

I came to a ramshackle door at the front of the house and knocked firmly. I received no response, so I went around to the rear of the abode where I found a courtyard so overgrown with weeds that they pressed up against the low, rusty gate before me.

In the near distance, the back of a shed faced me, but from the other side, which I could not see, I heard a man's voice singing softly. It was not a studied performance, but rather an incidental accompaniment to another activity.

"Hello? Superintendent Blay?" I called out.

The singing stopped.

"Hello?" I said again.

A head looked around from edge of the shed and I was astonished. Framing his face like a starburst was a shock of perfectly white hair. I guessed his age to be late sixties, but he could have been older than he looked. At any rate, he was a trim, smallish man wearing a soiled white T-shirt and a pair of ragged khaki shorts. He held a block of wood in one hand and a chisel in the other.

"Superintendent Mensah Blay?"

His brow creased. "Yes?"

"I'm Inspector Desmond de Souza. Please, may I come in?"

Blay nodded and gestured me in. The gate squeaked as I opened it against the foliage.

"Can I help you?" Blay asked.

"Please, I would like to talk to you about . . ." I trailed off, not sure what approach would be most persuasive.

"About?"

"About a murder case I've been working on without success. I work at CID Headquarters."

"I'm retired," he said abruptly but dispassionately. "I no longer involve myself with police cases."

"Please," I stammered deferentially. "I've come all the way—"

"From Accra," he said, sounding impatient. "Yes, I know."

I was momentarily confused. "You know, sir? Em, please, were you expecting me?"

He shook his head. "Not at all."

"Oh," I said, still not getting it.

"The paper stub sticking out of your breast pocket is the bottom of a toll ticket dated today," Blay said, "which means you've traveled from another region. I heard on the news this morning that the Greater Accra Region had had a sudden and unseasonal rain shower that resulted in flash flooding in the city, which was duplicated nowhere else in the country. You have fold marks at the bottom of your trousers as if you rolled them up for some reason—to prevent them getting them wet, for example. The specks of mud spatter on your trousers are consistent with your splashing through some flood water, very likely placing you in Accra."

It was an extraordinary, all-around picture: this little man with a crown of white around his head and what appeared to be—at least for the moment—an uncanny talent for deduction.

"Nevertheless," Blay continued, "you are not originally from the Greater Accra Region. You are a Fante from the Western Region, are you not?"

I smiled. "Yes please, I am. But that one was easy. My surname shows I am descended from the colonial Portuguese who settled in the Western Region."

"Nor did I claim my simple observation to be more than that," Blay retorted.

He began to turn away from me and I had a flash of panic. "Please, will you listen to my story, sir?"

He shook his head. "I've already given you an answer."

"Okay, sir," I said, "but then will you at least mend one of your toys?"

Blay whirled around. "Which toy?"

From my pocket, I produced a miniature VW Beetle and held it out to the superintendent. "I bought it for my little boy a couple of years ago. He takes it with him wherever he goes."

Blay's face softened as he took the miniature from me and regarded it with the smile of a parent beaming at a favorite child. "One of my originals," he said. "I see it's the left rear wheel that's coming off. I can fix that for him at no charge. It's no problem. Come along, Mr. de Souza."

I followed him to his workspace in the open courtyard under the shade of a canopy. Blay pulled a chair up for me, and I watched him in silence as he worked on the toy with much dexterity and skill, only once using a small power tool. Meanwhile, I racked my brain for a way to persuade him to listen to my story of the case and, hopefully, help me with it. He said nothing at all as he repaired my son's toy, and then he presented it to me with only a hint of a smile.

"Thank you very much, sir," I said.

He nodded.

"Goodbye," I said, rather mournfully.

As I walked away dejected, he called out to me. "Who was the murder victim?"

At this point in my tale, the palm soup was ready to be ladled into a large, shared bowl over plump mounds of fufu. Nothing bonds friends more than partaking in a common dish. After we had washed our hands and begun the feast, Prosper urged me to continue my story.

Wiping my lips to continue, I told him how thrilled I had been that Superintendent Blay had changed his mind and decided to assist me with the baffling case. It appeared that my giving him my son's toy to repair had touched a soft spot within him. Blay invited me into his home and we sat down together. After I had expressed my profound gratitude, I began my tale.

In the Sakaman District of Accra where the Blue Lagoon Road meets the Busia Highway, there is a large expanse of land called Gacy Park. Both a recreation and event space for weddings, parties, ceremonies, and so on, it is a beautiful area of manicured green lawns and symmetrically planted palm trees. All of this gigantic property is—or, I should say, *was*—owned by Peter Adjetey Gacy, a millionaire and entrepreneur. To say that he had a reputation for ruthlessness in business would be an understatement, and, of course, he had some enemies, personal and otherwise. This was relevant because on the morning of the tenth of March, Gacy was found murdered in his study.

Gacy lived in a sprawling mansion on the premises of his park in a secluded area that few people know about. In fact, he had built two mansions not far from each other. A family man, he loved to have members of his nuclear and extended family around him—the ones he liked, I should add. Living in the same large house were Gacy's wife, Efua, their daughter, Celine, and the older of their two sons, Robert. The younger son, Edgar, resided at the Airport Hills Estate.

On the ninth of March, Celine Gacy was married to Matt Roos, the son of the Swiss Ambassador to Ghana. The wedding, held on the grounds of Gacy Park, was lavish and almost certainly excessive. The after-party lasted well into the late evening. Celine and her new husband went off to the second mansion for some much-needed rest in advance of their honeymoon.

Gacy hosted three close friends, Jacob Baah, Solomon Damptey, and Cleophus Ferguson, for an overnight stay. The three guest rooms were next to each other on the ground floor of the mansion. On the second floor were Gacy and his wife in the master bedroom, and their son Robert in the far bedroom on the opposite side of the landing.

Everyone had retired to their respective bedrooms by midnight, but as was his habit, Gacy went to his study on the ground floor to do some work. He was a night owl and a compulsive worker who thrived on only three or four hours of sleep—as if his riches would evaporate as he slumbered.

When Efua woke in the morning, she was surprised to find her husband wasn't in bed. This was unusual, since Gacy usually returned to bed before dawn. As she got dressed, she heard an awful, animallike scream of terror downstairs, followed by a high-pitched wailing.

Following the sound, Efua ran downstairs and across the family room where she found Ama the house girl collapsed and shrieking in front of Mr. Gacy's study door, which was firmly shut. On the floor were her abandoned housework items—a rag, furniture polish, and a broom.

It took Efua barely a second to understand what had given Ama such an appalling fright. Hanging by a string from the top of the door was a hideous figurine. About six inches in length, it was a revolting caricature of a man with protruding eyes and misshapen limbs. The color of tar, it was splattered with a crimson substance that was almost certainly blood. The string by which it was suspended was wrapped around its neck. Efua was frozen at the sight. It could be only one thing: an ominous, evil juju object or a fetish.

At that moment, Baah and Ferguson emerged from their rooms to see what the commotion was about. "What is happening?" Baah said.

"Look!" Efua exclaimed, pointing at the door.

"My God," Baah said, taking a step back.

Efua snapped out of her horrified paralysis and went up to the door to call out her husband's name. Receiving no response, she tried the door, but it was locked. She hammered on it and shouted. "Peter! *Peter*! Are you in there?"

Just then, Robert and Damptey came in from the front terrace on the other side of the house where they had met to talk.

"What's going on?" Robert asked. Then he saw the hanging figurine and his face registered his revulsion. "What the hell is that thing?"

"That's what Ama found when she came to clean the office," Efua said tremulously, looking at the house girl, who nodded in confirmation.

"But where is Dad?" Robert said, thoroughly confused.

"I don't know," Efua said in distress. "He must be in the study, but he's not answering to our knocks."

In an authoritative manner, Robert went to the door and began to pound it with his fist as he bellowed, "*Dad*! Are you there? Open the door! *Open the door!*" He turned to the men present. "We must break down the door. We have no choice. He could have had a stroke or heart attack and be lying in there unconscious."

"Is there no window we can force open from the outside?" Baah asked.

Efua shook her head. "The room is completely sealed off."

Robert and Damptey, the largest of the men, put their shoulders to the door multiple times until the lock began to weaken. Both men almost fell as the door abruptly gave way with a crack and went flying open against the wall to the side.

Everyone crowded in the doorway to look. Efua screamed.

Slumped forward in his executive chair, Gacy was face down on his broad mahogany desk.

Robert was the first to reach him. "*Dad*! Dad?" He lifted his father's head and let out a hoarse cry of horror at what he saw. Gacy's face was discolored and bloated twice its normal size.

"What's happened?" Efua wailed. "What's wrong with him?"

Crying and babbling incoherently, Robert began to shake his father as if to rouse him.

Pushing Robert aside, Baah addressed Damptey urgently. "Help me get him on the floor so I can do CPR."

Together, Baah and Damptey struggled to ease the dead weight of Gacy's corpulent body onto the carpet and Baah began chest compressions as Damptey looked on and Robert paced the floor whimpering in shock. Gacy's eyes were open and staring to one side.

Efua, standing some distance away near the door, was weeping uncontrollably.

Ferguson came to her and put his arm around her. "Come, let's go outside. You must not see this."

He guided Efua back into the hallway and handed her over to Ama. "Take her to lie down in the sitting room and get her a drink of water."

As the other men watched with growing horror, Baah continued to pump on Gacy's chest, but it was no use. Exhausted and pouring with sweat, Baah finally gave up and fell back in defeat. He began to weep. "He's gone," he said, burying his face in his hands. "He's gone."

At this point, I paused in my account. Prosper, who had finished his meal, was staring at me with rapt attention. "So then," he said, "how did Mr. Gacy die? You said it was murder?"

"Yes," I responded. "Ligature strangulation and asphyxiation were confirmed in the autopsy results."

"Was the ligature found?"

I shook my head. "No trace."

"Something is bothering me," Prosper said. "Is it certain that the door was locked?"

"It is," I responded.

"Then it's obvious that the murderer had a spare key," Prosper declared confidently. "On leaving the room after committing the crime, he must have locked the door behind him."

I shook my head. "Efua Gacy told me that her husband—who was prone to absentmindedness except in financial matters—had lost the key to the room long ago and they had never had a spare, nor did they ever change the lock. So, the door could not be locked from the outside—only the inside."

"If that's the case," Prosper said, "I can only conclude that the killer locked the door after murdering Mr. Gacy and remained inside the study. Why have you not told me where the murderer was hiding?"

"No one else was in the room besides Gacy," I assured my friend. "Where would the killer hide? Under the desk? Behind the one armchair in the room? Those would hardly conceal him—or her."

"No hidden passages behind the walls?" Prosper persisted. "What about an opening in the floor?"

I chuckled. "You have been watching too many movies, my dear Prosper."

My friend shook his head. "Something is very wrong with this story. And what was the significance of the bizarre juju object hanging outside the door?

"I believe it was a ruse meant to make people believe that this murder occurred supernaturally, or 'spiritually,' as people say."

"You don't believe it?" Prosper asked skeptically. "Then how do you explain the door being securely locked with no other access in or out of the room? Only juju can explain this!"

"That's what Efua and a few others speculated," I said, "but I do not believe that. Neither did Superintendent Blay."

"What about the juju figurine? What more do you know about it?"

"We found it to be a wood carving painted with ordinary black acrylic paint. The red splatter over the black was also painted on—not blood, as it had first appeared."

Prosper scratched his chin. "The question now is who would have wanted to strangle Mr. Gacy to death."

"Correct," I agreed. "I uncovered some interesting pieces of information. For example, Efua felt that notwithstanding Baah being Gacy's friend, Baah had all along been a carpetbagger. Earlier on the wedding day, Efua stated she overheard her husband arguing with Baah. It appeared he had wanted a high executive position in the company, but Gacy had refused. Gacy cut the quarrel short by telling Baah, 'We will discuss this later. Now is not the time.' So perhaps Baah had motive.

"Another person with a possible reason to kill Gacy was his older son, Robert. Gacy preferred his younger son, Edgar, who had always been the brainy one, the 'good' boy—obedient and studious. Robert was an underachiever, erratic and blasé about most things. Robert was jealous of Edgar and angry with his father, with whom his relationship had soured badly."

"Did no one hear any commotion during the night?" Prosper asked. "Like sounds of a struggle?"

"No one. Not surprisingly, because the study is on the other side of the family room and the farthest away from the other rooms."

"I see," Prosper said. "So, this is not only a mystery of who did it but how was it done. The room was locked from the inside. It seems impossible, Desmond! And you say you solved the case?"

"Only with Superintendent Blay's assistance," I said.

"Then tell me, man! Don't keep me in suspense."

I laughed. "Okay," I said. "I'll continue. After I had told the superintendent what I've just related to you, he wanted to see three things: pictures of the study in general and the desk in particular; a photo of the juju figurine; and a photo of the study door the men had smashed open to get to Mr. Gacy. I have the pictures on my mobile, so I can show you."

Prosper eagerly took a look. The study was well-appointed with a tidy bookcase and luxurious furniture, but the desk against which Gacy's head had fallen was in disarray, indicating a physical tussle. Papers, a pair of scissors, pens, pencils, a tape dispenser, a pair of spectacles, and framed family photos were scattered, some cast to the floor.

The picture of the door showed how, as a result of its being forced open, the wood had split vertically along the grain around the body of the lock and the strike plate. The door had a conventional handle on both sides and a dead bolt lock operated from the outside with an ordinary key (long ago lost) and by a lever on the inside.

"So," I said to Prosper, "this door cannot lock itself. On exiting, you must use a key, and after entering the study, you must turn the lever you see in the photo. It would be impossible for Mr. Gacy, after being strangled, to get up, lock the door, and then return to his desk to sit down in that slumped position."

"How can you be one hundred percent certain?" Prosper said cynically. "Stranger things have happened."

I shook my head. "We dusted the dead bolt lever for fingerprints. None. Gacy could not have touched it at any time in the recent past."

Prosper grimaced in frustration. He still hadn't scored a point, but not for lack of trying.

Finally, I pulled up the image of the juju figurine with the string attached. Prosper shuddered. "What a horrible object. What was the superintendent's assessment of it?"

"He didn't offer one to me initially," I said, "but he did ask me if I could provide him with the actual juju object. I hurried back to CID and signed it out from the exhibit room that evening. I returned to Superintendent Blay the following morning. He took measurements and several photos of it and gave it back to me. He then instructed me to come back in four days, which I did. At that time, he gave me a small, sealed cardboard box, the contents of which he would not divulge. He told me I must have a courier deliver it to Cleophus Ferguson, and then just wait."

Prosper was intrigued. "How strange. Did you have any idea what might be in this box?"

"No clue," I said. "Nevertheless, I went ahead and had the box delivered to Ferguson. After four or five days, nothing had happened, and I called Superintendent Blay to let him know that. He was very short with me. 'I told you to wait,' he said, and ended the call. Then, after almost a week had gone by, I was sitting in my office when one of my junior officers knocked on the door and showed a man in. It was Mr. Ferguson. I was surprised to see him and asked him to have a seat. For a while, he seemed to have trouble telling me why he was there, but then his face crumbled and he burst into tears and began to speak unintelligibly. I made him slow down and start again. What he then said stunned me. He told me he had killed Peter Gacy."

Prosper was startled. "What? Really?"

I nodded. "He confessed he had been having an affair with Efua Gacy for over a year. He was deeply in love with her and begged her to leave her husband. But over and again, Efua had told him that as long Peter Gacy was alive, there was no way she could, or would, leave him. Ferguson began to seethe, obsessed with having Efua for himself. All the while feigning friendship with Gacy, Ferguson started to plot how he could kill him. During visits to Gacy's home, Ferguson familiarized himself with the layout of the study and also took note of the curtain ties in the sitting room. Sturdy yet flexible, the ties were the perfect length for an effective and satisfactory strangulation.

"But when would he have the opportunity? The answer came when Gacy issued an exclusive invitation to Ferguson and two other friends to stay over on the wedding night. Ferguson now saw his chance. He knew that Gacy invariably stayed up late at work, sometimes into the wee hours of the morning. Ferguson was betting that Gacy would do the same thing, even on the wedding night of his daughter.

"Meanwhile, Ferguson began preparing. A superstitious man, he went to see his juju spiritualist to request an amulet to protect him from any curses that enemies might place on him. The juju-man gave him a miniature sculpture in the form of a grotesque, misshapen man and instructed Ferguson to keep it with him at all times. Over the next few days, it struck Ferguson that he should attempt to make the murder seem not only impossible, but as if juju was involved. He understood that Ghanaians' fear of juju is so widespread and profoundly ingrained in the subconscious, that any appearance of juju causes general befuddlement, even in the minds of the police authorities that would ultimately investigate the murder.

"On the joyful wedding occasion, celebrations lasted until close to midnight, and finally everyone retired to bed—except Gacy. Ferguson, standing at the slightly ajar door of his guest room, saw Gacy pass into the family room on his way to the study. Giving enough time for Gacy to settle in, Ferguson went to the sitting room, where he removed one of the ties holding back the heavy curtains.

"Returning silently to the study, Ferguson peeped around the door to see Gacy seated at the desk in his executive chair with his back to the doorway. Softly playing in the background was classical music, which Gacy very much enjoyed. Deeply engrossed in his work, he neither saw nor heard Ferguson come up behind him. Ferguson quickly looped the curtain tie around Gacy's neck, crossed it behind the strut of the chair's headrest, and pulled with tremendous force. As the ligature tightened and held fast, Gacy kicked and thrashed around, but Ferguson slowly rolled the executive chair back on its wheels, preventing his victim from gaining any leverage or traction. After what seemed like several minutes, Gacy finally stopped breathing and moving. Ferguson wheeled him back to his desk and removed the ligature, allowing Gacy's body to slump forward.

"Now, Ferguson had to act quickly. On Gacy's desk were the tools he needed: a pencil and tape. He attached the pencil with the tape to the dead bolt lever in the unlocked position. To the bottom end of the pencil, he tied a length of string that he passed over the top of the study door to the outside. He then exited and shut the door, pulling the string firmly but gradually. That applied torque to the end of the pencil and hence the lever to which it was taped, thereby engaging the dead bolt. For the finishing touch, Ferguson tied the other end of the string around the juju figurine. The last step was to put the curtain tie back where it had come from. In the morning, upon discovery of the body, all Ferguson had to do was be sure he hid the pencil attached to the lever before anyone saw it, and he succeeded in doing that."

"Diabolical!" Prosper exclaimed. "But your account is far from over. How in the world did the superintendent get Ferguson to come in with this full confession? I suppose it had to do with the contents of the mysterious package delivered by the courier?"

"Yes, you are correct, Prosper. In the box was a figurine identical to the one Ferguson had left hanging on the door. With his superior carpentry skills, Superintendent Blay had fashioned the identical object, except that he detached the head from the body and placed both in the box. Added to that, he placed a length of string, a roll of tape, a pencil, and a note that said, 'Unless you confess, the juju will turn against you.'"

"My God!" Prosper exclaimed, both shocked and thrilled. "But how did Blay know to put those items in the box, and how did that result in Ferguson's confession? How did he even know whom to send the box to?"

"First," I rejoined, "Superintendent Blay told me that the solution to a mystery is almost always right in front of you. Often, the offender will use what is already available at the murder site, because the less he can bring with him and the less he has to take away, the better. That's why the superintendent asked to see the photos of the room, the desk, the door, and so on. Superintendent Blay figured out how the pencils, tape, and the string on which the figurine hung could be used together to engage the dead bolt from the outside. He tried it out at his own home, and it worked.

"The superintendent told me something else: what you see at the crime scene tells you much about the offender's belief system. Since Gacy's murderer chose to insert a juju object into the scene, whether he used it as a misdirection or not, he almost certainly had at *least* a trace of belief in juju. There's a saying that if you mess with juju, juju will mess with you, and all juju practitioners know that if you take on more than you can handle or if you use juju inappropriately, it can turn against you.

"When Ferguson received the box and saw the contents, he rushed in a panic back to the spiritualist to show him the beheaded figurine and the ominous note that came with it. Putting two and two together, the spiritualist asked Ferguson if he had committed a crime, and Ferguson confessed he had, although he did not say which. And here, I will try to reproduce the conversation as Ferguson reported it to me:

> "Have you kept the talisman on your person at all times as I instructed?" the spiritualist asked.
>
> Ferguson lowered his gaze. "No, please."
>
> Anger flashed to the spiritualist's face. "Why? Now, you see what has happened? Someone is turning the juju back against you because you haven't used the talisman correctly."
>
> "Can you help me?" Ferguson implored.
>
> "Bring a sheep to sacrifice and I will plead your case to the gods," the spiritualist said, "but now that you have thrown everything into confusion, I cannot guarantee your safety."
>
> "'How will I know if the gods have saved me and everything is okay?" Ferguson asked fearfully.
>
> "If the gods protect you, nothing will happen, and it shall be well."
>
> "And if they don't?"

The spiritualist shrugged. "Then you may die."

"So, what should I do?" Ferguson wailed.

"What do you want me to say?" the spiritualist snapped angrily. "The only thing you can do to be one hundred percent sure that nothing bad will occur is to do as the letter says. Whatever crime you have committed, you will have to confess."

Ferguson burst into tears.

"So that's how he came to the confession," Prosper said. "He was terrified of the same juju he tried to plant."

I nodded. "Yes."

"But what I still don't understand," Prosper said, "is how Superintendent Blay knew it was Ferguson who had committed the crime."

"Well," I said, "After Efua and the four men entered the room, it was vital for the murderer to remove and hide the pencil and tape before anyone saw it all. Recall the sequence of the men's entry into the office. Robert went to his father's side first. Next came Baah, who asked Damptey to help transfer Gacy to the ground. Baah performed CPR with Damptey and Robert looking on. We know Ferguson stayed behind them and escorted Efua out of the room in order that she shouldn't witness this terrible event. This gave him time to remove and hide the objects while the three other men were occupied."

"Ah, I see now," Prosper said. "And Efua Gacy? Is there any evidence that she knew what Ferguson was going to do?"

"She has denied it," I said. "If she did—well, we may never know, but there isn't any evidence connecting her to the crime and, short of a confession, we can't charge her as an accessory."

"Thank goodness for Superintendent Blay," Prosper said, stretching out his legs and looking at the dark, starry sky. "Will you use him in the future?"

"If need be," I said, "I will certainly approach him, but he is a most taciturn gentleman, and there are no guarantees what he will agree to do."

# WHAT MY FATHER NEVER TOLD ME

## *by Tess Gerritsen*

The room is dark when I wake up, and for a moment I am so disoriented I don't know what time it is, or where I am. Then, through the hotel window, I hear city traffic and pedestrians laughing on the street, and I remember.

*I'm in London. With Daddy.*

Packed in my suitcase is the wooden urn containing my father's ashes. A box of merely two hundred cubic inches contains all that remains of the man who rocked me to sleep when I was a baby, who held my hand at my mother's funeral, who danced at my wedding and dried my tears after my divorce. Tomorrow, I will scatter his ashes on a field somewhere in the Surrey hills, near the village where he was born.

*I'm bringing you home, Daddy. Just as you wanted.*

Something rustles in the darkness and I turn on the lamp to see that an envelope has just been slipped under my door. I assume it's merely a welcome note from hotel management, but when I open it, I find a heavy correspondence card with a handwritten message:

*My deepest condolences on your loss. JSW.*

I stare at the card, baffled. I don't know anyone with those initials. In fact, I don't know anyone in London, and I've told no one in this hotel why I've come to England, for fear I'll violate some law by scattering human ashes in the countryside. For a few moments I sit on the bed, struggling for an explanation, and finally just toss the card on the nightstand. I'm too jetlagged to solve this mystery right now, and too hungry. The last meal I ate was breakfast, after I'd arrived on the overnight flight from Boston; it's time to hunt down supper.

When I step out of the hotel, I'm overwhelmed by the bedlam of Covent Garden. It's a Saturday night in May and the streets are riotous with honking horns and rowdy laughter and the *clip-clip* of countless high heels on pavement. I thread my way through the crowd and catch savory scents that waft from the restaurants I pass: fish and chips and curries, pizza and kebabs. Whatever cuisine you crave, in London you can find it. I spot exactly what I'm looking for right across the street: an Italian restaurant. Pasta and salad and a glass of wine. Yes. A bus is rumbling toward the intersection, so I halt on the curb to let it pass.

That's when a hand lands on my back. It's not merely a touch but a brutal shove that sends me toppling forward onto my knees in the street. Time freezes to a standstill. Headlights rush toward me. Brakes shriek.

Someone grabs me by the collar of my jacket and wrenches me back onto the sidewalk.

Time suddenly leaps ahead. I see faces, so many faces, open-mouthed and staring at me. The driver jumps out of the bus and shouts: "Miss? Miss, are you all right?"

I'm barely able croak out an answer. "I—I'm fine. I think . . ."

Someone in the crowd snorts: "Aw, it's just another Yank, looking the wrong way."

*But I didn't look the wrong way.* Already the crowd is dispersing, and no one hears me when I say the words aloud: "I *didn't* look the wrong way. Someone pushed me!"

"I know," a voice says.

It's the man who pulled me out of the street. The man who saved my life. In his tweed jacket, his black hair streaked with silver at the temples, he looks like a distinguished college professor, not someone I'd expect to see wandering among these late-night revelers.

The man glances up and down the street. "He managed to slip away, but I doubt he's gone far."

"You *saw* him?"

"And not for the first time. Come, we need to get you out of sight." He raises his arm to flag down a taxi. It pulls over to the curb and he opens the door for me. "Hurry, Eve. Before he returns."

*He knows my name.* I hesitate, staring into the shadowy interior of the taxi. "Where are we going? I don't even know who you are!"

"Forgive me, I should have introduced myself. Julian Watson. I was going to pay you a call in the morning."

*JSW.* The initials on the card. "Should I know your name?"

"Your father never mentioned me?"

"No."

"Then you have a great deal to catch up on." He gestures urgently toward the waiting taxi. "Please. We may not have much time."

I step into the taxi.

Watson slides onto the seat across from me, and as the taxi navigates the maze of London streets, he studies me intently. The facing seats leave me exposed to his gaze, and I have no choice but to stare back at him. Lit by the intermittent flashes from the streetlights we pass, his face is all sharp angles—jutting cheekbones, a wedge of a chin, a prominent brow. He obviously knows me, so I must have *some* memory of this man, perhaps one that's been tucked away since my childhood, but I cannot retrieve even a wisp of recollection.

"You have your father's eyes," he observes.

"You sound as if you knew him well."

"I saw him only three months ago, the last time he was here in London. I can't believe he's gone."

"Why did he never mention you?"

"It seems there's a great deal he never told you." He scans the roadway, checking to see if any vehicles are tailing us. "I'm afraid that's placed you in a dangerous situation."

"I have no idea what you're talking about."

"Do you know how your father died?"

"It was an accident. He was on a business trip in Brussels. The police said he slipped in the hotel bathroom and hit his head."

"Yes, that's usually how it's done. Made to look like an accident."

"You're saying it wasn't an accident?"

He looks out the window again. "Here's where we get out."

The taxi has brought us to a quiet residential neighborhood where I don't see a single soul. Watson climbs out, but I hesitate to step out onto the eerily silent street.

"If you want to know the truth about your father, if you want to know who you really are, come with me." He holds out his hand.

After a moment, I take it.

We slip through a locked gate into a private garden that's enclosed by high walls and dense shrubbery. The grass is overgrown, and the scraggly hedges appear long neglected. As he unlocks the door of a stately house, I notice dead leaves scattered across the front steps, a sign that no one has been here in some time. When we step inside, I smell dust and dank air that has been trapped inside far too long.

He turns on the lights and I blink in surprise at what I see. Everywhere I look in this cavernous room, I behold wonders: A medieval tapestry of a lady and a unicorn in a bower of trees. An Egyptian funeral mask, agleam with gold. The mounted head of a monstrous canine, its citrine eyes glaring at me. I cross the vast room to peer into a cabinet of curiosities and marvel at intricate ivory carvings and mounted birds with brilliant plumage. On one shelf is a speckled snake, posed by the taxidermist as if it's about to strike.

"Is this a museum?" I ask.

"No. This was your uncle's house."

I turn to him in surprise. "What uncle? I have no uncle."

"Your father never told you about his older brother?"

"No. What happened to him?"

"His name was Colin. Twenty-seven years ago, he fell from the tenth-floor window of his London office. His death was deemed a suicide." He gazes around at the room, where dust layers every surface. "His house still stands empty. Waiting for someone to return."

I shake my head, stunned by this new information. An uncle I never knew about? A father whose death was not an accident? The room suddenly tilts around me. Or maybe it's jetlag and hunger that sends me reeling toward a green armchair. Legs wobbling, I sink onto the velvet cushion and sit shivering.

He lights the gas fireplace. Flames suddenly leap up in the hearth, bright and cheery, and I hear the squeak of a cabinet being opened and the clink of glassware.

He hands me a crystal tumbler of whiskey.

"When your uncle Colin died, your father was already living in America. He believed he was safe there. He never thought they'd bother to hunt him down. Perhaps that's why he never told you about his brother or about his family. He must have thought ignorance would protect you."

"Protect me from what?"

He pours himself a glass of whiskey and sits down in the chair facing me. The silver hair at his temples flickers with reflected gold from the firelight. "What do you know about your birth name, Eve?"

"Moriarty?" I shrug and take a gulp of whiskey. "The name is Irish, I think. Not a particularly unusual one."

"True, there are Moriarty families scattered all around the world. But there's only one Moriarty bloodline that's directly descended from your ancestor."

"Which ancestor?"

"You may have read about him. Professor James Moriarty."

As the heat from the whiskey seeps through my bloodstream, everything I've seen and heard tonight suddenly snaps together, like the pieces of an absurd puzzle. Professor James Moriarty. Julian Watson. The mounted head of the giant hound on the wall. The speckled snake in the cabinet.

"Oh, for god's sake." I stare at him. "This is a candid camera prank, isn't it? Some *stupid* media stunt."

"I assure you, everything I've said is absolutely true."

"Right." I'm so annoyed, I slam down the whiskey glass. "And now you're going to tell me this so-called Professor Moriarty died at Reichenbach Falls."

"He did. Pushed off the cliff by Mr. Sherlock Holmes."

In disgust, I rise to my feet. "I'm going back to my hotel."

"That would be most unwise."

"What, are you going to stop me?"

"I can't stop you. But I will point out it's not safe for you to leave."

"Hey, is someone filming this right now?" I look around the room and yell: "You can turn off your camera! I'm leaving!" I head toward the door.

"Please, Eve. Stop and think," he says, his voice perfectly calm. "If this is merely a media stunt, would we risk your life by pushing you in front of a bus?"

My hand freezes on the doorknob. Slowly I turn to look at him. He's made no move to follow me and he sits relaxed in the green velvet armchair, his long legs crossed, his hands casually joined to form a steeple. There's nothing to prevent me from walking out the door and calling a taxi back to my hotel. Nothing except the logic of what he just said.

Someone *did* try to kill me tonight.

He seems not at all surprised when I quietly return to the chair and sit down. "I knew you'd see reason," he says. "Just as your father always did."

"How can I believe anything you say?" I tell him. "These names you talk about—they're the names of *fictional* characters, invented by a storyteller. Sherlock Holmes never actually existed."

"I assure you, Holmes was real. As real as you and me."

"And Dr. Watson? Professor Moriarty?"

"Also real. But they were nothing like the characters described by Arthur Conan Doyle. His stories twisted the truth and libeled good people. He portrayed Professor Moriarty as a monstrous criminal, when the real James Moriarty stood for all that was right and decent."

I rub my temples, struggling to absorb this upside-down view of everything I'd read in the Conan Doyle stories. "Then who was the real Sherlock Holmes? Are you saying he wasn't a brilliant detective?"

"Oh, Holmes was definitely brilliant. Far more brilliant than that gullible Conan Doyle, who never questioned the falsehoods that Holmes told him. Falsehoods designed to smear Moriarty's reputation and justify his murder at Reichenbach Falls. No one mourned James Moriarty because everyone believed he was a criminal mastermind who deserved to die. When in truth, the real mastermind was Sherlock Holmes himself."

Dazed, I reach for the glass of whiskey but it's empty. He refills it and patiently waits for my next question.

"And Dr. Watson? He was your ancestor, I presume?"

"Yes. And like James Moriarty, also a victim."

"Holmes again?"

He nods. "A few months after Moriarty fell to his death at Reichenbach Falls, John Watson met his own death on a London street, when he fell under the wheels of a carriage. It was declared an accident. Just as your death tonight would have been. But Holmes didn't know that John Watson had been keeping meticulous diaries, documenting in painstaking detail all of Holmes's criminal enterprises—names, dates, aliases, account numbers. Incriminating evidence that could expose the real Sherlock Holmes."

"What happened to those diaries?"

"Years after Dr. Watson's death, his son found them hidden in his late father's study. He immediately shared them with Professor Moriarty's son, who happened to be a good friend."

"Surely the sons set the record straight?"

"They tried to, but no one believed them. By then, Conan Doyle's stories had already been devoured by millions of readers and the legend of Sherlock Holmes was as good as carved in stone. Nothing could dim his sterling reputation. The sons of Watson and Moriarty were dismissed as jealous frauds, and they eventually dropped out of public view. Meanwhile, Holmes's criminal enterprises expanded, nurtured by his descendants. They will do anything to avoid exposure, anything—including murder—to hide the criminal origins of their wealth. That's why our two families, the Watsons and the Moriartys, formed an alliance. It's for our own survival."

"Even now, after so much time has passed?"

"We're still dangerous to them, because we know the truth. And we're the guardians of John Watson's diaries."

"Then you should publicize them! Share them with the world!"

"That's exactly what your uncle Colin tried to do. He sent copies of the diaries to half a dozen journalists, but no one dared follow up on the story. It took only a few threats, and then your uncle's death, to scare everyone off. It scared off your father, too. It was years before he dared return to London."

"Is that when you met him?"

"Yes." He gazes up at an iron chandelier hanging high above us in the shadows. "This house is where the three of us would meet. Your father, my sister, and me. This room is where we mourned our losses and debated our next moves. And that chair where you're now sitting—that's where he'd sit, sipping whiskey." Sadly he shakes his head. "Now your father's gone. And Jane and I are the only ones left."

I hear the pain in his voice. The echoes of loss after loss. "What will you do now?" I ask.

He sighs, then shakes off his gloom and sits straighter in his chair. "We'll do what we've always done. We'll fight to be heard. We'll keep gathering evidence. And we'll try to stay alive."

*Alive.* I stare at the flames in the hearth and mull over everything that's happened to me tonight: the shove on the street, the bus careening toward me. I think of my father and my uncle, whose deaths were not accidents. "Now I'm part of this, too," I murmur. "Or they think I am."

"It's obvious they think you know the truth. Even if you return home, you will be tracked. Are you prepared for that?"

I take another gulp of whiskey, hoping it will steady my nerves, but when I set down the glass, my hand is shaking. "How does one prepare for something like this? I have no idea what to do next. Or where I should go."

"That's why I brought you here. My sister, Jane, is on her way now, to meet you. This house should be safe for you, a place to shelter while we catch you up on the facts. Where you can train for whatever might come."

"So I can't go home."

"Not until you're ready to face them. But I promise you won't be facing them alone. The Watsons and the Moriartys have always stood together. We've always fought together. You have no choice now, Eve. You're one of us."

I see both sympathy and inevitability in his eyes. He knows I did not ask to be part of this embattled alliance. I did not ask to be born a Moriarty and inherit the burden that comes with my bloodline. Yet here I am, following in the footsteps of my father, and his father before him.

I take a deep breath and I hold out my hand to shake his. "Teach me," I say. "Teach me everything I need to know."

He grasps my hand. "Eve Moriarty, welcome to the war."

# THE CASE OF THE WAILING GHOSTS

*by Joe R. Lansdale and Kasey Lansdale*

It ran on all fours.

It was fast.

I was proving pretty swift myself.

I ran like the goddamn wind, and it ran faster, and when I reached the end of the long walkway, as I leaped into the big, protective pentagram Dana had drawn, I felt it as it rose on its hind legs and its shadow fell over me and made me weak. I tumbled into the pentagram just as Dana Roberts raised the shotgun she was holding and fired.

That seems like the heroic moment in a story or film when the terror is vanquished, but I have to tell you, it wasn't all that heroic.

Let's back up.

It was a property in Colorado that was mostly trees and winding lanes, about two hundred acres of it. There was a big house there as well. It was three stories and sprawled over a vast amount of acreage, with outbuildings, a tennis court, and an empty swimming pool.

I kept both hands in my lap for fear of somehow getting my essence on the cream suede couch where Dana and I sat. I was now glad she had fought me about leaving my raspberry icee in the car, though I would never tell her that.

"My great, great grand-pappy struck it big during the gold rush," Eustace Frankland said.

He sure did, I thought. I looked around the room at the expensive decor. The rugs were lush and appeared freshly vacuumed, and the art that hung on the walls was a far cry from what I'd bought at Bed Bath & Beyond for my place, which had felt like a splurge.

"We've had this property in my family for generations now. Good thing is, I can afford to hire some help around here. For me and the grounds. Got a manager who makes sure everything is up and running. Had a chef, and there's Patty. She was my live-in nurse. But the bad thing is, no amount of money has been able to help with this thing."

Eustace Frankland gestured to his right shoulder with his chin and broke into a sad, crooked smile, rivaled only by his crooked back. He shifted a bit, taking the large hump with him. It sat snug on his back and against the side of his neck and pressed into his cheek slightly. It had to be painful just for him to sit. Eustace was a spindly man, with cotton white hair and a matching white beard that clung to his face in patches. I guessed him to be in his late seventies. He noticed me looking at his scattering of beard, and said, "I have a hard time getting the razor close, for obvious reasons."

I nodded, embarrassed. "Can hardly tell."

"But I've not asked you here to discuss my shaving habits, I know your time is valuable." He looked at Dana as he said it. I tried not to take that personally. "Short of it is, I've got ghosts."

"Ghosts?" I asked, "As in, multiple?"

"Four to be exact." He didn't really look at me, though. His attention was on Dana. "I've read your books, Ms. Roberts, and I know that most of the time you find that ghosts, supernatural activity—excuse me, *supernormal*, as you call it—is usually nothing but an overactive imagination, bad digestion, banging shutters, and creaking doors. 'No ghosts need apply,' I think you said in one of them."

"Don't forget rats and mice," I said. "Those things get a lot of people confused, with their squeakings and scratchings. And they leave little turds everywhere."

Dana gave me a hard stare.

"They do," I said.

Eustace laughed a little. "I see that you, Jana, are the comedienne of the two." Dana didn't give me time to respond.

"Sometimes what people think is from the beyond, is actually something from here and now, but not always," Dana said. "If you've read my books, you know that. 'This agency stands flat-footed on the ground,' as an ancestor of mine once said."

"It's why I'd like to hire you," Eustace said, and leaned back at an angle in his brown leather La-Z-Boy as he thought about it. His wiry legs stretched far beyond the extended footrest. Then I watched as his face grew taught.

"Every one of them is distinct looking. They're a horrible sight, cut up and covered in blood and who knows what else. They come out of the walls at night, all four of them. I've never been so scared in all my life. In the beginning, I thought maybe I was losing my mind, but eventually Patty saw them, too. Same as me. She left in a hurry, quit the next day."

"Anything else?" Dana said.

"There was only one at first. Then two. Three. And now four. And they seem to have become more insistent, for lack of a better word. Used to see only a glimpse, but lately they seem more solid and more dramatic. They always show around midnight, stay visible for a while, and then suddenly they're gone. The hallway, which turns cold and foul-smelling when they're present, grows comfortable and the stench goes away when they do. The doctors have suggested that this thing on my back and neck may somehow affect the blood to my brain, might cause hallucinations. Then again, they don't quite understand my affliction; it seems unique to them. As for hallucinations, my employees—especially Patty—weren't sharing my hallucinations."

Dana reached up to tuck her blonde hair behind her ear, concealing the white forelock mixed within. I could also see where her little finger on that hand was missing the tip. An encounter with something wicked from beyond this world had bitten it off, but that's another story.

"Tell me about Patty."

"Patty Abner. She's about my age. My nurse, as I said, but she is also a good friend. I have a lot of money and a lot of items, but not many friends. I need her back most of all. Sooner we can take care of things here, the sooner I can get the both of us back home."

"You're not staying here?" I asked.

"At night I'm at a motel in town. I leave before the ghosts show up. Even if I don't go in the hallway, I can feel their presence. It is uncomfortable to say the least. At the motel someone checks on me and brings me meals, even if it is just takeout. It's not like they have a five-star restaurant there. What they have is a refrigerator unit where you can buy a soda or an ice cream. Not too bad a commute, as the town backs up to the edge of my property."

"No one else is around during the day?"

"The property manager, Jimmy Monroe. He's the only one who hasn't abandoned me entirely. I pay him for the trouble, I can assure you. He takes care of basic needs, maintenance, et cetera. Place this big, there's always something. Sometimes he drives me down to the motel, sometimes I take a taxi, and now and again I drive myself. But he doesn't stay here at night, either."

"You can drive without any problem?" Dana asked.

"Driving or riding in a car for any great distance is uncomfortable. But at least I'm sitting. Standing is another story. It's like lugging a thirty-pound boulder around. Still, I prefer not to drive."

"If you don't mind," Dana said, "What exactly is the source of your . . ."

"Hump? It's alright, you can say it. No one knows. As I said, doctors are stumped. I wasn't always like this, you know. Didn't appear until I was grown. Late twenties to be exact. Was the result of some sort of unidentified disease or underlying condition that the doctors gave up on figuring out a long time ago. My great-grandfather, Sherman T. Frankland, had the same deformity. Supposedly it was the result of a Native American curse for him defiling their lands, killing buffalo, perhaps murdering people of their tribe. To be honest, I'm not sure exactly. Some of it is family legend, so I suspect. The curse is supposed to be passed from one member of the family to another, but if that's true, it waited a while to get to me. My grandfather, my father—neither had it. I've accepted it as just how things are. I don't have a lot of choice."

Dana and I nodded in unison. I could tell Dana was considering everything he said intently by the way her eyebrows furrowed and her usually full lips stretched into a thin, pink line. She could remember things I would forget seconds after they were said, but that might be because I was thinking about things like what we might have for lunch later.

"I think the best way to explain what's happening here is to have you ladies stay the night. See for yourself. If you aren't convinced, I'll pay the full rate anyway."

Eustace wiggled himself up to the edge of his chair with great effort, let out a ragged breath, and said, "Do we have a deal?"

Eustace extended his hand toward Dana. She leaned out from her position on the couch and shook it. His body jostled, the hump wobbling in response.

"We do have a deal. I'll give you a full report tomorrow. But fair warning, you may not like what we find."

"Understood."

Already at the edge of the chair, he kicked his heels into the footrest and locked it into place. After several tries, he used momentum to rock himself up to a standing position, assisted by the cane he had leaned up against the recliner. I wanted to help him to his feet, but I sensed that doing so would be a slight to his pride. I looked away as he steadied himself, suddenly finding great interest in the framed photos over the fireplace mantle.

There were various photos of him. Some in the present day with a woman I assumed to be Patty, due to the scrubs she wore, and several others from his younger days before the hump had taken hold. He stood straight and handsome in these photos. There was a group photo of him hugging a pretty Hispanic woman surrounded by two other couples in various poses, and other photos featuring some of the same people, those taken when the hump had clearly just started to form. As he aged and the hump progressed, the number of people in the photographs lessened.

Eventually, Eustace steadied himself on the cane, then shuffled over slowly toward the front door. It hurt to watch him move.

"It'll be getting dark soon enough," he said. "I best leave you ladies to it, car's waiting. I've left written instructions about where things are. Food. Your room. I wrote out some detailed notes about when and where the ghosts are seen, what to expect. I'll check with you tomorrow morning. I come back to work in my office, going over papers, real estate deals, all manner of investments that I try to keep going. I may have money, but it takes work to keep it."

"Of course," Dana said, and she was one to know. She had more money than Midas from all her bestsellers and film deals, as well as her spook-hunting business. She would work for clients with little or no money if she felt an investigation was needed, but she frequently worked for clients who had paid her richly, like Eustace Frankland.

Eustace struggled through the doorway and hobbled outside, moving as if he had one foot in a ditch and the other on high ground.

"I'm surprised you took this case," I said, peeling myself from the couch. "I mean, really, four ghosts? You get this stuff all the time, and it's rarely anything more than faulty plumbing."

"Don't forget the rats and mice."

"Right. But this doesn't seem like the kind of case you would take on, ghosts or not. Not a lot of call for investigation, clues, deductions. Besides, you usually like something with more gristle, something that puts my life in danger."

"I do not put your life in danger."

I stared at her silently.

"Sometimes things get a little tight," she said.

"That's one way of putting it."

"You'll be fine. We'll both be fine. This case, though, there was something about Eustace that intrigued me, and a few things popped to mind that might make this situation more interesting than the usual: find the grave of the ghosts, sprinkle them with salt and iron shavings, do a spell, and it's over. Boring. I have a feeling there's more to this."

Don't you just hate it when people say, "I have a feeling"? It doesn't mean squat. Well, it doesn't for most people, but truth to tell, when Dana says she has a feeling, what she's really saying is, "I have experience as well as research knowledge that makes me think this event could be more than merely interesting."

"We have a few hours before the ghosts are said to arrive," Dana said. "First, I'll find the notes he left for us, and in the meantime, you can quit looking at your phone and find a contact for Patty Abner."

"Here it is," I said. "Did you think I was looking up dog and cat pictures?"

"You've been known to."

"Because they are so cute. There's one with some donkeys that's special, too. But what I was looking up, Miss Know-it-All, was Patty."

I put my cell phone in front of Dana so she could see the Facebook profile of a smiling, round woman with bright, red-orange hair, likely an at-home dye job gone awry.

"How can you be so sure that's her? We have to be thorough."

"Says right here, see?" I pointed at the detailed list of Patty Abner's former jobs, former schools. Of course, on the job list was home health nurse for Eustace Frankland. She had been at that the longest.

"Definitely her," I said. "Plus, I saw her in the photos on the mantle."

"We need to talk to her as soon as possible. Certainly before tonight."

"Already on it, boss. She's responding on instant messenger. I told her who we were. Says she won't come here to speak, but will do a video call."

"Instant messenger?"

"Well, it's faster than a carrier pigeon. We can talk to her right now."

I looked at Dana, expecting some signal of approval. When she didn't respond, I hit the small blue video camera icon in the corner of my screen and held the phone away from me several inches and spun in circles as I searched for the best light.

Patty answered on the first ring. Her face appeared along with her bright, red-orange hair in all its flaming glory.

I gave her a smile. "Patty, thanks for this, I know it's a bit—"

"Oh, honey, I don't mind. Anything I can do to help Eustace. Short of coming back to that house. He's a good boss and a good friend, but I don't do ghosts. I'll fight an axe murderer with my fists, but a ghost, oh no, baby. I stay away from that freaky mess. Where's the famous Ms. Dana Roberts?"

Suddenly I felt like yesterday's fish at the meat counter.

I put the phone in front of Dana so that both hers and Patty's face were visible on the screen. She then smiled her million-dollar smile.

"Oh, honey," Patty said. "You are way better looking than your photos."

"Thank you," Dana said, and ever professional-like put the squash on the chitchat and got right down to business. "What exactly did you see?"

"This may sound cray-cray," Patty said, "and I understand if you don't believe me. Now keep in mind, Eustace, he's been seeing these creepers in varying numbers for years. But only now and then. He claims they've gained intensity. Before, he thought he might be having hallucinations. Just decided to stay out of the hallway. He said first there was one, and then there was two, and so on. I've been with him for years, and to be honest, before just recently, I didn't see a thing. I was figuring he might be having some mental problems, or emotional ones. His doctor had suggested that, and I had an uncle that had a knot on his head, and well, that knot was some kind of tumor or something, and poor Uncle Henry, he could hear birds singing in a well and watch fish swim in the sky. He told me once his best friend was a blue hippopotamus that came to sit on the edge of the tub when he went for a bowel movement. I once told him he ought to train it to wipe his ass. He thought that might be a legitimate plan. Poor Uncle Henry.

"So, I'm thinking, maybe that thing on Eustace's back and neck might be causing something like that. He'd talk about sensing and seeing ghosts and such, but all I ever experienced was some cool air, a stink, an uneasy sensation, and a strong desire to avoid that hallway. Figured I was being a little goofy about it, letting Eustace influence me some. I mean, cold air isn't exactly a terrorizer. It's a feeling I bet is similar to being in a morgue, walking along with dead people on either side in meat lockers. I always went the long way around to go to the kitchen, and I'd use a different bathroom, even if I was close to the one in the hallway. It's hard to do your natural business when you have a chill running up your spine like a wet rat."

"If only you had your uncle's hippopotamus," I said.

I wasn't in front of the phone, but I heard Patty crack up. Dana gave me a look like I had spit in the water supply.

"Well, one night I was helping Eustace out of his chair, as he has to take small walks a few times a day to keep the muscles strong, or he'd get so weak he'd never be able to get up. I'd kept him company until late, which wasn't rare for us. I'd sometimes read to him, or we'd talk, or just sit quietly together while I'd knit and he read to himself. The clock in the study started banging midnight, and he decided he wanted to walk to the kitchen and have a glass of milk, or some such. I got him on his feet, and away we went. Normally, we go through the other door and take the long way around. We don't talk about that, just do it, avoid the hallway, which is lengthy enough to put in a subway line.

"Looking back, I think now he was testing things, seeing if he could see the ladies again, as he called them. He wanted me to walk with him, and I think, too, he wanted to find out if I might be able to see them. I believe he was beginning to think he was slowly tumbling over the sanity cliff. He didn't go down that hall often, but when he did, he normally chose to do it alone. Couple times he started out that way, then a few moments later returned, hung on the edge of the doorway, like he'd just swam the English Channel, all pale and weaker than usual. But this night he had a badger's determination."

I saw Dana nod to her, prompting her to go on.

"Now, I wasn't convinced there were ghosts, not on the surface anyway, though, as I said, I had some uncomfortable feelings now and then, but as we stepped into the hallway, I knew I wasn't just avoiding that path to the kitchen because it made me cold. Still, I bucked up, and down the hallway we went. We were right close to one another, and as we stepped forward it got so cold and stinky in there it was like we had stepped into a slaughterhouse. It made my nose quiver and my stomach flip. My breath was frosting in the air, and when I looked at Eustace, the growth on his back seemed larger, and his limp became more pronounced, like something had borrowed his ankle bone."

There was sudden silence, except for heavy breathing.

"Anything else?" Dana asked.

"I can tell you what I saw, but no way can I tell you how I felt. The smell and the cold and the sight of them—Guess I'm trying to avoid talking too much about them, and, of course, that's what you want to hear about, as you're the ghost lady."

I saw Dana tense up. If there is one thing she hates being called it's the ghost lady, or the ghost hunter, or anything like that. She thinks of herself as an investigator of the supernormal, the unexplained and unfathomable that may be a slippage between dimensions.

"My goosebumps had goosebumps when we were walking down that hall, then all at once, the wallpaper trembled and peeled, and the blue-green designs seemed to move and run together and twist and rip open wide. Then, everything got hazy, and if you had a stinky-as-shit meter that went from one to ten, this was about a twelve.

"As for the ghosties themselves, there was a long leg, really a skeletal leg with rags of flesh on it, and it poked out of the wall, and a bony foot touched the floor, then the whole ghost slid into view. I can't really remember it separating from the wall. It just did. It stood there and looked at us. And when I say looked at us, there wasn't anything more than a skull, some strips of flesh and hanks of hair dangling from the bone, and those rags of clothes, enough you could tell those rags were once bell-bottoms. Seventies-style clothes, and there was enough hair there to see it was cut the way Farrah Fawcett wore hers, feathered and long, but in this case, tattered as well. It was like her image shifted from being a mess, to almost looking human, then back again. All but those empty eye sockets.

"They seemed full of something more than darkness. It lifted its skeletal arm and pointed a bony finger and came right at us. Then came another lady. Out of the same wall, shorter, nothing but a shell that rattled as it came into the hallway. It was wearing one yellow shoe, and something about that one shoe made it seem all the more terrible. Like that was the last thing left of it that was tied to its previous life. There were only a few strands of hair on this one, but the eye sockets were the same as the other, little black pits that gave the sensation of being so much larger and deeper."

As Patty talked, we moved into the hall, and I could see Dana looking at the walls, touching them gently. I felt the kind of discomfort Patty had mentioned; a malaise of the soul, if you will. Patty kept talking.

"Across from those two ghosts, the wall opened on the other side, and this less rotted corpse floated out, and, yeah, I mean floated, and moved toward the center of the hall and settled, jewelry on her wrists and around her neck clattering like chains on a dog, enough hair for me to see it was in an Afro style. Her fingers were crumpled up like broken sticks. And if those three ghosts weren't enough, I knew there was one more of those things behind us. I knew by the way my back felt. I swear, my spine wiggled like it was made of jelly. My knees went weak as crumbling crackers, and me and Eustace leaned into one another. Odd, what I remember most in that moment was looking at him, seeing the swelling on his neck and back, and I swear, that lump actually throbbed under his housecoat, fluttered as if it were full of birds. We slowly turned and looked behind us."

Patty's face had gone so white it almost seemed translucent. It was as if her bones were trying to push out of it and show themselves. Her lips were thin as the edge of a knife blade with blood lipstick on them. Her moist blue eyes were deep, dark pools.

"That one was the worst in my view. I collapsed to the floor when I saw it. I didn't even know I had fallen right away, and by the time I realized it, the ghost was moving toward us. It had a limp and wore a ponytail that grew out from a skull that was partially covered in withered flesh. I closed my eyes after that. Could sense the ghosts crowding toward us. Well, more accurately, I could smell them. The odor had become so intense it could have worn a coat and tie and done a job interview. They were making an awful wailing sound, and that was enough to make me want to crawl away like a lizard, but I couldn't even open my eyes, let alone crawl.

"I felt faint. Eventually, with extreme effort, I opened my eyes to see them standing around us pointing, like they were saying, 'We want you,' and not in a good way. Then there was a feeling as if someone was pulling an ice-cold wet sheet right through me. They reached out and touched Eustace, and then they whipped away, like someone had filmed paint being thrown out of a bucket, then reversed it. They were thrown backward and into the wall, and then they were gone. And the wall, why, it was solid again. No rips. No breaks."

"They didn't actually harm either of you?" Dana said.

"No. But I felt they might. Soon as they were gone the air warmed a smidgeon. I got up, got Eustace out of there and in bed, then I went home. Haven't been back since."

"Is there anything else?" Dana asked.

"Just this. Tonight, you go in that hallway, you might want to double up on the panty liners."

When Patty signed off, Dana moved farther down the hallway, past the restroom there, and to the door at the end. She opened it. I could see into the kitchen. Dana closed the door. She walked back, touching the wall as she went.

"Come here," she said.

I went to her, like a trained dog.

"Touch the wall," she said.

I did. It was cold to the touch. Almost painfully cold. There was also a faint stench, like a dead rat in the wall.

"Damn," I said.

"Yes, damn," Dana said. "You know what the big question is?"

She loved putting me on the spot like that.

"Oh. Oh–I think I got this," I said. "Where did they come from, and what do they want, and why are they so intense, and why are they pointing at Eustace? What has this to do with him?"

"That's the question all right," Dana said, and I felt for a moment like a star student. "Something that we can label as the Big Bad is building up to fruition, and we need to stop it, and pronto. Let's go back into the living room."

"Gladly."

Stepping from the hallway into the living room, closing the hall door behind us, was like stepping off a sinking ship. I felt a sense of relief.

I said, "Okay. What now, Sherlock?"

"What I'd like you to do is see if you can find out if there have been any missing women in this area. That kind of thing. Date it back as far as you need to date it back, but check and see."

"All right. I get the feeling you've got other plans while I'm researching."

"That's right. I have to get my hands on a sledgehammer."

The fact that I didn't ask why Dana needed a sledgehammer is proof enough I've become a little too accustomed to this weird job, and it doesn't surprise me it might involve a sledgehammer.

I got my laptop and set it on the table in a sitting room that was just off the living room, and which I would better define as more living room, with a larger table, but, hey, I didn't design the house.

I started researching murders in town, and, of course, I came across a few as I checked back over the years, but there were four that caught my attention. I reached into my laptop bag, pulled out my notepad with pink and blue bunnies on the cover and a pen I'd gotten for donating money to animal rescues, and wrote down notes about those murders, things I thought might intrigue Dana. I won't lie, I was still trying to impress her, which was a little like showing a professional magician the card trick your drunk aunt Louise taught you one year at Thanksgiving.

Across decades, police in three of the four situations said witnesses had seen a dapper looking individual in the area. Well-dressed and carrying a cane like he was in a Victorian novel. But no one had associated him with the murders at the time. I looked at the artist's rendition of one of the witnesses' descriptions. He looked dapper indeed. Handsome even. The last mention of the man seemed to fit the original description as well, but then it occurred to me. They all said he was youthful. How could that be, all those years apart? It had to be the same person, the way he was described each time, but it couldn't be. Someone identical, over several decades, dressing in a dapper outfit with a cane—when the first and last murder were forty years apart?

Another curious mention was that at least two witnesses, one who was in the vicinity when the first murder happened, and another who was in the motel parking lot where the third murder had occurred, said they saw what they thought was a wild animal dragging something into the woods, some kind of wolf, one said. The other thought it looked like an ape. A short time before that, they both saw the dapper man with the cane. Both descriptions were thought to have been fueled by alcohol and street pharmaceuticals.

Other similarities were that all of the murdered women were described as prostitutes, not as victims, and you got the feeling that their deaths weren't exactly on the law's or the public's tragedy meter. All I could think was they were someone's daughter, sister, or maybe even mother. It kind of made me sick the way it was all reported. Worse, none of the women seemed to have relatives, or anyone who cared about them. They were as forgotten as ancient literature.

Most curious of all, there weren't any actual bodies at any of the incidents, just blood everywhere. The first in an alley behind the motel, the others not far from it. For each discovery, there were intestines, organs, and bits of jewelry or clothes that identified the victims known to those in the area, but the bodies were gone.

I don't know how long I was researching, but it was awhile, and what brought me out of my investigative trance was a booming sound from the hallway that suggested our ghosts had taken up bowling.

I cautiously slipped over to the door that led into the hallway, cracked it, and there was Dana, now dressed in tennis shoes, jeans, and a T-shirt, wielding a sledgehammer. Swinging it into the wall and sending wood and plaster everywhere.

Even dressed like that and swinging a hammer, she somehow looked elegant. Though she couldn't swing a hammer worth a damn.

"Remodeling?"

She paused, rested the head of the hammer on the floor and leaned onto the handle.

"How did the research go?"

"Oh, fine. How are you?"

"Come on, Jana."

I spelled out what I had found.

When I finished, Dana nodded, said, "There's another hammer in the kitchen. Get it and help me."

"Eustace might not find this renovation to his liking."

"I don't care. I'm going to bet it's almost ten years from the day of the last murder. Am I right?"

I thought about my research for a moment. "Wait."

I went away and came back carrying my bunny notebook. I flipped it open and read my notes. "Wow. Ten years to the day. Tonight."

"I had my suspicions."

"How?"

"I'm experienced. Right, now, grab the hammer."

"Hold off on the sledgehammer a moment, boss."

I went over to the wall where she had made several large holes, bent down, and looked through one of the openings. There was just more wall.

"It's doubled," I said. "You and Andre the Giant would take a week getting through that. If those bodies have been put in there one at a time, there has to be an easier way."

"The opposite side of the wall is stone. The entire wall in there is stone."

I walked along the wall, tapping it in places. I hit one spot and there was a noise like a snare drum. I used my fingernail to scratch along the wall there and snagged the edge of the wallpaper where there was a crease. I looked more carefully and saw that what looked like part of the pattern, a line that went from floor to ceiling, was actually a thin gap in the wall.

"Honey, hush," I said.

I used my fingernail to poke into the gap, and then I pushed, and a part of the wall slid aside. It was a secret doorway.

"You can forget that hammer," I said.

Dana came over carrying the hammer.

"You constantly surprise me," she said.

"I'm a problem solver. I thought, if someone actually put someone in the wall, which makes sense, they probably didn't tear the wall down each time to do it."

"That is kind of smart."

"That is real smart. As for you, you got some serious holes in the wall to pay for, boss. The nine-tenths of the law thing. You break it, you own it."

Dana crouched and looked through the gap the open door made. She pulled her little key ring penlight from her pocket, flicked it on, and slipped inside.

"I'll just wait out here," I said.

"No, you won't. Come on." Her voice already had an echoing sound.

I made a trip to the living room, took my own penlight from my purse, rushed back to the hallway, turned on my light, and followed her inside. It was narrow in there and smelled acrid, and I could see dust motes moving in the light beams. It was high enough inside to stand comfortably.

"As I suspected," Dana said.

I scooted up behind her and looked over her shoulder, covering my face with the crook of my elbow to try and lessen the smell. In a heap on the floor was a pile of rotting cloth and old bones. A skull, easily identifiable as human, sat perched atop the mass.

"I guess we know why they couldn't locate the bodies," I said.

Dana bent down, shining her penlight on the floor. "Seems they were murdered, eviscerated, and their torsos were brought here and put in the wall. There's some real psychopathy at work here, Jana. The killer likes to have his victims nearby."

I looked behind me. Not far away was another pile of bones, and beyond that I could see a long rack against the wall with wine bottles in it.

Dana said, "That explains the hidden room, narrow as it is. It's liquor storage, and my guess is it was built during prohibition, maybe by Eustace's father, and then forgotten. There's probably a door on the opposite wall of the hall, too, where the other ghost came out."

"You're starting to sound like you think Eustace is responsible? And I admit, a lot of things point that way. But he can barely walk, let alone murder someone."

"It's not Eustace."

"So you know what's going on?"

"I'm not quite ready to say. I'd rather play my hand and let it be revealed."

"I'm confused."

"You've dealt with confusion frequently. You'll be fine."

Dana had me use the flash on my phone while I took some photos of the bones and the bottles, then we made our way back to the hallway. It was uncomfortable there still, and I was glad when we entered the living room.

"What I'm going to do," Dana said, "is I'm going to contact Eustace, try and convince him to not stay at the motel tonight."

"You know, I realize it's close by, but still. A man like him in a motel is odd."

"I think it's the same motel where the murders have taken place. While you were busy, I went over for a look. It's seedy, Jana. One step up from a cardboard box, right next to the highway. All along that drag is where druggies and prostitutes ply their trade. The motel has been there maybe fifty years, and it shows every year and looks to have, at best, been upkept by a band of angry monkeys. The money he has—close or not, why would Eustace stay there?"

I was starting to have an uncomfortable idea why.

"Shouldn't we just call the police? Show them what we've found?"

"And tell them we think there are four ghosts in the wall from previous murders, and another is taking place tonight, and a man without the ability to move about briskly, that couldn't outrun a mummy, appears responsible?"

"Maybe Eustace sneaks up on them," I said. "Plays the kindly old, hump-backed gentleman, and when he gets close, he beans them with his cane. Did you consider that, Miss Smarty Pants?"

"Miss Smarty Pants did. And I thought about him ripping a body up and pulling it into the woods, across his property, and back to here, and that didn't seem likely. He doesn't have a car with him, so you can't exactly have a taxi pack your murder up in the trunk like it's luggage and drop you and it off at the house."

"Oh. Good point."

Dana pulled out her phone, and walked away from me as she called Eustace.

When Dana came back, she was carrying her work bag. "He's coming. I asked him to be here at 11 P.M. This will give us time before midnight. He didn't like the idea, and seemed quite frustrated by it. But I told him it was necessary for him to be here for us to solve our supernormal puzzle."

"I have no idea what you're doing."

"That doesn't surprise me. Before he arrives, we have some work to do. Come help me with a salt circle in the hallway. In fact, you do that. I'll do the windowsills. Don't do the doorways, not yet."

"We haven't even seen any ghosts yet," I said.

"If we wait to see them, it may be too late for the next victim. I believe Patty. And there's the cold wall and the stench. We experienced that."

Dana removed a plastic baggy from her spook fighter bag and gave it to me. I knew from previous supernormal run-ins that it was red brick dust. The dust contained some protections against evil, and like any of the things we did to hold back the dark, it was never certain. It depended on the strength and determination of the Big Bad.

She also handed me a large cloth bag I knew contained salt.

"Pour the salt and brick dust along the edges of the corridor. We don't have to know exactly where the ghosts appeared, we just need to try and put a safety on the hallway. If there's enough dust—I know there's enough salt—pour it from one end of the corridor to the next. But again, don't block the doorways. Make a spell on the walls. You know the one."

"So, just us, a spell, some salt, and brick crumbs to hold back the Hellmouth? Are you sure that's enough? It feels a little more powerful than that, way you're acting."

Dana gave me a look that said she would throw me to the Hellmouth if I didn't get moving.

"You will know in time. Don't try and move beyond your pay grade."

"Right."

As I poured the red dust along the baseboard using one hand, I traced my finger up and down the wallpaper, forming the omega shape from the Greek alphabet with the other. I said the protection spell she had taught me. I didn't know what the words meant, or even what language they were in, but I had them well memorized. I did this on both sides of the corridor, avoiding the doorway that led from the living room, and the one that led into the kitchen.

I finished that, then grabbed the bag of salt she had given me and placed salt on top of the brick dust. The idea that salt and dust could keep out certain forms of evil seemed quaint, but I had seen it work on more than one occasion. Still, this seemed a bit more than the usual demons and monsters and ghosties and such. Dana was acting cool, but underneath that cool exterior I sensed a slight trace of nervousness.

When I finished, Dana met me in the living room. She had been working on the windowsills, maybe even the upstairs. I wasn't certain.

"When he gets here," Dana said. "We'll gather in the living room. I'm going to explain some things to him, and then I'm going to go to the bathroom."

"What?"

"Not really. But when I say that I am, know that I'm going outside, and I'll be laying a path of brick and salt and spells all along the walkway. More powerful than the ones you just laid. Give me about twenty minutes. I'll try and time it so I'm done before midnight. You keep Eustace talking, and then, well, something will happen."

"Something will happen?"

"Yes. If I'm correct, you'll need to run for your life."

"Pardon?"

"Go through the living room door, down the hallway, and through the door at the end. I'll have it open. That leads to the outside and then the walkway. The spells in the hallway might not stop it, but it will protect you from the ghosts, though frankly, I don't think they mean any harm. As for the other spell, what you'll be running from, will slow it down at best. You run down that path fast as you can go, toward the edge of the property line."

"How far is that?"

"Not that far. Just follow the walkway toward the trees. I'll be waiting at the other end in a pentagram I've put down, one made of grave dirt and ashes and so on. A little different than I usually make. It'll be my masterpiece. You need to leap into the pentagram before it reaches you, but don't think of it as completely safe ground. You may need to move again, and quickly. At that point, you'll be following my lead."

"Shoot that by me again."

"It'll be alright."

"Aw, shit."

"Yeah. You won't want to mess around. You need to go full tilt."

"What if this thing is faster than me?"

"I've seen you run. I have faith."

"I hate you," I said.

A little after 11 P.M., I heard Eustace Frankland open the front door, followed by the clomp and shuffle of his feet and the tap of his cane as he rambled inside and to the living room where Dana and I were waiting.

"Uber's are quite nice," he said. "I've never taken one before."

"They can deliver food, too," I said.

"Oh," Eustace said. "That's helpful."

Dana gave me an exasperated look.

I couldn't help myself. I had only learned this recently and it seemed like an interesting bit of information to spread around.

"Thanks for coming, Eustace," Dana said. "Can Jana get you anything? Everything is yours, after all."

Eustace declined, and, with great effort, made his way to the same recliner from before.

"Is the motel comfortable?" Dana asked.

Eustace looked at her, surprised, but said, "As you might expect. It's not exactly the comfort I've grown accustomed to. I stay there from time to time when needed because it's close."

"About every ten years?" Dana said.

"I suppose." He seemed a little confused by both the question and his answer, as if he had never given thought to why every ten years he parked himself overnight in a place Dana said looked as if it were maintained by monkeys.

Eustace sank down further into the depths of the recliner.

"We spoke to Patty," Dana said. "Nice woman. Chatty."

"She is that," Eustace said, his face softening at the mention of Patty's name.

"From what we can tell, it seems that the ghosts aren't here to actually hurt anyone, which I admit, is not what we usually run into."

"How can you be certain?"

"I'm not certain, but it's a suspicion. And for that suspicion I need you here. For a while."

"I hired you so I wouldn't need to be here."

"You feel driven to leave, though, don't you? I don't mean merely to get away from the ghosts. You feel a need."

"Haven't thought of it that way. Now that you mention it, maybe so."

"Because you're not the one doing all the thinking."

"Are you saying that the ghosts are somehow manipulative? Messing with my mind?"

"No. I don't think it's the ghosts. In the spirit world, frequently, ghosts are harbingers of death. They are trying to warn the living."

"What exactly are they warning us of?"

"The next victim is being planned. They may not have been picked yet, but tonight, if I'm not able to do what I need to do, there will be a murder, and there will be another body in the wall."

"What?"

"Parts of her will be found near or in that motel you're staying in. The one that you've stayed at for each of the murders. It's part of an ancient ritual. Of course, if I do things right, that won't happen. Fact is, I do them wrong, the murder might take place quite nearer to home. Here."

I got her drift, and I didn't like the sound of that.

"What the hell are you talking about?"

Eustace was quite angry now, and he was starting to try and rise from his chair.

"Stay there, Eustace. For your life, and for a woman's life that might be taken tonight if you don't. Truth is, we are all in danger."

"I'm confused."

"That's alright. You would be. But, Eustace, though you are not personally responsible for these deaths, there is something about you that is."

"Something—what?"

"The hump."

"I beg your pardon."

"Some would think of it as a supernatural entity, but in my belief it is merely something we don't quite understand yet. Let's call it a parasite."

"You're referring to my hump? Young lady, I didn't hire you to come here and insult me."

"I assure you I am not. I could be wrong, but that's unlikely."

"Yeah," I said. "She's pretty much always right."

Dana glared at me. "Hush, Jana."

I made a motion of zippering my mouth.

"Listen to me, Eustace. I want you to know that it's not you that kills women and puts them in the walls."

Eustace lifted his eyebrows. "I never thought it was. Wait. Women in walls? You mean the ghosts."

"Ghosts have a source, Eustace."

Dana glanced at the clock. It was about twenty minutes after eleven. She turned her attention back to Eustace.

"Have you ever heard of something called a fetch? Or skinwalker? Doppelgänger?"

"Doppelgänger, yes, the rest, no."

"In some ways they are all related. They can exist due to many reasons, but one way—that's less known—is you can be born with. Let's call it a condition."

"Let's say you jump right to the point."

"Somehow, in your genetics, and I suppose some might say it could be the Native American curse passed on to you from your great-grandfather. Whatever he did to be cursed is a curse of the blood, the flesh, and the bone. Why your father and grandfather didn't have the curse, I can't say. Like genetics, sometimes a trait doesn't follow the next generation, or even the generation after. Occasionally, it's that way with a curse. That appears to be the situation."

Eustace snapped his cane against the floor and almost stood up. "I call that bullshit. It was just family lore."

"You hired me to solve your problem, and I hope to do just that, tonight. This genetic propensity, call it a curse if you will, is not actually a double, but a companion of sorts."

"Parasite," Eustace said. "Companion. Ridiculous."

"The condition you have, with the growth on your back and neck, the one the doctors can't explain, is that parasite."

"What has this got to do with my ghosts?"

"Everything. They are here to inform others of their deaths, and they are here to warn anyone they can of impending doom. It's unfortunate that those warnings are confined to that hallway, and unless you've spent your life researching and dealing with this sort of thing, it would be difficult to interpret."

There was that Dana Roberts confidence. She knew if she stepped in horseshit a winged pony would appear. I sat down on the couch where I had left my bunny notebook and pretended I was looking through it for something important. Watching Eustace try and understand what Dana was getting at was as uncomfortable as discovering your kindergarten teacher liked to do striptease at a retirement home on a walker.

"Every ten years, like clockwork, your dependent must fulfill a need," Dana said. "You are no longer enough to feed on. It has to satisfy a ritual to stay alive."

"What kind of ritual?"

"There is power in ritual, curses, symbols. And this thing needs to kill every ten years, and for whatever reason, call it supernatural if you want, it leaves you and commits murder and then returns home to its host."

"That's ridiculous. I would know if something left me. Doctors would have seen something in the scans."

"It is in a kind of cocoon when it's in you, then it blossoms, commits its horror, and brings the body here while you slumber in a stupor. It has human shape, needs, and abilities for a while. It can breathe the air and see the moon. For a moment, it can have the joys humans have. But only for a while, a few hours, perhaps. After it hides away its victims, enjoys its moments of truly feeling alive, it returns to its host. You."

Eustace sat there in stunned silence.

I glanced at the clock. It was right at eleven thirty. I looked back at Eustace. He had turned an unhealthy shade of gray and the part of his neck where the growth was visible had started to throb. The veins stood out in his neck like thick blue cables.

"I think you should go," Eustace said.

"That's the part of you that knows what's about to happen speaking," Dana said. "Down deep you know something happens. We are here to help you."

"I'm firing you," he said. His voice was as thin as a leaf's edge. "Go away."

"Not going to do that, but I'm going to excuse myself for a moment to your restroom. I'll be back."

Eustace stared at Dana as if she were a jockey in the middle of a horse race that had just decided to take a tea break. He tried to speak, but all he could do was let out a little air.

Dana picked up her bag, glanced at me, and left the room by way of the ghostly hall, leaving me with Eustace, who had begun to wheeze. I could hear

Dana out in the hallway, kicking around debris from the hole she had made in the wall earlier.

Eustace's eyes locked on me as I laid my bunny notebook aside and came over to stand near him. I was supposed to keep him busy, but I wasn't sure how.

"Hey," I said, "you heard the one about the two priests and the donkey?"

Then I remembered that was the kind of joke that would make a longshoreman blush.

"That's not a good one after all," I said. "I know. What are you reading these days? Another Dana Roberts bestseller? I tell you, that woman has made more money off those books than Genghis Khan has descendants."

"You don't need to entertain me with your inane jibber-jabber," he said. "Soon as I feel strong enough, I'm calling the police to have you removed. What was I thinking, hiring ghost hunters? You're charlatans. Fools."

By this time Eustace had exhausted himself. His face had begun to pop with beads of sweat about the size of driveway gravel. He rocked forward and removed his coat, loosened the top button on his shirt, and then the one below it. He was breathing too hard. I felt I should call an ambulance, but then I considered Dana and thought better of it. This was all part of it. Part of what, though, I was a little uncertain.

Eustace closed his eyes and practically melted into his chair, then, with a final wheeze, was still.

Okay. That was good. He was asleep and no longer appeared to be in pain.

I went back to the couch and sat and hugged my bunny notebook to me like it was a shield. I sat there in silence for what seemed like eternity. Then there was a noise that came from Eustace like someone gargling marbles, then a cracking sound, and then silence.

I saw the veins in Eustace's neck ripple, like before, and then there was something dark moving under the skin of his neck. I saw his shirt move a little.

"Eustace," I said. I called his name several times. It was like talking to Lot's wife after the whole pillar of salt fiasco.

I glanced at the clock. Three minutes until midnight. Suddenly he opened his eyes, and said, "Where's Miss Roberts?"

Talk about being startled.

"Shitter."

A smile crawled across his face and fell off into a frown. He closed his eyes again, shifted in the chair, the hump following behind like a mound of Jell-O rolling under his coat. His body started to vibrate. His eyes popped open again.

He tried to stand with the use of his cane, which was no harder for him than a drunk trying to build a skyscraper with an erector set. His brows glistened and sweat dripped off his face and splattered on the floor in greasy plops. He didn't make it out of his chair.

The air became cold and sticky, like refrigerated honey, and then his coat and shirt ripped and a wet squirming mass of bile-like lava oozed from the bulge on his neck and back, tearing through the thin film of his skin like a hot knife slicing through butter.

The ooze became something dark and taloned, and finally it had a face. It was Eustace's face, and it glistened in the light.

Eustace fell out of his chair onto the floor with all the finesse of a sack of potatoes, his cane clattering on the hardwood. I heard a screaming sound loud enough to crack mirrors, then realized it was my own voice.

This thing, this gelatinous mass with claws and Eustace's face was still crawling out of him. Eustace's hump was falling flat. There was no blood, just a thin, pale liquid flowing from him and onto the floor, mixing with the thing that had his face and some nasty claws.

Just as the critter on the floor began to morph and stand into what could be loosely called a human shape, like Eustace's twin brother but darker and meaner and with claws, the clock banged the first of twelve strikes toward midnight. The air smelled like rotten eggs.

I caught my breath. Three more bangs.

Get on the goddamn horse, I told myself. But my feet felt as if they were nailed to the floor. I stood there frozen, listening to the clock.

The thing transformed again, twisted and bent, and lost all resemblance to Eustace. It looked animallike, but not in a cuddly way. There was a popping sound as it bent forward and its hands touched the floor. It was on all fours now, hairy in spots, gristly in others, enough glistening fangs hanging out of its mouth for three crocodiles. It was neither human nor animal or reptile.

It was demonic with a big D.

My feet came unnailed, and I did a kind of jump around and bolted for the open door into the hallway like someone had stuck a roman candle up my butt.

Down the hall I went, and it was shivering cold in there, full of the ghosts Patty had described as well as that spoiled meat locker smell. The harbingers of doom.

My breath puffed in white clouds as I ran. The ghosts were howling and wailing, pointing at the thing behind me.

Yeah, girls, I know. Thanks for the warning.

The ghosts that might have frightened me at any other time didn't faze me at all. It was the thing behind me I didn't want to deal with. I ran right through the ghost with the afro and I could feel its ectoplasm congeal around me like wet cobwebs. She swirled into a blue and white mist and was gone. That was the salt and brick dust working, making them weak. I wasn't so sure if it was affecting what was behind me. I didn't have a lot of time to consider. By then I was well on my way to hauling ass through the door Dana had opened for me at the end of the hallway.

The thing behind me was close. I could hear its claws clattering on the floor, and amid the cold air I could feel its hot breath on the back of my neck. I feared if I glanced back I'd be looking at its dentition.

My legs burned as I darted across the kitchen and out the door that led to the walkway. Once there, I ran, trying to dodge the extended limbs of the decorative shrubs. Whatever spells Dana had laid down along the walkway were about as effective as an honor system at a prison. I could hear pops from the spells, like light bulbs blowing, and when I finally ventured a look over my shoulder, that thing was still coming. Its shape and appearance continued to morph into something ugly and impossible to describe. Teeth and claws and burning red eyes, however, were prominent features.

I felt my legs shred against the rose bushes and loose gravel snapped up from under my shoes and struck me like shrapnel. I ran until I thought my feet would fall off and my lungs would explode, and all the while I could hear and sense it gaining on me.

I finally made it to the edge of the property where I saw Dana waiting inside the pentagram, which was white with chalk and goofer dust and who knew what all. She stood in the center of it, poised with a double-barreled shotgun at the ready. I didn't even know she owned one, let alone had it with her.

"Run!" I heard her yell, and wondered what it was she thought I was doing. I reached the edge of the circle and leapt with such height and projection, pole vaulters around the world wept with envy.

Just as my feet left the ground and one leg was inside the circle, I felt a brush of air against my unprotected ankle and realized the thing had reached for me and had missed by micro measurements. I leapt so far inside the pentagram, I almost came out on the other.

I screamed like a five-year-old girl afraid of spiders, which I still don't like.

Dana cut down on the monster with one barrel, and the blast caused my ears to ring and my innards to shake. That shotgun was loaded with more than buckshot, that's for sure—silver, lead, spells, and totems were crammed into those loads. A shot meant to send that thing straight to hell and assign it chores.

The beast started to smoke and stumble as it threw its weight against the barrier of the pentagram. It sizzled and lurched forward several more times and let out a banshee cry, then, all at once, it collapsed into a pile on the damp earth, steaming like fresh manure.

Dana stood there, the butt of the shotgun pressed tightly against her right shoulder, the length of it steady in her left. She was prepared to cut down on it again with that extra barrel.

My knees, no longer able to support the weight of my own terrified body, buckled and sent me to the ground within the pentagram.

I watched as the monster flailed about, howling, morphing back and forth from the creature to the younger version of Eustace. It collapsed in a pile of flesh and fur and bone and black gooey mass, then it morphed itself together again, trying to rise. It managed to do just that, then stumbled about and collapsed, crawling on hands and knees.

And damned if it didn't get up again.

Dana, doing what she always told me not to do, stepped out of the pentagram and cut loose on it with the other barrel. The blast was fiery and the stench stronger than steam and sulphur.

With one final shriek, the monster, skinwalker, doppelgänger, fetch—whatever—collapsed into a pile again, and then into the shape of the maggot that had first crawled out of Eustace. It sizzled on the ground like bacon in a skillet. The air stank.

I looked at Dana, who still had not moved from her position. Then we both watched as the thing smoked and cracked until it finally faded into the dirt leaving only a trail of mist and a foul-smelling stench that faded rapidly away.

Acid inside my guts churned. I worked my way slowly back to standing. Dana, having finally dropped the gun by her side, stepped back into the pentagram to extend a hand to help me to my feet.

I took it, and once I was standing, I said, "It almost caught me."

"Not at all."

"Yes. It almost did."

"You are very fast."

"Damn you, Dana. I am not your guinea pig."

"Of course not, you're my assistant. And with the big check I'll get from Eustace, you are due a raise."

"Oh. Okay. A big raise?"

"Of course. Let's go back to the house."

When we went down the hallway there were no ghosts, and in the living room we found Eustace. He was still in a wad on the floor and was attempting to get up.

"Stay where you are, Mr. Frankland," Dana said.

I wanted to rush over to help him, but stopped when I saw the deep wound on his shoulder throb.

We stood there and watched as the gaping hole in Eustace's neck and shoulder bubbled and scabbed over in front of our eyes. After the next ice age passed, Eustace managed to his feet. He took an awkward, stiff-legged step forward, and stumbled, but didn't fall. His eyes darted wildly around the room.

"It's going to take a moment. Your gait will have changed after all this time." I looked to Dana, trying to discern the message behind her voice.

I could see the wheels turn in Eustace's mind as his eyes stared off at a faraway memory. He reached up and touched his bare neck, then the part of his shoulder that had torn open. A clear liquid was dripping from the wound.

I went to him and, on the wound-free side, offered my body as a prop to take him back to the chair, but he gestured toward the couch. We hobbled to the edge of the sofa. "Should I lay down a towel, or. . . . It's a nice couch."

Eustace rebuffed my offer with the wave of a hand. I watched as he slid from my shoulder to sit in the center of the pristine cushions, me being just able to rescue my bunny notebook before he ended up on top of it. He looked noble sitting there. Different, but in need of a closer shave and a new set of clothes and a wash down.

Still stunned, Eustace said, "I haven't been able to sit anywhere comfortably but that damn recliner for almost forty years." He paused a moment, then buried his head in his hands, "I know now. I had no idea before, but now I know. It's like a dam has been unblocked. The memory of it, my connection to it. I know everything I did."

Dana said, "You know what *it* did, not what you did. Technically, it wasn't your fault. You must embrace that. You will most likely have ugly flashes of what your passenger did, but in time, that too will fade. And even if it doesn't, it wasn't you, Eustace. Listen, I'm going to suggest something. We don't call the police on this one. No way could we explain all this to them. No way they would believe it. We took care of it. I say that's enough. I recommend we remove those poor women from behind those walls and give them proper burials. Not one of them has had a family member look for them after all these years. They are discarded humans. I suggest Jana digs them graves and we bury them properly."

"The ground is kind of hard this time of year," I said.

No one paid attention to me.

"I will place spells of contentment within each grave, so as to free their spirits, though the death of your passenger has pretty much achieved that, I suspect. Jana will cover them and there will be no more ghosts, because they are settled and respected. See your doctor about the change in your condition, but explain nothing. Let the healing scabs and the loss of your growth be a mystery to you as well as them. Only in their case, it will be a true puzzle. You know something of the answer."

We left Eustace there on the couch, sobbing gently, and went into the kitchen to prepare coffee. An excuse to let him have some dignity and quiet time to digest it all.

Walking down the hallway to get there, it felt like nothing more than a path. No cold. No smell. No ghosts.

In the kitchen, Dana said, "See if you can find a nice tray, Jana. We'll present coffee and cream and sugar in style."

"You mean *I* will."

"Of course."

"When I die, I will come back to haunt you."

"I know how to take care of that."

"Yeah. Guess you do."

I searched for a tray.

There's not much more to tell. Dana actually didn't have me dig any holes. Said she was just messing with me, so I used one of her lipsticks. She'll find that out next time she gussies up. I will feign ignorance, but she will know, and that will be good enough for me.

We visited with Eustace over the next few days. He was learning to walk again, and better, though still with the cane.

Patty and his other employees came back to work. He was especially glad to see Patty. But before they returned he hired a backhoe to dig trenches for roses, and when it was finished and the backhoe driver was gone, Dana and I took the bones from inside the walls and wrapped them in blankets and Dana cast spells over them. We placed them gently in the holes, and then I did, in fact, fill the holes in using a shovel.

Dana and Eustace went into the house to have coffee and doughnuts that Dana had ordered. I suspected the jelly ones with the powdered sugar would be gone before I could finish, though likely not at Dana's hand. She actually didn't eat doughnuts. But I had a suspicion Eustace was an old hand at doughnut consumption. Takes one to know one.

I covered the graves carefully, patted them down with the shovel. Roses would indeed be planted on top of the graves.

That would be nice. A rosebush is better than a headstone.

I stuck the shovel into the earth and went into the house to wash my hands and scavenge for whatever sort of doughnut might be left.

I mean, hell. We have to take it all in stride, because terror is our business.

# THE TWENTY-FIVE-YEAR ENGAGEMENT

## *by James W. Ziskin*

(From the reminiscences of John H. Watson, M.D.)

During the time of my early acquaintance with Mr. Sherlock Holmes, I confess that, now and again, his vanity inspired in me flashes of pique that tested my equanimity. It is understandable, of course, that two intimate friends lodging together in close quarters might suffer bouts of discord in counterbalance to the good cheer they normally enjoy. And while on occasion I found myself prey to such ill humors—tame though they were—Holmes remained immune to similar agitation in his attitude with me. The inevitable outcome of these episodes was, of course, a return to harmony and respect for my companion.

Reflecting on our long collaboration, through all the adventures and investigations I've chronicled over these many years, I can recall no incident that so well exemplified this subtle peculiarity of our friendship than the Case of the Twenty-Five-Year Engagement.

A late-November gale was raging outside our shared rooms in Baker Street, cooling any eagerness we might have felt for venturing into the night in search of a meal. The rain thrashed against the windows in waves, as fierce squalls rose and fell, whistling down the chimney and through the rafters, causing the gaslight to dance on the walls. With such inclement conditions, we decided to ring the landlady, Mrs. Hudson, who delivered to us the remains of a toothsome steak-and-kidney pie from her larder. We made short work of the dish, rinsing it down with a serviceable claret I'd procured from the wine merchant. Alas, without advance instruction, Mrs. Hudson had prepared no pudding. Our appetites nevertheless tolerably sated, we repaired to the sitting room where I intended to dive into a yellow-back book of sea stories. I drew up the basket chair and settled before the hearth, a dash of brandy and soda within easy reach. My companion placed his post-prandial pipe on the mantelpiece and took up his violin at the music stand. After a moment's attention to the rosining of his bow and the tuning of his instrument, he began to play.

He was soon lost in a rapture of transcendent euphony, an aspect—I noted—not dissimilar to the vacant look of satisfaction he displayed when under the spell of one of his cocaine solutions. Yet at no point on that cold and rainy November evening had he injected himself with a stupefacient or consumed a medicinal concoction of any kind. The source of his delight was, I knew well, vainglorious, not chemical. It was, in fact, pride at his own musical talents that inspired his contented mood. Truly, so enchanting was the melody he summoned from the violin that, despite the bother I felt at his satisfaction with himself, I closed my book, folded it in my lap, and chased all thoughts from my mind, save for the enjoyment of the recital. The music coursed along merrily for a few minutes more until, in the midst of a particularly energetic burst of spiccato, Holmes fell victim to what I can only surmise was overmuch zeal. Basing my conclusions on the visual and aural evidence available, I arrived at the most logical interpretation, namely that the extreme friction produced by his bowing had caused the A-string of his violin to snap. A man possessed of lesser sangfroid would surely have abandoned his performance forthwith and restrung the instrument. But not Sherlock Holmes. He carried on—I presumed—out of native contumacy and the desire to demonstrate the full measure of his considerable skill. Without hesitation, he contrived a mysterious solution that veiled from the listener the loss of the A-string altogether. Once he'd brought the piece safely into port with a stirring tremolo at the finale, I forgot the annoyance that had beset me earlier, and I begged him to enlighten me as to what clever artifice he'd employed to accomplish the feat with only three strings.

"Simplicity itself, Watson," he said, lighting his pipe. "As the D-string lies adjacent to the A, I needed only elevate the pitch of the former by a factor of one-fifth to produce the notes usually dispatched by the latter. An unorthodox but effective fingering method, I'll allow, though one that should be within the abilities of even the most prosaic fiddler."

"Well done!" I ejaculated. "Had I not witnessed it with my own eyes, I would never have believed it."

"Thank you, Watson. And now, I would ask your indulgence as I intend to recount a singularly fascinating case that was presented to me recently. As you will have no doubt observed, for some time, I have been wanting of a challenging investigation to stimulate my interest. And, so, it was with great relief that Thursday last I received in these very rooms an attractive visitor of middle age.

"Taking her coat, a seal plush jacket bearing hints of wear at the elbow, I invited her to sit before the hearth, in the very spot you occupy now. The snugness of her Kersey vest, worn over a pearl-shaded blouse topped by a frilled *haut col*, made it abundantly clear that she was belted into a tight-fitting bodice underneath. Such a sartorial choice, when considered along with her ample bustle and the peculiar passementerie brocade adorning her skirt, convinced me that her wardrobe was, perhaps, four or five seasons out of fashion. That conclusion served to substantiate my initial approximation of her age, which I had placed between forty-eight and fifty. Still a handsome woman by any popular standard, she was making every effort, I inferred, to reclaim by means of the restrictive garment the trim silhouette she'd sported in years gone by. Vanity exacts its price at the expense of comfort. The fabrics and workmanship were of a fine quality, indicating that she circulated among the more privileged classes of our city, even if newer costumes appeared to be beyond the limits of her purse.

"She introduced herself as Mrs. Lavinia Biddlecombe, and while her surname suggested Somerset to me, her speech indicated otherwise. To wit, East Anglia or the Fens. She confirmed my suspicions and informed me that she had been born in Lincolnshire. Biddlecombe was her husband's good name. The scion of a wealthy family of Taunton, Charles Henry Biddlecombe was deceased, she explained, having died in a shooting accident twenty-six years before in his native Somerset.

"'It was a wet November, much like this one,' she told me. Her husband tripped in the mud and fell on his gun while hunting otter. The weapon discharged and he was killed instantly.

"I offered condolences, calculating silently that she'd been widowed at the age of twenty-three or -four. As she was still using her late husband's name, I deduced she had not remarried in the intervening years.

"The lady cast her eyes downward and thanked me for my kind words. Then, as if to sweep away the memory of her husband's premature demise, she asked me how I had managed to ascertain her origins, given that she had resided in London these past thirty years, all the while endeavoring to adapt her diction to her surroundings."

"Excuse me, Holmes," I interrupted, "but has her provenance anything to do with the case? Or is this simply more of your usual brag and bounce?"

"My dear Watson, I am attempting to paint a picture for you," he said, having taken no offense at my gibe. In fact, he seemed eager for some friendly sport. "Clearly my spellbinding powers of narration have intrigued you so that I have strained your patience to hear the conclusion."

I chuckled despite myself, even as I bristled at his capacity for self-congratulation. Holmes, smiling, dug into the Persian slipper where he stored his tobacco, and, having filled his pipe again, he lit it and puffed blithely before continuing his tale.

"I asked my visitor the motive of her visit, and she, reaching into her purse, produced a letter, which—she informed me—had arrived in the morning post a fortnight earlier. Examining the envelope, I observed that the Penny Lilac had been affixed artlessly, askew, with no thought to symmetry or parallel lineation. And the handwriting was coarse, almost infantile. Now, Watson, you will surely recall that, inspired by one of Rosa Baughan's clever tomes, I once made a deep study of graphology and the character traits observable in handwriting. Armed with that science, I concluded that the letter in question had been written by a left-handed man of the laboring classes—approximately sixty years of age—of below average intelligence."

"All that from his handwriting? Really? Nothing more?"

"Only that the author suffered from advanced arthritis of the gonorrheal variety."

"But surely that's impossible," I cried. "Never mind that you are not a pathologist or, for that matter, a physician of any sort. How can you possibly know that this man was afflicted with gonorrheal arthritis?"

"Simple graphology, my dear Watson. The swelling of the distal joints of his left fingers trailing the pen was discernible in the ink smudges on the page, indicating a severe arthritic condition."

"Yes, but gonorrhea? Can you be sure it was not rheumatoidal?"

"Tumescence of the distal joints is rarely symptomatic of rheumatism, as you must be aware. I once wrote a monograph on the subject of arthritis and the venereal diseases among the criminal classes. You would no doubt find it instructive. For now, however, I shall describe the contents of the letter in question, and my reasoning viz a diagnosis of gonorrheal arthritis, I trust, will become plain to you at the conclusion of my report.

"A Mr. Feargus Cheswick, late of the Sixty-fourth Regiment of Foot, was the author of the letter, in which he described his experience in India shortly after the Great Mutiny had begun. The year, of course, was eighteen fifty-seven. The regiment had recently shipped back from Persia to Bombay, whence it was immediately sent marching to relieve the siege at Cawnpore. I need not tell you, dear Watson, that the Sixty-fourth failed to arrive in time to save those poor British souls—men, women, and children—from their fate at the hands of the mutineers. It was during this campaign that Cheswick befriended a comrade in arms by the name of Edward 'Ned' Plunkett.

"Now, addressing once more your objections to my diagnosis, I remind you that the Great Mutiny preceded by several years the Cantonment Act of Eighteen Sixty-four, which, as everyone knows, imposed strict prophylactic controls on the dens of iniquity in that far corner of the Empire. Before the enactment of such regulations, British soldiers frequenting such establishments on the subcontinent routinely fell victim to all manner of venereal contagions. Gonorrhea is the most likely culprit in cases of arthritis of the hand."

"Still, Holmes," I said, raising one last protest, "you'll understand my irritation. What evidence have you that this Cheswick fellow visited brothels in India?"

"It is but an inference, my dear Watson, but perhaps we shall find confirmation of my theory before the night is through. Now, to continue my tale, Messers Cheswick and Plunkett became thick, as they say, after the latter saved the former's life at Ahwera. Young Plunkett bayoneted to death a charging sepoy who, musket lowered, was poised to blow Cheswick's brains out. Cheswick, in turn, pledged devotion to his savior from that day forward, and stuck to him like a burr. The two men shared rations, water, wages, and even the details of their sentimental histories, a point upon which Cheswick insisted in his letter.

"After two months on the march, the relief force finally stood ready to enter Cawnpore and free the British hostages held there. We both know that chapter of history turned out otherwise. And so it did for Ned Plunkett, as well. He was cut down by a mutineer's bullet in the chest just outside the city. Cheswick cradled his wounded friend in his arms, comforting him in his last moments. Before going to meet his Maker, however, Plunkett asked Cheswick for one last kindness: a promise to deliver a token to the woman back in London whom he loved and had intended to marry upon his return. And so, with Cheswick's solemn oath to fulfill the commission, Plunkett placed a small leather pouch into his friend's hand. 'This is a ring I found in Bombay,' said he. 'It was to be Lavinia's wedding ring, and I wish for her to have it.' Plunkett died an instant later."

"And now Cheswick is here to honor his promise? Twenty-five years later?"

"That appears to be his intention, though Mrs. Biddlecombe is not persuaded of the fact. Citing woman's instinct, she fears a nefarious motive on his part."

"What is it she suspects?"

"She declined to say, explaining instead that she only wanted me to attempt to recover the ring, if the ring exists at all. I could not fault her for her caution. A strange man emerges from the mists of the past, claiming to have in his possession a token from her long-deceased betrothed? It is suspicious. She is a woman of some means, after all, even if she is not wealthy. Naturally she fears this Cheswick may be after some other quarry."

"Blackmail?"

"A possibility. And if so, I can only surmise that it involves the bygone romance Ned Plunkett described to him. Mrs. Biddlecombe was, I noted, keen that I not think her the wrong kind of woman. She explained that she was already widowed when she agreed to Plunkett's proposal, which had come in a letter he'd posted from India upon learning of Charles Biddlecombe's death."

"But why such worry?" I asked. "Surely no harm can touch her reputation now."

"It would seem not. Although the swift proposal might well have prompted vicious gossip at the time. I advised her to meet with this man to gauge his intentions."

"A logical course of action."

"But Mrs. Biddlecombe objected. She neither wanted to confront the man at his Shoreditch lodgings, as he'd suggested, nor would she entertain the idea of his visiting her in her home. As my interest was stirred, I proposed a rendezvous here. If she was averse to meeting Cheswick face-to-face, she could wait in the next room while I recovered the ring from him. And, provided the heavy weather has not dissuaded them from the appointment, the meeting will happen this very night at nine."

I consulted my watch and remarked that it was nearly nine already.

"Indeed," said Holmes. "And despite the gale outside, I perceived just now the distinct clopping of a single horse's hooves in the street below. A hansom cab, no doubt. I expect the bell to ring at any time."

And, in fact, it did. Moments later, Holmes ushered into the sitting room an attractive lady of about fifty years of age. He introduced her to me as Mrs. Lavinia Biddlecombe and assured her that any confidence she shared with him was secure with me.

"Mr. Cheswick will arrive before long," he said. "When he does, you will conceal yourself in the next room. There is an armchair for your comfort." He fished in his pocket for a small enameled etui. "Keep these pastilles at the ready in case you feel the urge to cough."

"I was told I could count on you, Mr. Holmes," she said. "Thank you for indulging the whims of a foolish, frightened widow. I'm sure my suspicions will prove to be groundless."

Holmes smiled and assured her he would get to the bottom of the matter.

In due course of time—barely ten minutes later, in fact—the bell sounded again. Lavinia Biddlecombe slipped into the next room. Presently, my friend and I nestled into our chairs in the company of a ragged man of an indeterminate age.

"Am I correct to presume that I have the pleasure of addressing Mr. Feargus Cheswick?" asked Holmes.

"You are," he said in a gravelly voice. "Mind, I wouldn't rightly call it a pleasure, leastways not for a gentleman such as yourself." Then he glanced in my direction with an air of uneasiness.

"You may put your worries to rest," said Holmes. "This is my colleague, Dr. Watson. He enjoys my full confidence and, provided you do not seek some undeserved or illegal gain from my client in this matter, you may speak freely in our presence without fear of consequences."

Holmes considered our guest down his long nose. Cheswick, for his part, fidgeted under the scrutiny. His black overcoat, soaked through by the rain, threw off an odor typical of the larger breeds of hunting dog. The bloodhound came to mind, and one that had just tramped through a bog, at that. I repeat this last detail with some vexation, given Holmes's extensive knowledge of the properties of soil and mud around London and, indeed, across the British Isles. His habit of advertising his mastery on all matters involving clay, loam, peat, and the like annoyed me. I confess that the subject of mud—along with that of the distinguishing qualities of various types of cigar ashes—figured among the least enjoyable in my many colloquies with Sherlock Holmes.

But I have strayed from the subject at hand, which was the outward aspect and manner of the man seated before us. So wasted and bent was he that I found myself unable to estimate his age. He may have been an infirm pensioner of sixty years, or a relatively hale-and-hearty grandfather of five-and-eighty. A grizzled beard, matted and tangled upon itself, obscured much of his face, though not enough to disguise the ravages of a hard and diseased life. Holmes endeavored to put him at his ease, offering him some tea. But Cheswick, having spied the decanter on the sideboard, affected a shiver and remarked he wouldn't object to a peg of brandy instead.

"It's a raw night out, indeed," said he, licking his lips and showing a toothless grin. "I shouldn't wonder if I catch my death."

Holmes obliged and served up a generous portion of the spirit. I studied Cheswick's hands, which shook from avidity as he took the glass. He drained half the liquid in one gulp, before swallowing the residue with similar dispatch mere seconds later. Observing him closely, I had to admit that his swollen fingers and puckered, bilious eyes, which squinted at the low light as if distressed by it, provided little evidence to contradict my companion's earlier diagnosis.

"Now, Mr. Cheswick," said Holmes once he'd refilled the man's glass, "I have read the letter you sent to Mrs. Biddlecombe and, before any other discussion, I have an urgent question to put to you."

"You want to know why I waited so long to keep my promise to deliver the ring," he answered. "You won't be surprised to learn, Mr. Holmes, that I have led a life of cold coffee and gruel. My earliest recollections are of my dad floggin' me for the sin of bein' handy when he was worse for the drink. 'Course he up and died one fine day when I was not yet twelve. I come home from the factory and my mum tells me it's broxy and ale for dinner 'cause we're celebratin'. 'Father's went to his eternal reward,' says she, 'and begone and good riddance.' Sure but she never pined after the blinkers and bruises he give her, and she shed no tears at his demise neither.

"You see, Mr. Holmes," he continued, "my earliest miseries led me to a life of disgrace and hardship. A thief from a young age, then a factory boy for slave wages and a bent spine. And, when I was a mere lad of thirteen, my mum was knocked down by a speeding Brougham in the street, leaving me an orphan. For a few years, I moiled and toiled, stealin' and runnin' for the swell-mobsmen, buttoners, and gang leaders around the docks and the Rookery. That's when I acquired a taste for the pleasures to be found in the company of the fair sex. And I've paid dear for those enjoyments, with more doses of shameful maladies than a decent man ought to admit."

My friend glanced at me and raised his eyebrows, a subtle signal to indicate that Mr. Cheswick had all but confirmed the diagnosis of gonorrheal arthritis. I had to concur, of course, though not without a sting to my pride.

"Pray, go on," said Holmes to our guest.

"After several quarrels with the law, I decided I was ill-suited to the life of a thief. I'd heard tell that there was fortunes to be made abroad, so I joined the army and spent the next seventeen years with a musket on my shoulder, trampin' about the world for queen and country. From the Cape of Good Hope to China and Burma and Afghanistan, I seen a healthy portion of the Empire, I did. But I never made my fortune. I limped from one payday to the next, fritterin' away my wages on women and drink, never layin' by a farthing away for a rainy day. The only luck I ever had was to steer clear of the worst horrors of war. Until the Mutiny, that is."

"And that's where you met Mr. Plunkett, isn't it?" asked Holmes.

"It was on that hot march from Bombay to Cawnpore we became fast friends, Ned and me. Not for long, true enough, but never have I known a finer mate. Saved my life, he did. So watchin' him die in my arms near broke my heart. The hardest thing I ever saw was that handsome lad gaspin' for life, and me with nothin' I could do to help him. The hardest thing ever, I tell you. Until the next day, that is. What was waitin' for us inside the Bibighar drove many a brave man to tears. And then to rage. I ain't proud of the justice we give 'em as repayment for the butcherin' of those women and children, but if you'd seen what we had, well, I'd wager you'd have ne'er a word to say against us. We took eyes for eyes and teeth for teeth, and then some more for good measure."

Outside the wind continued to keen, dashing more rain against the windows, intensifying our sense of dismay at the memory of that distant tragedy and its murderous aftermath. Holmes puffed silently on his pipe. Cheswick sipped his brandy and wiped away a tear with his rough, knobby hand. At length, my companion suggested a return to the subject of Plunkett and the ring.

"He was fadin' fast," said Cheswick. "I could hear the blood gurglin' in his chest as the life drained out of him. But he had enough strength left to reach into his pocket for a small pouch. There was a ring inside. Sterling silver, he said."

"May I see it?" asked Holmes. Cheswick produced the pouch and held it out to my friend. "A peacock," observed Holmes, turning the ring over in his hand. "Fine workmanship. And a great, red eye. A garnet."

"So Ned told me. Said it cost him every penny he could steal or borrow. Bought it in Bombay for Lavinia. Made sure I committed her name to memory so as to deliver it on my return to England."

"I see," said Holmes, giving the ring and pouch back to his guest. "What else did he tell you about his beloved?"

"That she was a widow," said Cheswick. "He told me she'd married a cold-hearted man who ill-treated her. But fate smiled on her and the husband died young. A hunting accident, he said."

"And when was that?"

"November of fifty-six. Mere days after Ned shipped out for Bombay, as it turned out."

Holmes put down his pipe. Gazing at the ceiling, fingertips pressed together, he seemed to be putting some data in order. At length he spoke.

"Tell me why it took you so long to deliver this ring to Mrs. Biddlecombe."

"I was keen as mustard to honor my promise. It was never my intention to delay. But I served five more years after Cawnpore. Then I was drummed out of the corps and locked up in a Singapore jail for a misunderstanding involving a gent and his purse. Took me this long to do my time and raise the sum for my passage home."

"Very well, then," said Holmes. "I now have all the information I require, good sir. You may go."

Cheswick was caught off his guard by the dismissal. He managed, nevertheless, to recover his wits and pour the last of the brandy down his throat. Then he stood—crooked—and bowed to his host and to me.

"What about the ring?" he asked from the landing.

"Keep it," said Holmes, causing me great surprise. "I shall contact you in the days to come if Mrs. Biddlecombe wishes to have it. Good night, Mr. Cheswick."

Once the door was closed and we'd heard the man's footfalls melt into the night, Holmes called to Mrs. Biddlecombe to come out from her place of hiding.

"Your interview took longer than I would have imagined," she said. "Did he have the ring?"

Holmes lit a fresh pipe. "Yes, he did. And I left it in his charge. He has kept it safe for twenty-five years. Surely a few days more will do no harm."

"I don't know what to say, Mr. Holmes. I feel let down by you."

Just as the lady uttered those words, the bell rang once more.

"Who can that be at this hour on such a night?" I asked.

"That will surely be Inspector Lestrade." said Holmes. "Earlier today I invited him to come once Mr. Cheswick had departed. Mrs. Biddlecombe, Inspector Lestrade is the finest detective—so called—that Scotland Yard has to offer. I am certain he will be useful in the resolution of this case."

Looking quite waterlogged and in foul temper, the inspector soon joined us in the sitting room. Holmes attempted to placate him with some brandy and a seat near the fire. Still, Lestrade wanted to know what the mystery was all about. My companion began sketching out the details of the letter, the ring, and the interview with Mr. Cheswick. Before he could finish, however, Mrs. Biddlecombe interrupted to make clear a point.

"I agreed to marry Ned Plunkett, but before you judge me wrongly, I must insist that we became engaged only after my husband had passed away. And, of course, we were determined to observe all proper conventions of mourning and wait at least three years before pursuing any plans of marriage."

"Then your husband was indeed dead, as Mr. Cheswick described, when you accepted Plunkett's proposal?" asked Holmes.

Mrs. Biddlecombe blushed scarlet. "Of course he was. I would never have given my heart to him if not free to do so."

"Still, you will allow that the courtship was a brief one?"

"Ned and I were acquainted from a young age in Lincolnshire," she said with a huff. "There was a sympathy of spirit between us, but nothing base or tawdry. After Charles died, Ned declared his long unrequited love for me in a letter and asked for my hand. I agreed to his proposal, but insisted that we must keep it secret as long as I was in mourning."

"Quite right. And when did you learn of Mr. Plunkett's demise?"

"In September of the following year, fifty-seven. I remember because word of Ned's death reached me on my birthday. A tragic coincidence."

"You are quite sure of that date?"

"One does not easily forget such a horror on one's birthday."

"I would imagine not," said Holmes. Then, addressing Lestrade, he continued. "Edward Plunkett died, shot through the chest by a mutineer's ball, at Cawnpore on the sixteenth of July of fifty-seven, just as our brave boys in arms were retaking that forsaken outpost. His dying wish was that Cheswick deliver a silver peacock ring to his betrothed, this very same Lavinia Biddlecombe."

"A touching story," grumbled Lestrade. "But hardly worthy of dragging me out on a night such as this. You must have something more up your sleeve."

"Indeed, I have. I summoned you here this night to arrest Mrs. Lavinia Biddlecombe for the murder of her husband, Charles, twenty-five years ago."

"That is a lie!" she exclaimed. "I did not murder my husband. The verdict of accidental death was confirmed by the coroner's inquest."

"I am sure it was," said Holmes. "And I would wager there were no witnesses to his death besides yourself."

Reluctantly, the lady admitted there was none.

"At our first meeting, you told me your husband died while hunting otter in November of fifty-six. And yet, Mrs. Biddlecombe, your husband could not possibly have died shooting otter at that time of year. As any hunter knows, otter is only in season from April to mid-September."

"Clearly, I misremembered the game," she said with a stammer. "Perhaps he was stalking hind instead."

"The species of the game is unimportant. What matters is that my suspicions were aroused by the mere mention of otter-shooting in November. It caused me to question your entire story, so I decided to start at the beginning. With your husband's hunting accident.

"I made my way to the General Register Office in the Strand where I consulted the death indices for the year eighteen fifty-six. But it was the oddest thing. I could locate no record of a Charles Henry Biddlecombe among the deaths in the fourth quarter—or any other quarter—of that year. Perplexed, I searched the indices for eighteen fifty-five and eighteen fifty-seven, even though I thought it unlikely that you would have forgotten the year of your husband's death."

"I was in shock, Mr. Holmes. You can hardly hold me at fault for this discrepancy if some doctor or clergyman neglected to register the death."

"Ah, but there was an inquest. Which means your husband's death would have surely been registered properly at the conclusion of the proceedings."

"Then how do you explain the absence of his name in the index?" she asked.

"It baffled me for some time. I confess that I smoked several pipes, brooding over the mystery, before a simple path to the solution finally occurred to me this very morning. As I breakfasted alone—my fellow lodger, Dr. Watson, was sleeping late, as is his custom—I had a revelation. What if Biddlecombe actually had been hunting otter when he died, as you told me?

"I pulled on my waterproof and hat and dashed back to the Register Office. As I'd already consulted the years from fifty-five to fifty-seven with no result, I decided to expand my search to include the second and third quarters of eighteen fifty-eight, when otter was in season. My persistence paid off in a trice. I discovered that Mr. Charles Henry Biddlecombe of Taunton, Somerset, died on May thirteenth, eighteen fifty-eight. The cause of death was recorded as an accidental gunshot wound to the chest. And, according to the index, the informant of the death was Mrs. Lavinia Biddlecombe, widow of the deceased."

"Can this be true?" asked Lestrade. "Are you certain there is no mistake in the registration date?"

"Perfectly certain," said Holmes. "Fearing such a question might arise, I dispatched a wire to St. James's Church in Taunton this morning as soon as I left the Register Office. St. James's is, of course, the oldest church in Taunton and, as such, I thought it most likely to have been Biddlecombe's parish. My instinct proved correct. The vicar's reply arrived at teatime this afternoon, confirming the date of May thirteenth, eighteen fifty-eight, graven into Charles Biddlecombe's headstone in the churchyard there."

Holmes let his words echo in the room for dramatic pause before continuing. "Now, Mrs. Biddlecombe, how was it possible that Ned Plunkett believed your husband dead in a hunting accident in November of eighteen fifty-six—and informed Feargus Cheswick of as much in the summer of eighteen fifty-seven—when your husband did not, in fact, die, until May of eighteen fifty-eight? The explanation, of course, is that Ned Plunkett knew of your intentions to murder your husband. But something must have disrupted your plan. Illness, perhaps? An inconvenient witness? Lack of opportunity? Whatever the reasons for the delay, you were unable to communicate them to Plunkett, as he was aboard a ship bound for India in November of fifty-six. So, with no option, you left Ned to assume the murder had gone off according to its original timetable."

Lavinia Biddlcombe fixed her blazing eyes on her accuser but uttered not a word.

"You must truly have despised your husband," said Holmes, "to have waited so patiently to shoot him dead long after Ned Plunkett was gone."

Lestrade cleared his throat to speak. "I would urge you to unburden your conscience," he said, addressing the lady. "But I must also inform you that your words will be taken down and may be used against you."

"My husband was an odious, miserly man," she answered. "Even if I hang for it, I have no regrets. You may not believe that twenty-five years free from his cruelty is worth the price to be paid at the gallows, but I tell you—for me—it is a fair bargain."

"Your powers of deduction are without peer," I said once the inspector had led the lady away in handcuffs.

Holmes threaded a new A-string onto his violin and commenced to tuning the instrument—plucking and tightening—as he spoke. "I dare say, Watson, that, while fascinating, this was one of my simpler cases. It was the otters that first sparked my doubts about her. Cruel sport, that, shooting otters." He paused to reflect. "Or, when you come to think of it, shooting men."

A shiver ran down my spine as I considered Lavinia Biddlecombe's singular determination. "It is a hard-hearted woman who will murder her husband and coolly bear false witness before the coroner's inquest."

"True enough. And yet, I detected in her bearing today emotional turmoil whenever Ned Plunkett's name was mentioned. No more than a tinge of melancholy in her eyes, but it betrayed what I am certain was authentic sorrow and yearning for the lad she lost so long ago. Perhaps that is why she never remarried."

"Who would have guessed that, of all the characters in this sordid tale of murder and otters, a man as outwardly vile as Cheswick would play the noblest part?"

"The poor man has led a life of misfortunes, some of his own doing and others resulting from the conditions of his low birth. Yet I have seldom witnessed such genuine devotion in one man for another. And now his health is failing. I doubt he is long for this world. My fervent hope is that he will pawn that accursed ring and use the money to find some little joy in the time he has remaining."

"I fear he will only spend it on women and drink," said I, all thoughts and recriminations for Holmes's arrogance behind me, replaced by the usual warm affection and admiration I felt for him. "But let us think of pleasanter things."

"Quite right, Watson," said he, the A-string now in place and tuned to his satisfaction. "Shall I play something sweet, that we may forget—for a short while at least—faithful Cheswick and his troubles?"

# WHEN YOU HEAR HOOFBEATS

*by Robin Burcell*

The murder of John Watson had me stumped for the better part of a week. Two suspects, both accusing the other of lying, and nothing to prove otherwise.

In desperation, I brought the case to my former colleague—and rival—retired San Francisco PD homicide detective-turned-PI, S. Barker. He was a logical thinker, and right now I needed logic.

I walked into his office that afternoon, the place smelling of shrimp and fried rice, no doubt due to the proximity of the Chinese restaurant just downstairs.

"I have to admit," he said, dropping a carton with the remnants of his lunch into the overflowing wastebasket, "I wasn't expecting a call from one of San Francisco's finest."

"Can't say I was expecting to be here myself." I sat in the chair. "How've you been?"

"Existing." He studied me a moment. "I take it this isn't a social call?"

"I have a case I'd like to run past you. I feel as though I can toss a coin between both my suspects to decide who is and who isn't telling the truth. I've even wondered if they're both in it together. And . . . there's the zebra—"

"The what?"

"One of the suspects, Joseph Bell, says he saw a zebra appear on the wall at the time of the murder."

"Is this . . . vision significant?"

"I couldn't say. Possibly an early attempt to claim diminished capacity, should we arrest him. He's apparently addicted to opioids from a previous back injury and was under the influence."

"What's the relationship between him and the victim?"

"Bell is his partner and long-time friend who moved into a guest room over the garage after his wife booted him out a few days ago. My other suspect happens to be the victim's wife, Mary Watson, who was drinking at the time, per the officer's report, moderately intoxicated. She says there is no zebra on the wall, and never has been, insisting that the zebra is proof that Bell is lying. Each are accusing the other of being the killer."

"Gunshot residue?"

"Both positive. It seems Mary Watson and Dr. Bell spent the morning skeet shooting at a club they belong to. They're on a competition team. The murder happened that night."

"What sort of murder weapon?"

"Saturday Night Special. No serial number."

Barker's chair squeaked as he leaned back, steepling his fingers beneath his chin. "Definitely intriguing. Tell me about your victim."

"Dr. John H. Watson shared a lucrative plastic surgery practice with suspect number one Dr. Joseph Bell. Watson was murdered in his car, in his own driveway. He'd just come home from a business trip, one that Bell was supposed to have accompanied him on but cancelled due to the skeet shooting competition. Watson had just pulled into the driveway, stopping short of the garage to answer a call on his cell phone from Bell less than thirty seconds before the murder. Judging from the surveillance video, Watson saw the killer moments before he was shot."

I gave him the factual details as reported to me by both suspects: "Mary Watson says she was in the backyard, having imbibed in a couple of cocktails earlier in the evening. She had just stepped out of the hot tub when she heard a gunshot. She immediately ran through the house and out the front door in time to see the silhouette of Bell in the headlights of her husband's car as her husband backed it into a drainage ditch near the street."

"Did she say what Bell was doing?"

"Running into the garage from the driveway, she thinks into the side door to get back into the house without being seen. She called the police on her cell phone just as Bell came out of the front door behind her, asking what happened. She, in turn, asked him what he'd been doing in the garage—the question was recorded on the nine-one-one call."

"Did Bell respond?"

"He did, and I quote: 'What are you talking about?' Any further conversation between the two ended when the operator asked what the emergency was. That's pretty much it from her point of view."

"I take it that Dr. Bell's statement contradicted Mrs. Watson's?"

"It did. He admitted to having taken OxyContin and an alcohol chaser prior, both of which were found in his bloodstream. He reports that he awoke from a sound sleep due to a loud noise, unsure if what he heard was a gunshot or a car backfiring, followed by tires screeching. When he saw the giant zebra painted on the wall, he figured he must have been hallucinating from the drugs, because he didn't recall seeing it when he'd retired to the room about twenty minutes earlier. He hurried downstairs and then through the house, only to find Mrs. Watson already outside, calling the police. And, yes, he denied having been in the garage."

Barker picked up a pad of paper, taking notes. "What about this phone call Watson received?"

"Definitely a red flag," I said. "Bell made no mention of the call in his initial interview. When I confronted him with the records from the cell phone company, he insisted he must have dialed Watson's number in his sleep. Which is rather convenient, considering that the call came moments before the murder."

Barker was quiet a moment. "I take it they both have motive?"

"So far, only Mrs. Watson. Her husband had recently discovered she was having an affair with her skeet shooting coach and threatened divorce. That's about the extent of it."

"Can I see the surveillance video?"

I pulled out a laptop from my briefcase, brought the video up, and showed it to him.

The surveillance video screen was divided into quadrants: the front, back, left, and right sides of the house. There was a time/date stamp on the lower portion of the screen. Dr. Watson's Mercedes pulled into the driveway at precisely 9:23 P.M. The alarm company log showed the garage door had opened at the same time. Instead of pulling into the garage, he stopped to answer his phone, the call lasting less than ten seconds. He opened the car door. Two more seconds passed before he stood then looked up suddenly in the direction of the garage, presumably at the shooter who stood just out of sight, parallel to his open car door. Watson shook his head, then scrambled into the car, the driver's door hanging open, the headlights sweeping across the pavement as he quickly backed away. The vehicle came to a standstill at 9:24 when the right rear wheel and backend of the car dropped into a shallow ditch at the end of the drive. The twin beams of headlights went askew, one of them shining into the camera mounted over the garage door, obliterating the picture until 9:25 when the vehicle slid farther back into the ditch. The light shifted off the camera, revealing the mortally injured Dr. Watson slumped over the steering wheel. It was shortly thereafter that Mrs. Watson and Dr. Bell both came running toward the disabled vehicle, Mrs. Watson on her cell phone talking to the police.

The first patrol car arrived a few minutes later, its red-and-blue emergency lights reflecting off the windows of Dr. Watson's Mercedes. The responding officer pulled the victim from the car, his CPR efforts fruitless.

Barker watched the video a second time, pausing it at the point Dr. Watson stopped the car then answered his phone. He jotted down the time of the call. "That's either an amazing coincidence or Dr. Bell was watching for Dr. Watson's car to pull into the driveway."

"A call that effectively makes sure Dr. Watson's attention was diverted, while the killer picked him off? As I said before, I can't help but wonder if they were both in this together."

"An interesting prospect."

"Unfortunately," I said once the video ended, "the responding patrol officer didn't turn up any evidence other than the he-said, she-said between the business partner and the wife. Sadly, neither have I."

"About this zebra . . . ?" Barker asked. "You're sure there was nothing that could be mistaken for a striped horse anywhere in that house?"

"The responding officer found no zebra anywhere."

"Do you think Mrs. Watson will allow us to have a look?"

"I'm sure it won't be a problem. She's been extremely cooperative."

The Watson house was located in the country, about twenty miles north of the city. There were no sidewalks or gutters, just a ditch where the water drained down one side of the road then through a culvert beneath the Watsons' driveway. Since there was very little traffic, I parked on the street and we walked up the drive past the shallow drainage ditch, the tire marks where the Mercedes's rear wheels slid off still evident.

Barker stood there a moment, looking at what had been the vehicle's point of rest, then glanced toward the two-story, white-stuccoed house. Neatly trimmed boxwood hedges bordered the front. There were at least half a dozen windows on the top floor overlooking the drive, and on the ground floor, two large picture windows. White, wide-slatted blinds on both the top and bottom floors were lowered and closed. I saw someone lift one of the slats in the picture window on the ground floor, looking out at us. Less than a minute later the front door opened.

It was Mary Watson, one hand on the door, the other holding a glass wet with condensation, filled with ice, sparkling liquid, and a slice of lime floating within.

"Sorry to bother you," I said. "But we were hoping to get a better look at the premises. For the report."

"So you said in your call." She glanced at Barker. "Who is this?"

I wasn't sure how to introduce him. After all, he was a PI, not a cop. I decided on a slight compromise. "Mr. Barker. Retired SFPD. He occasionally works as a consultant."

She said nothing, merely stared at us. Her lips pressed together as she looked from me to Barker then hesitated as though trying to decide if she should let us in. "It's the zebra, isn't it?" she said.

As good an excuse as any. "We were hoping to figure out where the zebra played into this."

She rolled her eyes. "He was ranting about it from the moment they started questioning him. What that has to do with my husband's murder, I couldn't say."

"Is there a zebra on any of the walls?" Barker asked.

"You're welcome to look for yourself. Come in."

I could smell the alcohol on her breath as we entered.

She closed the door, took a long drink, then set her glass on the entryway table. "This way."

We followed her through the foyer, down a hall, and up the stairs leading to the rooms over the four-car garage, passing by several cans of white paint, clean brushes, a paint tray, a ladder, and tarps neatly folded.

Barker nodded at the equipment. "Doing some painting?"

"That was the plan. Put on hold for now. We got as far as the rooms over the garage, where Dr. Bell was staying, until . . . my husband was killed."

"Exactly why was Dr. Bell staying with you?" Barker asked.

"His wife kicked him out. I should have known better than to let him stay with us. He's addicted to OxyContin from a back injury." She stopped at the first door, opening it wide. "This was the room he was in at the time of the murder. It was painted the day before my husband was killed. As you can see, no zebras."

I glanced inside, seeing a couch set against the wall, a window on either side, both with wide-slatted, wooden blinds lowered over them. Much like the rest of the house, the ceilings were coffered with white crown molding.

I walked over to the window on the right, the slats partly open and angled down, giving a clear view to the driveway at the front of the house. Barker moved beside me, looking out. Below us, scuff marks left by the tires were visible on the pavers below, as was the angry scar in the dirt of the drainage ditch where the vehicle had landed after Dr. Watson was shot.

Turning back into the room, we both took a closer look at the walls. I had no idea how difficult it might be to see the difference between fresh paint and old paint after this many days. Black stripes would take quite a few coats to paint over.

I walked up to the wall, touching it, casually using my finger to scrape the surface, and even moving close enough to smell.

There was nothing. No scent, no rubbery, uncured paint that might suggest a fairly new coat. The walls were a clean white. I couldn't remember the last wall I'd painted. I do remember my late mother painting the dining room red, then, a few months later, changing her mind. It took about three coats to return it back to white, mostly because the walls were textured. Years later, there was still red paint visible in the tiny nooks. I expected any black paint would leave similar telltale signs but found none.

Clearly, there were no zebras on the walls, nor any evidence that one had ever been painted on one of them. There was, however, a picture book on the sofa table, *On The Serengeti*. The photograph on the cover was of a herd of wildebeest and, scattered within said herd, a few zebras.

Barker nodded at the picture book. "How long has this been here?"

"I honestly couldn't say. My husband had always dreamed of taking an African safari."

"And you're sure this is the room Dr. Bell was in at the time?"

"Positive," she said. "The sofa turns into a bed. Because of his addiction—" She cleared her throat. "I wasn't comfortable with him staying in the main house. My husband and I were in counseling in an attempt to repair our marriage, and our counselor advised us against letting him stay here. I should have listened."

"Do you mind if I take photos?" Barker asked.

"Feel free," she said.

He took several. "And where were you when all this started?"

"I'd just gotten out of the hot tub. I'll show you."

Barker hit the timer on his phone, no doubt curious about how long it took to walk from this room to the front of the house as Mrs. Watson led us back down the stairs. "What's this door?" he asked at the bottom of the stairs.

"It leads to the garage," she said, without stopping. "That's how I think Dr. Bell got in and out of the house without anyone seeing."

When we reached the foyer, Barker stopped the timer, and started a second count as we followed her to the right, down another hall, and into the master bedroom, which was at the complete opposite end of the house, overlooking the backyard.

I'd done the exact same thing on my initial investigation, discovering the room over the garage was five seconds closer to the front door than the master bedroom—eight seconds closer if he took the side door into the garage. This fit with the scenario Mrs. Watson described: that Dr. Bell was already in the driveway when she arrived from the back of the house.

After we passed through the master bedroom, she pulled open the sliding door to a covered patio, and just beyond, a hot tub and a swimming pool.

"Nice set up," Barker said. "How many jets?"

"Twelve."

"How long were you in there for?"

"No more than ten minutes. I'd just turned it off when I heard the gunshot. I grabbed my robe and ran to the front door, but Dr. Bell was already there, running into the garage. I assume he went back into the house from there, because the next thing I knew, he was coming out the front door behind me."

"You didn't see the gun?"

"No. Not until the officer found it tossed into the bushes by the front door."

Barker nodded. "I appreciate your openness. Do you mind if we call if there are any more questions?"

"Of course not."

Our house tour over, Barker asked if he could talk to our second suspect, Dr. Bell, who had moved into one of the local hotels after the murder. I cleared it with Bell's attorney, who insisted we meet at his office so that he could be present during the interview.

"Look," Dr. Bell said when we arrived about an hour later. "I know it sounds insane. But when I heard the shot, I didn't move for several seconds. I was sort of out of it. And then I turned over and saw a massive zebra on the wall and ceiling. I must have looked at it for another couple of seconds before I registered that what I'd heard was a gunshot. That's when I ran downstairs."

"A zebra?" Barker said. "You're sure it couldn't have been moonlight coming through the slats of the blinds?"

"Absolutely not. The stripes were definitely black and white. I think if they were from ambient moonlight, they'd be pale blue. And . . . well, it was definitely a zebra. If you have a pen, I'll draw it."

Barker handed him a black pen.

"As crazy as it sounds," Dr. Bell said, sketching away, "I have near-photographic memory. *This* is exactly what I saw."

He was a fairly decent artist, drawing thick, black-and-white lines depicting the square snout, face, mane, and neck of a zebra.

Assuming the guy wasn't so high he'd imagined this thing, there was no way anyone could hide anything like that on the wall.

While I was once again contemplating the possibility of someone painting over the zebra in the few short days since the murder, my former partner looked at the sketch, saying, "If you hear hoofbeats . . ."

"Think horses," Dr. Bell replied.

"Pardon?" I looked at each for some sort of explanation.

"Medical school," Barker said. His late wife had been a physician. "If you hear hoofbeats, think horses, not zebras. It means more than likely there's a logical explanation. I do have one more question. About the phone call you made to the doctor."

"Accidental," he said. "I must have done it in my sleep."

"And yet, the video surveillance shows Dr. Watson actually speaking into the phone."

This was a bald-faced lie. It was too dark to actually see much of anything other than Dr. Watson putting the phone to his ear. I kept my expression neutral, but just when I thought Dr. Bell might answer, his attorney put up his hand, stopping him.

Barker wasn't having any of that. "Whatever that phone call was about, if it helps clear your client of murder, it'd be to his benefit to answer the question."

"I'm advising him not to answer."

"Okay, yes," the doctor said, earning a look of exasperation from his lawyer. "I did call him."

"About what?" Barker asked.

"He was going to turn me in to the medical licensing board for drug abuse. I wanted to beg him not to. It would ruin me."

"And then what?"

"He refused to listen. He just hung up."

"And then you killed him?"

"No! I was upstairs. I swear. I heard the garage open as he pulled into the driveway. That's when I called. It was right after that I heard the shot. And then I saw the zebra."

If Barker believed him, he gave no indication. He did, however, look at his watch, then me. "Do you think Mrs. Watson will give us access to the house once more?"

"As mentioned, she's been very cooperative. I don't see why not."

He turned toward Dr. Bell. "I think I can clear up everything, if you're willing to meet back at the house tonight, say nine-fifteen?"

"Absolutely not," his attorney said.

Barker pushed back his chair and stood. "Feel free to show up should you change your mind. We'll be passing on the same info to Mrs. Watson."

Dr. Bell glanced at his lawyer, who shook his head.

Bell gave a tepid smile. "Sorry. My attorney advises me not to."

"You realize he's an addict?" I asked Barker as we drove back to his office. "Assuming Bell actually saw a zebra, he was obviously hallucinating, or prepping for the diminished capacity defense."

"So it would seem. I'll need a few hours to put together some equipment. Better call Mrs. Watson and her attorney. Tell her we'll be there around nine-fifteen tonight. And bring a camera that will photograph in low light."

"Maybe Bell will change his mind."

"Not sure his attorney will let him."

Barker was already at the Watson home, standing at the back of his car, when I pulled up later that night. He lifted his hand, shielding his eyes until I shut off my headlights. "You brought the camera?"

I held up the canvas bag that I'd checked out from one of the evidence techs at work. "Right here."

He hauled out a large, hard-sided case from the open trunk.

"What's that?" I asked.

"Portable light." He nodded out toward the driveway, where the landscaping lights cast a dim glow across the scuff marks on the pavers. "I want to see what Dr. Watson saw that night. Do me a favor. Stand on the porch."

I did as he asked.

Barker found an exterior outlet, plugged in a long extension cord, then looked at the scuff marks on the driveway. "Approximating the position of where Dr. Watson stopped his Mercedes . . . it seems the left headlight of his car would have been shining toward the entryway . . ." He positioned his light on its stand then turned it toward me. "If you were going to shoot someone from just outside the front door, could you see?"

I squinted against the bright light. "Not from here." I moved out a few feet. "From here, maybe."

Barker nodded. "Don't forget the driver's door was open in the video. Since there was no broken glass, the killer had to have been standing inside the garage, out of sight of the camera. And in a position to shoot inside that open car door."

We both glanced in that direction, then up at the security camera mounted over the garage. Just above were the two windows of the room Dr. Bell had allegedly been occupying at the time of the murder.

Mrs. Watson opened the door, holding what looked like a gin and tonic. Judging from the look in her eye, it wasn't her first of the night. She saw Barker's spotlight on its stand, asked us what it was for. When he told her it was approximating a headlight, she said, "Wouldn't it have been easier just to pull your car into the driveway?"

"The stand is set to the same height, the spotlight the same lumens as a headlight on your husband's Mercedes." He looked past her. "Is your attorney here?"

"He's running late."

"When he arrives, we'd like to take another look at the guestroom where Dr. Bell was sleeping."

"Have at it. Who knows when he'll be here." She glanced out into the driveway at Barker's setup. "I'll be in the living room."

She left the front door open, leaving us to our work.

I returned my attention to Barker. "What is it you want me to do?"

"Go up to the guest room. When I call, stay on the line, and I'll tell you when to start the timer."

"We both already timed it."

Barker, setting up his spotlight in the driveway, glanced in my direction. "Humor me. Don't forget the lowlight camera."

I patted the case and headed inside, catching a glimpse of Mrs. Watson staring out the window as she sipped her gin and tonic. I continued down the hall, up the stairs, then entered the room over the garage.

Barker called my cell phone shortly thereafter. "Ready?"

"For what, I'm not sure."

"Start the timer and hang tight . . ."

I glanced out the window through the slatted blinds, seeing Barker moving his light toward the street. Suddenly I was blinded as he angled it up—I assumed to mimic the headlight that had shone directly into the security camera.

"What do you see?" he asked.

"Besides a blinding light?"

The phone to my ear, I looked away, my night vision effectively ruined by staring out the window into Barker's simulated headlight. As I turned back to the room, I stopped at the sight of a massive zebra on the wall, its head rising onto the ceiling exactly as Dr. Bell had described and sketched. It was clearly a pattern from the spotlight shining up into the room through the slats of the wooden blinds. "You're not going to believe this . . ."

"Stop the timer and take a picture. I'll meet you up there."

I did as he asked, checking the digital screen to make sure the photo recorded. I took another from the far side of the room to get the full effect, then brought up my copy of the zebra that Dr. Bell had sketched for us. "How'd you know?" I asked Barker when he walked into the room.

He leaned toward me, looking from the sketch to the zebra on the wall. "As I suspected, there had to be a logical explanation. Other than the zebra being an inverted version, I'd say his drawing is spot on."

It most certainly was. "So it proves he saw a zebra on the wall—"

"—caused by the left headlight of Dr. Watson's Mercedes."

"Which means what? Maybe he'd seen it before from another car. Decided to bring it up now as his excuse."

"I highly doubt it," Barker said, taking one last look then heading from the room. He glanced back at me as he stood at the top of the stairs. "That zebra proves that Mrs. Watson was lying."

"Lying about what?" Mrs. Watson said. She now stood at the bottom of the steps, her gin and tonic in hand.

"There was no way you could have seen Dr. Bell downstairs. He was up in that room, looking at a zebra."

"He must have gone out this door here to the garage," she replied.

I trailed down the stairs after Barker.

"Follow me to the driveway," he said. "I'll show you."

The three of us stepped out the front door, looking down the driveway to where Barker had set up his spotlight to represent one of the headlights of Dr. Watson's Mercedes after it had backed into the ditch.

Barker walked up to the light and stood next to it. "The only time Dr. Bell could have seen that zebra was after the shot was fired, after your husband's car had backed into the ditch, thereby raising the angle of the headlight."

"Then he must have run back upstairs, seen it, and run back down again."

"A physical impossibility in the time given."

I realized that Barker was correct. Dr. Bell would've had to have been in two places at one time in order to see the zebra *and* be the killer. "When you hear hoofbeats . . ."

"What does that mean?" Mrs. Watson asked.

I pulled out my handcuffs. "It means you're under arrest for the murder of Dr. Watson."

# MR. HOMES, I PRESUME?

## A BRIEF INTRODUCTION TO SHIT-TALK HOMES

*by Joe Hill*

The first Syd "Shit-Talk" Homes adventure, *Dying is Easy*, appeared as a series of five comic books, published over the winter of 2019–20. I wrote the scripts and Martin Simmonds provided the lush, neon-soaked visuals. Unless you happened to have read *that* story, you're coming to Syd fresh, and it might help to know a little about him before you start *this* story.

The Shit-Talk Mysteries take place in the midnineties, in the last years before everyone had a smartphone in their pockets (smartphones are a pain in the ass for fair-play mystery writers). Syd served twelve years on the police force of an unnamed East Coast city, three of them in homicide. He left trailing an ethical stink, got divorced, and decided to take a shot at his first love, stand-up comedy. Is he any good? That depends on what makes you laugh—if you enjoy bitter, grisly cop jokes, he's your man.

Syd's old habits die hard and he finds himself solving cases off the books to stay on top of his bar tab. In that way, he's a clear descendant of Lawrence Block's heart-worn and alcoholic ex-cop Matthew Scudder (the best of the Scudder stories might be a novel called *When the Sacred Ginmill Closes*, which I think should've won a National Book Award). But of course, there's also Syd's not-very-nice nickname, which is, of course, a deeply juvenile riff on Sherlock Holmes.

I grew up on Doyle's tales of murder by gaslight, when I was thirteen years old and nothing fired my imagination more. I had a deal with my parents: bedtime was at nine, but if I was in bed and reading, I could stay up until ten. I soon discovered I could read a standalone Holmes mystery in exactly an hour (it took four evenings to complete one of the novels). I finished the complete run of the tales in just over two months and immediately started again. Then I moved on to Holmes adventures by other writers. *The Seven-Per-Cent Solution* by Nicholas Meyer sticks out in my memory as a particular favorite. I never missed an episode of the Holmes adaptations that ran on PBS, starring Jeremy Brett, a man who could've stepped right out of one of the Sidney Paget illustrations that accompanied the original stories in *The Strand* magazine. I even had a deerstalker cap, and it's possible I sometimes wore it in the privacy of my own bedroom. Somewhere along the line I discovered there was a private club named The Baker Street Irregulars, after Holmes' private spy network of street urchins. Limited to just a few hundred members, the Irregulars met once a year for a feast and talks on Holmes-adjacent subjects: infamous 19th-century murders, undetectable poisons, Victorian conspiracies, and the like. There was a rumor the New York City branch held their meetings in a secret library that could only be accessed through a door hidden behind a bookcase.

As it happens, editors Laurie King and Leslie Klinger are quite the Sherlockians themselves. When they asked if I'd contribute a story to their new Holmes anthology, it only made sense to pull Martin Simmonds into things, and whip up a new mystery about our Syd. Besides, they could also offer me something better than money: an entrée to the Irregulars. When you have an opportunity to give such a gift to your thirteen-year-old self, I think you should always go for it.

I wish I could tell you if the Irregulars really *do* meet in a private library hidden behind a bookcase, but you don't go blabbing secrets about a secret society *this* interested in getting away with murder. Shit-Talk Homes can't help running his mouth. The author, however, knows better.

Joe Hill,
Exeter, New Hampshire,
May 2020

**DYING IS EASY**

*Shit-Talk Homes*, The Insulting Detective, in…

## *"RACHE" IS GERMAN FOR REVENGE*

Written by
Joe Hill

Illustrated by
Martin Simmonds

Lettered by
Shawn Lee

Edited by
Chris Ryall

RUTGER! WHAT THE FUCK?
CHRIST ON A CRACKER! JESUS, RUTGER.
WHY'D YOU GOTTA DO THAT TO YOURSELF?

SEPTEMBER 1995

RUTGER BöTTCHER? THE OLD GERMAN GUY? WHY?
DUNNO. NO NOTE. WE DON'T GOT MUCH TO GO ON...
...BUT WHAT WE DO KNOW IS CREEPY AS FUCK.
BöTTCHER CAME OUT HERE TO GO TO WORK... HAD ONE LOOK AT HIS CAR...
...AND WENT RIGHT BACK INSIDE TO HANG HIMSELF WITH HIS BELT.
IT'S GERMAN, YOU KNOW.
Hello friend
RACHE

FUCK'S IT MEAN?
"RACHE" IS GERMAN... FOR REVENGE.
LOOKS LIKE SOMEONE MADE HIM A SUGGESTION AND HE DECIDED TO TAKE IT.
MAYBE BECAUSE HE WAS MORE WORRIED ABOUT WHAT WOULD HAPPEN TO HIM IF HE DIDN'T.
OR MAYBE HE SUDDENLY REALIZED HIS CAR IS A FILTHY SHITBOX AND INSTEAD OF DRIVING IT TO THE WASH, HE SAID 'FUCK IT,' AND DECIDED TO TAKE THE EASY WAY OUT.
YEAH, I CAN RELATE.
I FEEL THE SAME WAY EVERY TIME ANOTHER CAR PAYMENT'S DUE.

YOU OKAY MILT?
I KNEW SOMETHING WAS WRONG. SOON AS HE WENT BACK INSIDE.
I SEE HIM EVERY MORNING. HE SITS ON THE BACKSTEP AND SMOKES ONE OF HIS LITTLE GERMAN CIGARETTES AND DOES THE CROSSWORD BEFORE HE GOES TO WORK.
SOMETIMES I HELP HIM WITH THE PUZZLE WHILE I'M STRETCHING OUT—BEFORE I GO FOR MY WALK.
"I WAS DOIN MY LUNGES WHEN HE FINISHED HIS BUTT AND GOT UP TO GO.
"BUT THEN HE JUST FROZE, STANDING NEXT TO HIS CAR. STOOD THERE STARING AT IT—AT THAT AWFUL SHIT WRITTEN IN THE DUST.
"HE DIDN'T MOVE FOR HALF A MINUTE. I WAS SCAIRT HE WAS HAVING A STROKE!"

I ASK'T HIM WHAT WAS WRONG. HE JUST HANDED ME HIS CROSSWORD AND TOLD ME TO FINISH IT FOR HIM.
HE WENT STRAIGHT BACK IN AND PUT HIS GODDAMN NECK IN HIS OWN BELT.
WE BEEN FRIENDS TWENTY YEARS... EVER SINCE HE MOVED HERE FROM MASSACHUSETTS.
WE HAD A LOT IN COMMON. WE BOTH WORKED CONSTRUCTION—HE USED TO POUR CEMENT, I USED TO HANG DRYWALL. WE DRANK THE SAME KINDA BEER!
WE BOTH HAD WIVES RUN OUT ON US. MINE TOOK OFF TO CALIFORNIA WITH HER PSYCHIC. HIS HOOKED UP WITH THEIR LAWYER AND DISAPPEARED.
WE BOTH LIKED THE FIGHTS. WE WATCHED 'EM ON THE HBO. WE BOTH WAS IN THE WAR... DIFFERENT SIDES, OF COURSE.
I USED TO RIB HIM, CALL HIM AN OL' NAZI, BUT HE WAS JUST REGULAR GERMAN ARMY. RADIO OPERATOR.
HE TOLD ME HE KNEW THE WAR WAS OVER WHEN WE GOT INTO IT. HE SAW LOUIS ANNIHILATE SCHMELING IN '38.
HE SAID GERMANS DIDN'T KNOW ANYONE IN THE WORLD COULD HIT LIKE THAT. LIKE AN AMERICAN.

OH, LOOK.
IT'S MY FAVORITE EX-COP, SYD HOMES, TAMPERING WITH EVIDENCE AND MEDDLING WITH MY WIT'.
Backyard excavation of a Brockton swimming pool unearths two corpses; police believed to have identified victims.
AREN'T YOU A FUNNY MAN NOW? YOU WANNA PRETEND YOU'RE STILL A COP, WHY'N'T YOU LAUNCH AN INVESTIGATION INTO WHY NO ONE LAUGHS WHEN YOU'RE ONSTAGE.
SUMMA US GOT CRIMES TO SOLVE.
DAILY NEWS
NATO LAUNCHES STRIKE
YEAH, HOW'S THAT GOING, HOWIE?
YOU FIGURED OUT WHO LEFT BöTTCHER THE SINISTER MESSAGE ON HIS CAR?
IN 20 YR OLD

RIGHT NOW, MY MONEY IS ON MOSSAD.
I THINK THEY WERE ABOUT TO DROP THE NET ON THE EVIL NAZI FUCK.
YOU KNOW WHAT "RACHE" MEANS IN GERMAN?
YEAH. SPEAKING OF MYSTERIES, YOU KNOW WHAT MYSTIFIES ME?
THE IDEA THAT JENNIFER ANISTON WOULD EVER DATE A HOUND-DOG-LOOKIN SAD-SACK-OF-SHIT LIKE DAVID SCHWIMMER. ONLY ON TV, RIGHT?
LET ME SAVE YOU THE TROUBLE OF CALLING MOSSAD AND EMBARRASSING YOURSELF.

YOU WANNA FIND THE SINISTER AGENTS WHO LEFT THAT HANGED MAN ON BÖTTCHER'S CAR? THEY'RE OVER THERE. GO GET 'EM, JOE FRIDAY.
THE ONE ABOUT YOU SMELLING LIKE A DOG...
THE ONE ABOUT WHEN I KILLED YOUR PET FROG...
LISTEN TO HER. SHE'S MAKING UP TITLES FOR FRIENDS... YOU KNOW, THE TV SHOW.
DAILY NEWS
NATO LAUNC
STRIKE
"RACHE" IS ALSO ONE LETTER SHORT OF RACHEL, THE ANISTON CHARACTER.
JESUS, YOU GUYS. THIS IS WHY BEAT COPS SHOULDN'T GET THEMSELVES CONFUSED WITH DETECTIVES. IT'S A GAME OF HANGMAN.
BÖTTCHER PROBABLY DIDN'T EVEN NOTICE IT.
HE WASN'T LOOKING AT THE CAR. HE WAS LOOKING AT HIS PAPER.
DAILY N
NATO LAUNCHES STRIKE

GRISLY EVIDEN
IN 20 YR OLD
MISSING PERSONS CASE
"BÖTTCHER MOVED HERE TWENTY YEARS AGO, FROM MASSACHUSETTS, AFTER HIS WIFE DISAPPEARED WITH HER LOVER.
Hello friend
RACHE
"HE USED TO WORK IN CONCRETE. HAVE A LOOK WHAT THEY JUST DUG OUT FROM UNDER A CONCRETE-LINED SWIMMING POOL IN BROCKTON.
"I MIGHTA JUST WRITTEN IT OFF AS COINCIDENCE, BUT THERE'S NO DOUBT BÖTTCHER'S FROM BROCKTON."
DAILY NEWS
NATO LAUNCHES STRIKE
CHECK OUT THAT ROCKY MARCIANO TAT ON HIS ARM. BROCKTON'S HOMETOWN CHAMP. FORTY-NINE AND OH.
IF YOU WANNA PRACTICE BEING A BIG TIME DETECTIVE, GO AHEAD AND FINISH TODAY'S CROSSWORD.
IT'S A MONDAY PUZZLE. THOSE ARE EASIEST.
SHOULD BE RIGHT YOUR SPEED.
THE ONE ABOUT HOW YOU AIN'T GOT NO CLUE...
THE ONE ABOUT HOW THIS TIME EVERYONE IS LAUGHIN' AT YOU...
DAILY NEWS
NATO LAUNCHES STRIKE
FIN!

# THE OBSERVANCE OF TRIFLES

## *by Martin Edwards*

### AN IRREGULAR BLOG OF SHERLOCKIAN ARCANA, CURATED BY FREDERICK PORLOCK

*1 April*

***Book Review: Five Pillows and an Ounce of Shag, by Shinwell Johnson (Hyperbole Press)***

The appearance of Shinwell Johnson's first new book in three years is a major event, not merely in the dusty libraries of Sherlockian scholarship but in the wider world of publishing. This is a book destined to sell by the dumpster-load to general readers with no more than a passing interest in the Sage of Baker Street, as well as to lifelong fans. We have these assurances on the authority of the publishers themselves, and for all that their name is well-chosen, I don't doubt that they are right.

Encomia from leading writers swarm across the back of the dust wrapper while Benedict Cumberbatch exclaims with rapture from the front cover. Unconfirmed rumours hint at Banksy's hand in the artwork that adorns the endpapers. The publicity blitz has encompassed not only tonight's book launch but also podcasts and promotional videos galore, to say nothing of a blizzard of advertising posters along escalators at London Underground stations. There is even an accompanying app, said to reflect Shinwell Johnson's fascination with computers and technology. As for the book's sly title, calculated to tease and titillate those casting a casual glance along the supermarket shelves, followers of this blog (a small and select band who are by definition well-read) will recognize Johnson's knowing wink at "The Man with the Twisted Lip."

Those same loyal students of Sherlockian arcana will forgive me if I deny (or spare) them a detailed survey of the contents of this weighty tome. Suffice to say that we have been presented with a specimen of classic Johnson. Notwithstanding florid claims in the press release of breathtaking erudition and original insights, this book offers the familiar eclectic brew of snappy one-liners, Delphic allusions, questionable assumptions, and encyclopedic footnote knowledge. We have come to expect nothing less from (I quote directly from Hyperbole's excitable director of publicity) "the world's foremost expert on fiction's greatest character."

Disguise is a recurrent theme in the book, just as it is the thread running through the colorless skein of Johnson's life. The true identity of the author is a puzzle. He remains unknowable to the millions who hang on his every word, and his refusal to make public appearances has added to the mystique of the man who hides behind the name of the ex-convict from "The Adventure of the Illustrious Client"—a man who had "the *entrée* of every night club, doss house, and gambling den in the town."

The moody black-and-white author photograph represents the latest variation on a well-worn theme. We glimpse a figure emerging from the shadows of a London alleyway, yet masked from us by a gauze of mist. The biographical note rounds up the usual awards and screen adaptations. As regards Johnson's personal life, we are led to believe that he divides his time between Baker Street and Bohemia. Only those unacquainted with *The Sign of Four* will take at face value the suggestion that his interests include miracle plays, medieval pottery, Stradivarius violins, the Buddhism of Ceylon, and the warships of the future. Truly he is a compound of the Busy Bee and Excelsior. Yet we are given no explanation as to why an essentially slim volume (despite the book's apparent heftiness, the font is large and there are acres of white space) took three years to write. Might it be that the powers of "the most imaginative detective fiction scholar of the 21st century" are on the wane?

I should, at this point, give a modest cough and declare a personal interest. My own name is included in the acknowledgments, tucked away without comment on the tenth of eleven pages, in the middle of a paragraph mentioning twenty-nine individuals. To borrow a question from one of Sherlock's saintlier rivals: where would you hide a leaf? In a forest, naturally. My contribution is submerged in the torrent of fulsome expressions of gratitude to friends and correspondents from all over the world. A minor grievance? Well, it has long been an axiom of mine that the little things are infinitely the most important.

Although the two of us have never met, our careers have run in tandem. When this blog began at the dawn of the present century, Johnson—then unknown to fellow Sherlockians—commented on my very first post. At once it became apparent that we shared a love of all that is bizarre and outside the conventions and humdrum routine of literary scholarship. It has always been my habit to hide none of my researches, either from Johnson or from anyone who might take an intelligent interest in them. For a time we corresponded daily. Or at least, I did.

Since then, I have followed his relentless rise with interest. I hear of Shinwell Johnson everywhere. As regards the interpretative bravado on display in *Five Pillows and an Ounce of Shag*, anyone who cares to make a close examination of the text may identify methods of analysis whose origins are to be found in my postings or in my private correspondence with him. Perhaps when a man has special knowledge and powers like my own it rather encourages him to seek a complex explanation when a simpler one is at hand, but Johnson once drove me to remark that I'd be lost without my Boswell. His response was a smiley face emoji; how characteristic of his pawky sense of humor. Since then, he has never communicated with me, never replied to a single email, whatever time of day or night it was sent.

In the early days, Johnson and I briefly debated meeting in person. Jokingly—or was it?—he proposed a remote Alpine pass as an appropriate venue. This came to nothing, since I am not a social animal. Johnson quipped that he had the impression that I was something of an automaton, a calculating machine, with something positively inhuman in me at times. The innuendo was plain, and I took it as a compliment. Admittedly, I am a little queer in my ideas, while my personality approaches to cold-bloodedness. When he borrowed yet again from *A Study in Scarlet* to imply that I was as sensitive to flattery on the score of my academic analysis of the canon as any girl could be of her beauty, I could scarcely muster a denial. If a touch of conceit is good enough for the Great Detective, perhaps it is good enough for . . . well, I am tempted to say, his present-day incarnation.

My first trifling monograph, in which I analyzed the implications of 160 separate metaphors in the canon, remains perhaps my most important work of literary detection, although it gained scant attention. Even the solitary five-star review on Amazon focused exclusively on the prompt delivery of the print-on-demand edition. Twelve months later, Johnson's debut study, *Three-Pipe Problems,* was nominated for literary awards extending over many nations and three separate continents. The lowest and vilest literary hacks do not present a more dreadful record of logrolling than the smiling and beautiful celebrities who lined up to heap praise on the newcomer's work.

I do not claim that Johnson plagiarised my blog posts, but I sense that he has no keener pleasure than following me in my literary investigations and admiring the rapid deductions, as swift as intuitions and yet always founded on a logical basis, with which I unravel problems of the canon. The similarities evident in his work—his grasp of botany is variable, his geology profound solely as regards mudstains, his knowledge of sensational literature and crime record *almost* unique—are suggestive, if not downright sinister. He mimics my insistence on the importance of sleeves, the suggestiveness of thumbnails, and the great issues that may hang from a bootlace.

Yes, circumstantial evidence is a very tricky thing, but you can tell an old master by the sweep of his brush. I find it significant that in the early days of our correspondence, Johnson described me as the stormy petrel of Sherlockian studies. Beyond a doubt, he knows my methods—and applies them. He does not associate himself with any literary activity that does not tend toward the unusual, or even the fantastic. The inspiration he draws from me is plain. I have trained myself to see what others overlook. Some people, without possessing genius, have a remarkable power of stimulating it. Shinwell Johnson has sucked the vital essence out of my life's work, robbing me of the credit I deserve.

Forgive me. I have gone too far. Whilst I cannot agree with those who rank modesty among the virtues, to my sombre and cynical spirit all popular applause is always abhorrent. Nothing amuses me more than to read online reports of awards ceremonies that result in triumph for the essentially orthodox bon mots of Shinwell Johnson. Life is infinitely stranger than anything which the mind of man could invent.

Meanwhile, I have labored night and day without thought of monetary reward. My life is spent in one long effort to escape from the commonplaces of existence. I think that I may go so far as to say that I have not lived wholly in vain. If my record were closed tonight, I could still survey it with equanimity. The world of Sherlockian scholarship is sweeter for my presence. In over a thousand blog posts I am not aware that I have ever used my powers upon the wrong side. And yet . . .

Like all great artists, I live for my art's sake; not least because I have no choice. Small digital presses have been prepared to convert my monographs into ebooks, if not to pay an advance or to forward the small change of royalties more often than biannually. Of course, I have always lived alone. All emotions are abhorrent to my cold, precise, but admirably balanced mind. As a lover, I would have placed myself in a false position. I seldom take exercise for exercise's sake, and I look upon aimless bodily exertion as a waste of energy, seldom bestirring myself save where there is some academic object to be served. I spend my days lounging on the sofa in a purple dressing gown, a tab of white powder within my reach. My diet is usually of the sparest and my habits simple to the point of austerity. I sink into reveries and devour sandwiches at irregular hours.

Hence the cocaine. What is the use of having powers, when one has no readers? It is one of the peculiarities of my proud, self-contained nature that, though I docket any fresh slight very quickly and accurately in my brain, I seldom make any acknowledgment of the pain I suffer. The paradox is this: as Johnson's star has risen, my own has fallen. Yet I cannot live without Sherlockian scholarship. To let the brain work without sufficient material is like racing an engine. It racks itself to pieces. And yes, my mind *is* like a racing engine, tearing itself to pieces because it is not connected up with the work for which it was built. What else is there to live for?

Why does Fate play such tricks with poor helpless worms? Is not all life pathetic and futile? Is not my story a microcosm of the whole? We reach. We grasp. And what is left in our hands at the end? A shadow. Or worse than a shadow—misery. What is the meaning of it? What object is served by this circle of misery and violence and fear?

To suggest that I am rancid with jealousy would be absurd. The emotional qualities are antagonistic to clear reasoning. The truth is more prosaic. My iron constitution broke down under the strain of research which extended over two months, never working less than fifteen hours a day. Perhaps it is true that the example of patient suffering is in itself the most precious of all the lessons to an impatient world.

Life is infinitely stranger than anything which the mind of man could invent. If Sherlockians could fly out of their windows hand in hand, hover over this great city, gently remove my apartment roof and peep in at the queer things going on, the strange coincidences, the plannings, the cross-purposes, the wonderful chain of events, leading to the most outré results, it would render the whole of *Five Pillows and an Ounce of Shag* with all its conventionalities and foreseen conclusions most stale and unprofitable.

I once proposed to devote my declining years to the composition of a textbook which would focus the whole art of Sherlockian scholarship into one volume, but of late I have contemplated writing another little monograph on the keyboard and its relation to crime. It is a subject to which I have devoted some little attention, but on reflection it seems simpler to articulate my thoughts in a blog post. The blogosphere is a most valuable institution, if you only know how to use it. And to be candid, I have always had an idea that I would have made a highly efficient criminal. A complex mind—all great criminals have that.

Perhaps this is a point which has escaped Johnson's Machiavellian intellect. Allow me to be blunt—the highest type of man may revert to the animal if he leaves (or is diverted from) the straight road of destiny.

I know well that I have it in me to make my name famous. No man lives or has ever lived who has brought the same amount of study and natural talent to the study of Sherlockiana which I have. And what is the result? I have been elbowed aside by a charlatan.

If I call Johnson a criminal, I am uttering libel in the eyes of the law—and there lie the glory and the wonder of it! The greatest schemer of Holmesiana, the author of all manner of devilry—that's the man! But so aloof is he from general scorn, so immune from criticism, so admirable in his management and self-effacement, that for those very words I have uttered, he could hale me to a court and emerge with my life savings as a solatium for his wounded character. Is he not the celebrated author of *Jezail Bullets*, a book which ascends to such rarefied heights of scholarship that it is said that there was no man in the Sherlockian world capable of criticizing it? (Other than myself, of course; but nobody ever thinks to seek my opinions.) Is this a man to traduce? Foul-mouthed blogger and defamed literary icon—such would be our respective roles! That's genius, alas.

Thus I have determined that tonight, Shinwell Johnson will die. I may be committing a felony, but it is just possible that I am saving my soul.

Why kill Shinwell Johnson? Surely the answer is plain. How could one compare the ruffian, who in hot blood bludgeons his mate, with this man, who methodically and at his leisure tortures my soul and wrings my nerves in order to add to his already swollen money bags? There are certain crimes the law cannot touch, and which therefore justify private revenge. I had rather play tricks with the law of England than with my own conscience.

The launch party will be held on the roof of The Baker Street Hotel, one of London's trendiest spots. Johnson will, as is his custom, turn up in disguise. By claiming to detest personal attention, he thereby guarantees it. Inevitably, he seeks to mimic the Master. At his past three book launches he has appeared, respectively, as an Italian priest ("The Final Problem"), an asthmatic old master mariner (*The Sign of Four*), and a drunken-looking groom ("A Scandal in Bohemia"). But my eyes have been trained to examine faces and not their trimmings. It is the first quality of a criminal investigator that he should see through a disguise, and tonight, it will be the first quality of a criminal. Sauce for the goose is sauce for the gander. I would have made an actor and a rare one. I shall attend the launch adopting the persona of an Italian priest: in the circumstances, a tip of the hat to "The Final Problem" is in order.

How to commit the deed? The less said, perhaps, the better. I have always been exceedingly loth to communicate my full plans to anyone until the instance of their fulfillment. Suffice to say that I have a remarkable gift for improvisation, and it will be as well to have my pistol ready.

But I am not blind to the dangers of my intended course of action. Although I am determined to kill Shinwell Johnson, I recognise the risk that I may perish with him. And so I have scheduled this post for publication at midnight, come what may.

The game is afoot!

## COMMENTS

*Wiggins, 2 April 7:30 A.M.*
Hope I'm right in assuming this is an April Fool!

*Mrs. Hudson, 2 April 8:10 A.M.*
Haven't you seen the news? *Tragedy at Book Launch*

*Wiggins, 2 April 8:15 A.M.*
Sorry, that link isn't working . . .

*Mrs. Hudson, 2 April 8:17 A.M.*
Glitch with my laptop, sorry. Anyway, the gist is that poor Fred died at the hotel. He fell from the rooftop during the launch party. Apparently the drink was flowing and there was a bit of a kerfuffle. He launched an unprovoked assault on an elderly bookseller and tried to fling him over the parapet, although his

physical frailty meant he couldn't manage it. An old lady tried to save him, but in vain.

*Wiggins, 2 April 8:19 A.M.*
Oh no! R.I.P. He was quite well-read. A bit eccentric, maybe, but aren't we all?

*Mrs. Hudson, 2 April 8:25 A.M.*
Yes, he was a one-off. Not that I knew him personally, of course. And I never expected him to troll the great Shinwell. Such a shame that he was so bitter. Why can't we all just get along?

*Wiggins, 2 April 8:50 A.M.*
You don't think this post is some kind of elaborate hoax, a sort of playful suicide note?

*Mrs. Hudson, 2 April 9:40 A.M.*
That never occurred to me, but perhaps you're right. How awful. I'm just glad Shinwell wasn't at his own party. The report says he never showed up. Perhaps Fred threw himself off the roof in sheer despair. This review suggests he became rather unbalanced toward the end. Not that I like to speak ill of the dead, of course.

*Lestrade, 2 April 10:30 A.M.*
I've never understood this sentimentality about speaking ill of the dead. Surely it's much less painful than humiliating someone while they are still alive?

*Anonymous, 2 April 11:00 A.M.*
How true. And how much Shinwell Johnson might have said about Porlock, had he been so inclined. Especially when, not for the first time, he hacked into his computer, only to learn that the old buffer was contemplating his murder.

*Wiggins, 2 April 11:15 A.M.*
Really? This is all very strange, very mysterious.

*Anonymous, 2 April, 11:30 A.M.*
It is a mistake to confuse strangeness with mystery. Singularity is almost invariably a clue. As a rule, the more bizarre a thing is, the less mysterious it proves to be.

*Wiggins, 2 April, 11:35 A.M.*
I don't understand.

*Anonymous, 2 April, 11:40 A.M.*
Porlock deluded himself into believing he was Sherlock Holmes, when in truth he was a poor man's Peter Jones. Tenacious as a lobster if he gets his claws into anyone, but an absolute imbecile in his profession.

*Wiggins, 2 April, 11:35 A.M.*
A bit harsh, surely? Over the years Fred has really done very well indeed.

*Anonymous, 2 April, 11:40 A.M.*
He missed everything of importance. His final and fatal mistake was to identify a harmless bookseller as his adversary. Detection is, or ought to be, an exact science. He should have remembered that women are never to be entirely trusted—not the best of them.

*Wiggins, 2 April, 11:50 A.M.*
You don't mean that *the* woman . . . ? Extraordinary!

*Anonymous, 2 April, 12:00 P.M.*
Elementary.

# INFINITE LOOP

## *by Naomi Hirahara*

I heard of Michael Tanner's disappearance first from his mother.

It was about 10:30 P.M. Saturday evening and I was sitting at my desk in my single room, attempting to figure out what medical schools to apply to.

My phone rang underneath some brochures.

"Hello," I said into the receiver after maybe the fifth ring. As I pulled the phone cord, I almost toppled over my open can of Tab.

"Is this Joann Wat?" The woman on the other end sounded out of breath, as if she had climbed too many stairs, and her voice had a weird gurgle like phlegm was stuck in the back of her throat. She identified herself as Mitzi Tanner. "I'm Michael's mother. I think he's missing."

"How did you get my number?" I asked her. After all, I was a university dorm resident assistant, not some summer camp counselor in charge of the kiddies.

"Oh, your number is listed. I just called information."

I cursed myself for being too cheap to pay extra for my number to be unlisted. But I was a scholarship student on a budget.

"Michael always calls me at nine. I haven't heard from him since last night."

Oh my God, I thought to myself. Your son is a freshman at Stanford, majoring in computer science. And you are going to call me, the R.A., because he hasn't verbally checked in with you? I was stunned and, to be honest, a little envious. My parents operated a Chinese restaurant in Orange County, and during high school, my brothers and I were free laborers every weekend night when we weren't doing schoolwork. No one was keeping tabs on our well-being, then or now.

"Could you just check his room and the rest of the dorm and call me back? We are in Hollister."

I wasn't sure how to answer her. On the one hand, checking up on the residents was part of my job description, but to do it on behalf of parents encouraged too much codependence, at least that's what we learned in the mandatory Peer Counseling class we took during spring quarter. I told her that I would do what I could, which was the best that I could offer.

I looked out my window and saw one of the other R.A.s. He was walking down the pathway with two freshman women, probably his main incentive to work in a four-class dorm. I was responsible for the first floor, which was much smaller than the second and the third. Curiously, all the women on my floor were juniors and seniors while the men were all freshmen. Except the one single on the end. That was inhabited by a male junior, Shel Rock.

Shel was a strange one—always wore black, his hair was a platinum white, and he usually wore sunglasses, even on the rare occasion the peninsula was overcast. He owned a Roland Jupiter-8 synthesizer, a huge keyboard that dominated his single room. Lately, during midterms week, he started to play some obsessive, fever-pitched Philip Glass-type music that reminded me of the film *Koyaanisqatsi*, forcing me to pound on the door to quiet him down. I didn't care for *Koyaanisqatsi* in the movie theatre, and I didn't need a reprise of it in the dorms at two o'clock in the morning. Not surprisingly, he was a computer science major; I thought that he might even be a T.A. in one of Michael Tanner's classes.

I sighed and went to Michael's room and knocked. No answer. Michael was a bit socially awkward. Almost too honest and a little uptight. He wore a metal chain with a cross pendant, which sometimes peeked out from the OP T-shirts he liked to wear. He roomed with Patrick, a light-skinned black man who came from a high-profile prep school on the East Coast, and Jason, a white man with a bowl haircut who was from West Virginia but had no trace of a Southern accent. They were a strange combination. I didn't think they had become that close.

I went into the lounge to see if the three roommates were there. I wasn't surprised to find it empty. We weren't a party dorm. The more social residents went over to other housing facilities to have fun on Saturday nights.

I then walked over to Shel's room. I heard Pink Floyd's "The Dark Side of the Moon" through the door. Although it was 1982, everyone at Stanford seemed to reject Top 40 songs for classic rock—The Rolling Stones, Crosby, Stills & Nash, Grateful Dead—and in Shel Rock's case, Pink Floyd.

I knocked.

No answer.

I knocked louder. "Shel," I said. "It's Joann Wat. The R.A."

"Yeah."

I tried to open the door, but it was locked. He finally opened the door, a haze of marijuana smoke emanating from his room. There was a line of bongs on his dresser. Prisms the shape of pyramids, reminiscent of one of Pink Floyd's record covers, were lined up on a high shelf on the wall. What the hell was this guy into? A part of me was fascinated by Shel's iconoclasm. I, on the other hand, had been always careful to toe the line, at least in public. I wondered what it would feel like to be more on the edge, to be surprising and dangerous.

"I wonder if you've seen Michael Tanner."

He said nothing and blew out a stream of smoke.

"Michael Tanner. You know him. He lives down the hall. The one with the curly hair." I'm sure you've seen him pissing in the urinal next to you, I thought. "I think you're his T.A."

"Michael Tanner. Lapsed Catholic who goes to Memorial Church on campus because the Episcopalians are the closest Protestant religious group to the Catholics. Only child who has an oedipal relationship to his mother. Wears unfashionable shorts that should be outlawed. I'm not his T.A. and I don't know where he is," he said and shut the door.

I shrugged my shoulders.

When I returned to my room, I called Mrs. Tanner back and her answering machine picked up. "Mrs. Tanner, it's Joann Wat. Michael is not around the dorm, but I'm sure he's alright. He may be at the computer lab. It never closes." The tape cut me off before I could say anything more.

It was going to be a long night. I took out my red electric hot pot and got ready to make some ramen.

The next morning at around 8:30 A.M., my phone rang. I fumbled for the receiver.

"Hello."

"Miss Wat, it's Michael's mother. No one's answering Michael's room phone."

Fuck.

"Michael's father and I will be leaving after Mass to drive over to the dormitory."

"Mrs. Tanner, I don't think that will be necessary. Many students let out some steam right now. It's Michael's first time going through midterms."

"But it's not like Michael."

If you're so damn worried, call the area hospitals, I thought, but Mrs. Tanner already had that covered.

"We've called the Stanford Hospital and other medical facilities in the area. No one fits his description. We'll be there around one."

Michael had told us ad nauseum about his hometown, Hollister—it was known as an intersection of two major fault lines and had been rattled by hundreds of temblors. I knew it as a drive-over territory in the middle of the

Pacheco Pass, which linked together the new Interstate 5 and the 101, on my drives to and from Stanford and Orange County. Hollister was about an hour's drive away from campus.

I walked outside my room in my sweats to brush my teeth in the women's bathroom across the way, muttering "shit" under my breath.

"No sign of him?" Shel stood a few feet away from me in his signature black button-down shirt and jeans and sunglasses.

I was startled. "You're up early," I said. In fact, I never remembered ever seeing Shel walking through the dorm during daylight. "His parents are coming. They'll be here at one." I went into the bathroom and began brushing my teeth at one of the sinks. I looked like hell, but that wasn't unusual. When I came out with my wet toothbrush, cup, and rolled-up toothpaste, Shel was waiting for me in the hallway.

"You have keys, right? To get into our rooms," he said.

"I'm only supposed to use them in an emergency. Maybe I should report Michael's disappearance to the campus police first." I should have also informed our resident fellow, a gay Marxist professor who didn't like to be bothered by matters like this any more than I did.

"Do you always play by the rules?" Shel challenged me more than inquired.

I figured that the Tanners would end up insisting that I open the door, anyway. I might as well know what I'm in for.

I found the master key and went to Michael, Patrick, and Jason's room, which was in the corner by the doorway to our lounge. I had gone in there a few times, first when they were moving in and later to inform them of a social activity or educational dorm program. I knocked loudly and called each one of their names. No answer. I took a deep breath and used the master key to unlock the door. Shel was right behind me as I walked in. It was set up like most of the dorms originally built in the 1970s. Two desks arranged in an L against the near wall. In the connecting room there was bunk bed on the left and then opposite it a long twin bed where Michael slept. His desk and set of drawers were right behind it.

It was relatively neat, at least neater than my single. Patrick had his Western Civilization books lined up on a proper bookshelf. I remember that he told me that he had read most of the classics in high school. Jason's engineering books were stacked on his desk. Michael had resorted to the old standard—cinder blocks and wood planks. Aside from the requisite dirty laundry piled on Jason's and Michael's chairs, the only visible eyesore was a pile of computer paper spilling from Michael's desk to the floor.

Shel checked the closets and studied the floor where shoes were piled up. Then he went to Michael's set of drawers. There was a Velcro wallet with a ten-dollar bill on top. And a set of keys attached to his Stanford ID. "He's left his wallet, keys, and school ID," Shel said. "That's a bad sign."

What the hell. What did he know about bad signs? Was he an expert on bad signs? On second thought, maybe he was.

Shel then took a look at the dot matrix printing on the multiple feet of continuous computer paper, holes along the edges. He studied the whole formula from beginning to end. "All infinite loops. The guy is a hopeless idiot or a genius."

I never took computer science classes, so I wasn't quite sure what Shel was talking about. My ignorance must have been apparent, because he added, "An infinite loop is when the computer programmer writes faulty code, mostly unintentionally. Here Michael wrote a program that causes a loop to start over from the beginning."

"So there's no end?"

Shel shook his head. "It's continuous. Sometimes you want that to happen, like in a video game."

"Well, maybe this means that he was in the computer laboratory last night," was all I could offer.

"He and his roommates partied last night. Ingested about a line of cocaine and smoked about eight joints between them."

"How do you know this?"

"Because I sold it to the preppy one. The black kid with the freckles. Patrick, I think his name is. He said he was buying it for Michael. I gave him ten bucks in change and the bill is here on his wallet."

For a second, I didn't know how to respond. Shel confirmed my suspicions and obviously wasn't worried about divulging his criminal activity to me.

Maybe because he had figured that I didn't want to rock the boat. I wasn't concerned with bettering Stanford undergrads' lives. I just wanted to earn my keep with the least amount of hassle while maintaining a high enough GPA to get me into medical school.

"You're responsible then. You sold him drugs."

"He bought it. I didn't force him, too. He could have just said, 'no.'" Shel quoted the First Lady's antidrug slogan.

I cursed again.

"So, what you are going to do? Report me to campus police? And then I'll report everyone that I've sold to, which includes about a dozen people in this dorm, including the R.A. on the second floor. It will be quite a scandal."

"Damn it," I murmured. "Well then, help me. We have less than three hours before the Tanners arrive."

We were leaving the boys' room when Jason appeared, his eyes bloodshot and his helmet hair unchanged.

"What's going on?" he said. I couldn't tell if he was wearing the same clothes from last night, because he was always outfitted in a nondescript polo-style shirt and jeans.

"Jason, have you been with Michael?" I asked.

"Why?"

"Michael's parents haven't heard from him since Friday. They're on their way to check up on him."

"Shit."

Shel intervened. "We know you three were partying last night. Tell us where you went."

"We kind of lost him."

"You mean you and Patrick," I clarified.

"We were at ZAP and he disappeared."

ZAP was a self-op housing unit on the other end of campus that was notorious for its laughing gas parties.

"And you didn't bother to look for him?" I asked.

"Well—"

"You were high," Shel said.

"Where's Patrick?" It was quite apparent that I wasn't going to get any work done today.

"In the dining room."

All three of us walked through the lounge to the cafeteria that fed residents from not only our dormitory but also other dormitories in Flo Mo, short for Florence Moore.

Patrick sat as clean-shaven as ever at one of the tables with some other male residents. On his tray was a bowl of Cheerios and a cup of black coffee. He quickly figured out by the looks on faces that something was wrong and got up with his tray. "What's up?" he said placing his bowl, still filled with milk and cereal, on the conveyer belt leading down to the kitchen. He held onto the white ceramic cup of coffee.

The four of us went into the lounge. "Michael is missing," I announced to Patrick. "And his parents will be here in less than three hours."

Patrick didn't seem bothered in the slightest as he sat on the leather couch. "He's not in our room?" he innocently asked, taking a sip of his coffee.

"Cut the crap, Patrick. We know you were all smoking pot and doing lines of cocaine."

"Just one line, and only Michael did it."

I widened my eyes. Patrick was not as smart as he thought himself to be.

"Okay, okay." Patrick placed his mug on the weathered coffee table. "Michael came from the computer lab a total mess. He kept saying that he was a failure and he couldn't get out of this infinite loop. I told him to calm down. I felt sorry for the guy. You know that his mother expects him to call every night at nine o'clock? I told him to fuck it. I suggested we get high. The three of us. We went over to ZAP because I heard that they were having a laughing gas party. I figured they wouldn't notice us getting high in a corner."

"And then you left him?" I took a seat on the couch beside him.

"He said that he was hungry. Once I noticed that he wasn't around, I went into the kitchen and he wasn't there."

"Wasn't in Terra, either," Jason added. Terra, the hippie self-op, was also located in the Cowell Cluster and known for residents baking fresh bread at strange hours. "You're not going to tell on us, are you, Joann?"

I looked at their faces and sighed. There was no easy way out of this.

I told Patrick and Jason to go back to their dorm room in case Michael returned. "We'll go over to ZAP to see if anyone has seen him," I said and went back to my room to get my car keys and wallet.

"I guess 'we' includes me." Shel had emerged from his room in his trademark black trench coat and was following me out the side door to the parking lot in the back of our dorm.

I walked up to my car, a tan Toyota Tercel. Shel seemed reluctant to get in. "This is an ugly vehicle."

I got into the driver's seat, with Shel pulling his long legs into the passenger's side.

Once I started the car, he started peppering me with questions. "So how long have you been dating your boyfriend?"

I gave him a side eye.

"You're in a long-distance relationship; it's obvious."

"How's that?"

"You're reasonably attractive and I don't see anyone coming out of your room late at night or early in the morning. I see you riding your bike to the post office regularly with a letter or package in your basket and also returning with a letter."

"Are you spying on me?"

"Just observing. I observe everyone. I wasn't quite sure if you were straight, lesbian, or bi, but based on this car, I figure you are straight. Only a straight person would own this kind of car."

I didn't get his logic on that one, but it's wasn't worth pursuing. "What else do you know about me?"

"That you really don't care about the students on your floor."

Now that shocked me. I steered the Tercel too close to the curb and quickly readjusted.

"I don't mean that as a bad thing. I'm thankful for it. You've never tried to stop my business transactions."

"I didn't know that you were selling drugs out of your dorm room."

"Well, you didn't really try to find out, either. You're pretty fixated on your personal future."

I tried to pretend what he said had no effect on me, but his assessment did sting. Mostly because it was true.

I pulled into the parking lot of the Cowell Cluster. Unlike the case of most living halls, the lot was fairly expansive, with a number of open spots.

We both got out and made our way to one of the wood two-story structures. ZAP was on the far end. It was past eleven, but it seemed like the residents were just getting up, dragging themselves into the light in furry bathrobes and red Stanford sweatshirts. The main living area looked like a war zone. Laughing gas cartridges littered the shag rug like metal flowers. I recognized one of the residents, a blonde chemistry major who was in some of my same classes. "Lauren—"

She lifted her head from the couch and cringed as if my voice was hurting her ears.

"Oh, hi, Joann."

"Listen, I'm looking for one of my freshman students who was here last night at your party."

"Hmmmm?"

Shel butted in to show her Michael's Stanford ID. That was good thinking on his part to bring that, I had to admit.

"Oh, that kid. Yeah, he was hungry so I told him to go to the Teahouse. You know, right by Okada House?" Okada House was the Asian American theme house in Wilbur.

As soon as Lauren mentioned the Teahouse and Okada House, I felt my stomach sink.

"I really don't want to go to that dorm," I told Shel as we left ZAP.

"You lived there freshman year."

"How the hell did you know that?"

"You mentioned it during one of the first dorm meetings. Back when you were peppy."

I had momentarily lost my mind and transformed into a cheerleading R.A. during the first week of the school year. My euphoria wore off by the second week.

We decided to leave the Tercel in the Cowell Cluster parking lot and walk to the Teahouse.

"Why are you selling drugs?" I asked Shel. "Do you need the money?"

"I like to fulfill a demand. It's basic economics. I have the supply; why not share it?"

"But what are you going to do when you graduate?"

"I may graduate or I may not."

"What is wrong with you? Don't you have any goals in life? I mean, you must have to get in here."

"I consult on the side."

"What kind of consulting?"

"I consult on whatever is needed. When companies or individuals need an outside perspective. A thinker for hire."

*Okay*, I thought, *whatever*.

"You don't have to go along with what's expected," he said.

"What do you mean?"

"Doctor. Chinese immigrants' daughter. Isn't that almost a stereotype?"

"That's some B.S. You don't know me."

"Do you know yourself?"

I gave him a hard look. I hated people who made those kinds of comments. "Let me go to the Teahouse solo. It'll work out better that way."

The Teahouse was located in a narrow space in between a couple of dorms. A student space for the Okada House, it served *char siu bao*, ramen, and almond cookies for students who had late-night food cravings. I didn't think anyone would be there, but the door to the Teahouse was open, revealing a tall metal coffee maker on the counter. A Japanese curtain was hung across the top of the doorway.

A lanky figure was pulling out plastic trash bags overfilled with paper bowls and cups. Of course, it had to be Rick Chang. Responsible, dependable Rick. He looked the same except for a couple days' growth above his upper lip.

"What are you doing here?" he asked.

"A freshman from my dorm is missing. I heard that he maybe came here to eat."

"So you are R.A.ing. Where?"

"Cardenal in Flo Mo."

"Oh, pretty mellow." Rick was still holding onto the plastic trash bag. "So does this take you back?"

I looked around nervously. I hadn't lived in Okada House since my freshman year.

"You still with him? The guy you met in England."

I nodded.

"He already graduated though, right?"

"He's in Missouri. Med school."

Rick shook his head. "Of course. What else? That's the thing about you, Joann. You never change."

His comment was meant as a criticism and was taken as such.

"Oh, by the way, that freshman from Cardenal—Michael something, right? He was here. He was high as a kite. Talking religion. That he needed to be baptized again."

I frowned. I hoped that his destination wasn't our campus man-made lake or a hot tub in one of the neighboring apartment units. I asked Rick some more questions, but he had nothing else to say about Michael.

"Hey," he called out to me before I left. "Don't be a stranger, okay?"

There was something in his voice that shook me. A yearning that I hadn't felt before.

"You seem a bit upset," Shel said as I joined him back in front of the dorm.

"I didn't want to come here, I told you." I was pissed. "Why did you have to sell Michael Tanner drugs?"

"You know that you aren't the center of the universe."

"Excuse me?"

"The world doesn't revolve around Joann Wat." He gestured with his spindly arms. "People do things that is in their interest. It may not serve your purposes but that's irrelevant."

What the hell? I wanted to pull off his stupid sunglasses and crush them underneath my Nikes.

"So what did your former boyfriend say?"

I ignored his reference to Rick. "He said that Michael found religion and wanted to be baptized again." I then gave voice to my worst fear. "Maybe he's drowned in Lake Lagunita."

"No, that's highly unlikely."

Shel's brash pronouncement managed to mollify me for a moment.

"It's too dark to get over there at night. He's more likely to get run over by a car."

"Thanks, that's comforting."

"You said that he wasn't found in any hospitals."

We had a difference of opinion on where to search next. I insisted that we go to Mem Chu—Memorial Church—the ornate cathedral that Leland and Jane Stanford built in memory of their dead son, the father's namesake. "You're the one who said he goes here," I said.

"He's not going to be in there right now," he said. We peeked in its majestic doors and sure enough, the Sunday service was in session. I saw a priest in a red robe standing on a high podium, the stunning stained glass of the crucified Jesus behind him. No sign of Michael in the pews.

Shel's choice was the Claw, the White Memorial Fountain, in front of the admissions building. Almost every Stanford student was dunked at least once in this fountain with its giant claw-like sculpture in the center; it was the closest thing on campus to a baptismal pool.

There was a pile of wet clothes on the side of the fountain.

"These are Michael's," he said.

"Are you sure?"

"Tan OP T-shirt with palm trees stretching out from a pyramid, a pair of cargo pants that is missing a button on its side pocket, standard Stanford sweatshirt size extra-large with the hoodie drawstring missing, and of course, tighty-whities. Jockeys."

I tried to separate the soggy clothing, T-shirt, cargo pants, and sweatshirt. Damn, were those men's underwear? Was Michael high and walking around Stanford butt naked?

"I have to go to campus police."

"The police—not to mention the campus police—won't be able to help you."

"I'm not going to mention anything about you," I told Shel. "You can stay in the car."

I wasn't sure if anyone would be in the office for public safety. I parked the Tercel in the lot for the basketball arena and spotted a campus police officer in her squad car watching for speeders.

Leaving Shel in the car, I approached the police car. "I'm an R.A. in Cardenal," I said. The officer was parked underneath a short palm tree and I could hardly make out her face. It was a woman with sinewy arms that were visible from the driver's side window. "And one of our students has been missing."

"For how long?"

"Uh." I thought back to when he was at the Teahouse. "Since maybe eleven last night. I just found his clothes around the fountain."

The officer offered no emotion. "So you are missing a male student who is walking around campus naked?"

I nod my head.

She brought out a clipboard from the back seat. "Fill out this form. We'll let you know if we find him."

It was about one o'clock when we arrived back at Cardenal. I noticed a large silver Oldsmobile in our parking lot with a "Stanford Mom" license plate frame. I tried to gird myself as we got out of the Tercel. This wasn't going to be pretty.

We entered through the side door—and the first thing I saw in the hallway was a curly-haired young man wearing a red robe that reminded me of the wardrobe of the Mem Chu clergyman.

"Michael!"

At the other end of the hallway, a middle-aged woman and man struggled with the door from the lounge. I pushed both Michael and Shel into the men's bathroom.

"Ah, hello, Mr. and Mrs. Tanner," I called out as they entered the hallway. Mrs. Tanner was an older, female version of Michael with her curly hair and broad build. "You didn't have to come all this way to campus. Your son is here, safe and sound."

"Where?" Mrs. Tanner's face was flushed pink while her husband seemed disoriented, even though this wasn't his first time in the dorm.

As I pointed to the men's bathroom, Michael eventually appeared, wrapped in a white towel instead of the monkish red robe.

"I've had a life-altering experience," he announced. "I'm dropping out of Stanford. I want to be a Jesuit priest."

Mrs. Tanner began to shriek. Her husband was frozen in place. Time for me to retreat.

I crept into my room, put on some earphones, and played the Go-Go's so loud on my turntable that it almost made me cry. After about an hour of this, I removed the earphones, turned off the record player, and returned to the hallway. Seated on the hallway floor across from each other were Patrick and Jason, their legs outstretched.

"What happened?" I asked.

"Michael told his parents that he had an epiphany this morning," Patrick said. "He went to Mem Chu to see a priest and it was confirmed—at least to him. He wanted to follow that path; he always had felt a calling. He didn't want to fight it anymore."

"He didn't mention anything about the drugs," Jason interjected.

"Maybe he is right for a holy path." Patrick crossed his legs.

"Michael's parents drove him home to Hollister. They said that they needed to talk some sense into him," Jason said.

"I don't think he's going to change his mind." Patrick almost seemed proud of Michael.

I walked down the hall to talk to Shel.

"Oh, he left," Jason called out.

"He did?" I figured that I'd see him in the dining hall for dinner that night, but there was no sign of him then.

While Michael did leave the university by Christmas break, Shel hadn't formally dropped out, although I never saw him in the dormitory. I considered using my master key to take a look around his room, but I had no justification to invade his privacy. I received no frantic calls about his whereabouts. During this time, Rick began coming around Cardenal. I first encountered him eating in the Flo Mo dining room, saying that he was meeting someone in his study group. Then he started hanging out near my dorm room. I'd plug in the hot pot and put in two packages' worth of ramen noodles.

One day, when I was at the campus post office to receive the latest letter from my boyfriend, I saw Shel. He was wearing his trademark black trench coat, dark jeans, and sunglasses.

A protest regarding the US government's intervention in Nicaragua had gathered around White Plaza. I thought that he was watching the protest, but I realized that he was looking right at me. I walked my bicycle over to him.

"I haven't seen you in a while. I thought that maybe you had dropped out."

"Had some consulting projects. Maybe you can help me in the future," he said.

Yeah, right, I thought.

"Extra money."

There was that.

He looked in my bicycle basket. "Mail from your long-distance boyfriend?"

I blushed, feeling guilty about my recent infidelities.

"And I suppose that you mailed off all your med school applications."

"You know, there's nothing wrong with things going along as planned," I said to Shel.

"That's one way to put it," Shel then laughed and began to walk through the crowd of protesters until he disappeared again.

I was annoyed as I completed my other errands at the Student Union. Why did I feel guilty for being responsible, going along with a plan that had been predestined for me since elementary school?

When I returned to the dorm, I heard the frenetic reverberations of the synthesizer coming down the hallway. In the past, the music was an irritant, but today it was more like Pied Piper's hypnotic tune—codes seeking to make sense and starting over and over again. Could I break my personal infinite loop? Did I even want to? I was going to fight to stay on course but as I put my room key in the lock, I didn't turn the doorknob.

# A SÉANCE IN LIVERPOOL

## *by Lisa Morton*

**LIVERPOOL, SUNDAY EVENING, OCTOBER 30, 1881**

The rented carriage clattered down Daulby Street, and Arthur Conan Doyle watched, startled, as his friend George Budd threw open the door to leap out before they'd come to a full stop. Conan Doyle considered following him, but decided to wait; it wouldn't do to have him, the newly hired ship's surgeon, board a steamer leaving Liverpool in twelve hours with an injured leg.

"Arthur, where's your sense of adventure?" Budd clapped a hand on his friend's shoulder.

"I'm about to spend four months on a barely seaworthy tub bound for West Africa; I'll get plenty of adventure, I daresay—" Conan Doyle broke off as his gaze traveled to the house in front of them. "Well, this chap's done rather well."

The house was brick, three stories, with landscaped grounds and a wrought-iron fence circling it on all sides. To Conan Doyle, who had recently received his medical degree but was too poor to set up his own practice, it looked like Buckingham Palace, despite being in Liverpool.

"You wait, my friend—we'll both be better off than this soon enough," said Budd as he led the way through the gate and up to the front door.

Conan Doyle bit back a laugh; although a year ahead, Dr. George Budd had fared only slightly better and also had a young wife to support. Conan Doyle had probably made more money off the short story "Crabbe's Practice," based on Budd's ludicrous (and yet not unsuccessful) stunts to create a clientele, than Budd had made in the last month, despite his recent claims at a vastly improved income. Conan Doyle doubted that his authorial abilities would ever provide him with a sole means of livelihood, but they'd kept him afloat while he'd struggled to find a permanent medical position.

As Budd straightened his suit and hair before pulling the bell at the front door, Conan Doyle asked, "Dr. William Hitchman, you said?"

"That's our man. Acclaimed Liverpool physician, member of the Royal College of Physicians, expert in homeopathy, and dedicated Spiritualist."

"And we're here for a séance?"

"Not just any séance but a séance with a medium who's supposed to be the next great thing."

"And we're paying *what* for this great privilege?"

Budd was prevented from responding as the door opened. "Good evening, gentlemen."

The man in the doorway was slight, young, with a narrow face that Conan Doyle couldn't help but think would be more at home on a weasel. His suit, Conan Doyle noted, was new but cheap, fitting badly in some places. The man squinted, eyeing them in the low light of the porch. "Ahh, Dr. Budd and his young friend Mr. Doyle, I presume. Please enter." He stepped aside and gestured them within.

Budd exchanged a look with his friend that indicated some amusement; Conan Doyle realized the man admitting them couldn't possibly be the esteemed and sixty-ish Dr. Hitchman. As they entered, they removed their outer coats and hats, which were taken by a maid who appeared from nowhere. The greeter extended a hand to each of them. "Good to see you again, Dr. Budd. And welcome, Mr. Doyle. I'm John King, Miss DeLisle's manager. This way, please." He indicated a sitting room off the main hall.

They followed his gesture, and Conan Doyle saw that the elegantly furnished and decorated room was already filled with a small company of two women and three men. King made introductions: there was a couple in their late fifties, Mr. and Mrs. Sidgwick; an elderly widow, Mrs. Bergen; the homeowner, Dr. Hitchman; and a tea merchant in his thirties, Mr. McCarthy, who was visiting from London.

When the introductions were completed, King took up a position in the middle of the room. "Thank you all, ladies and gentlemen, for coming tonight. Since we're all assembled, we'll begin soon. Our medium, Miss Daniela DeLisle, is even now preparing for this evening's séance, and we anticipate a gathering filled with the communion of many spirits."

Conan Doyle tried to drink in every word, already inwardly composing a letter to his mother, Mary: "For the night before I went to sea aboard the *Mayumba*—bound for Madeira and West Africa—you might have expected livelier proceedings, but instead I let George Budd, who I know you don't approve of, lead me into nothing less than a Spiritualist séance. Can you imagine? We're expected to believe that the spirits of the dead will leave their happy Paradise at the mere invitation of a very human medium. Still, Budd swears that the woman invoking the ghostly visitors is a new sensation and that we are almost certainly in for wonders untold. There's no denying that it seems appropriate amusement for the eve of All Hallows' Eve."

Conan Doyle's attention returned to King, who addressed the onlookers with great solemnity. "Before we convene tonight's gathering, I must receive assurance from each of you that you will abide by a few simple rules.

"First, Miss DeLisle assumes that you are all good Christian folk who will engage in prayer and hymn when instructed to do so."

The assemblage murmured approval, although Mr. Sidgwick snorted derisively; apparently he was mildly offended by the mere suggestion that he *might* not be good Christian folk.

"Secondly, once we have moved into the dining room and you are all seated, you will place your hands upon the table, where they will remain throughout the entire sequence of events, unless instructed otherwise by Miss DeLisle.

"Third, you will refrain from engaging the spirits in questions or conversation until instructed to do so.

"Finally, and most importantly, you accept the stipulation that you may not, *under any circumstances*, leave the room or break the circle during the séance, since to do so could lead to irreparable harm, even *death*, for the medium.

"Are you all agreed?"

Conan Doyle muttered along with all the others. King smiled and nodded. "Very good. Please wait here while I see if Miss DeLisle is ready to commence."

He left the room. Budd leaned into Conan Doyle and whispered, "Well, *that* dramatic rendering alone was nearly worth the two-bob each."

"Two-bob?" Conan Doyle blurted out, drawing surprised stares from the others. He realized that two shillings probably didn't seem like an extravagant amount to the rest, but to him it was a pie and a pint.

"Calm down, Arthur," Budd was saying, "I really can afford it."

Just then a servant entered with a tray of brandies, and Budd turned away from Conan Doyle to focus on the drink. Left to his own devices, Conan Doyle accepted a glass (grateful that at least the fee included this), sipped the warming liqueur, and studied his fellow séance sitters. He'd had little experience with Spiritualists, but pictured them all as slightly dotty seniors, which fit the Sidgwicks, Mrs. Bergen, and Dr. Hitchman well enough. However, he was slightly perplexed by the presence of the London tea-seller, Mr. McCarthy, who seemed too young to fit his admittedly uneducated view of Spiritualists. McCarthy was not just relatively youthful compared to the others, he was also tall, of athletic build, his dark suit of a cut Conan Doyle hadn't seen before, and he had a habit of stroking his short moustache (Conan Doyle, on the other hand, preferred to keep his moustache long and dashingly waxed). Curious, Conan Doyle approached McCarthy.

"You're from London, Mr. McCarthy?"

The other man turned a piercing gaze on him, and Conan Doyle had the immediate thought that this fellow was no simple merchant. "I am, Mr. Doyle."

"Actually, I prefer Conan Doyle."

The man nodded slightly. "My apologies, Mr. Conan Doyle. Mr. King didn't indicate your origins, but from that burr I'm guessing Edinburgh . . . ?"

"A fine guess, Mr. McCarthy. My friend Dr. Budd and I met while we both attended the University of Edinburgh."

"Yet he goes by 'Doctor,' while you don't."

Conan Doyle smiled, admiring the man's acumen; he reminded him slightly of his old professor, Joseph Bell, whose talents for diagnosing patients just by sight was legendary. "Quite right. We have the same degrees, but I've yet to achieve any placement in the profession. I hope to change that after tomorrow, when I begin a four-month tour as a ship's surgeon bound for West Africa."

McCarthy nodded, apparently satisfied, turning his eyes back on the other guests. Conan Doyle asked, "Are you a Spiritualist then, sir?"

The other man smirked slightly before replying, "Let's say I have a cultivated interest in séances."

McCarthy's focus shifted to the older guests, who were all carrying on a tense, hushed conversation. Conan Doyle followed McCarthy's lead and listened in.

". . . so tragic," the widow, Mrs. Bergen, was saying.

"And relatively young," Mr. Sidgwick added. "He was barely forty-five."

The host, Dr. Hitchman, interjected. "I once attended a séance with Colonel Barnes conducted by Daniel Dunglas Home."

Mrs. Bergen gasped, causing her voluminous gray bun to tremble. "I always wished I could sit with Mr. Home."

"He remains," Hitchman said, "the most astonishing medium I've encountered."

"Is it true that he can elongate his body and hold hot coals?" asked Mrs. Sidgwick.

Hitchman answered, “I personally witnessed him accomplishing both such feats, and more.”

Mr. Sidgwick asked, “So you knew the Colonel? Do you think it’s true that he used a laudanum overdose to take his own life?”

Hitchman frowned. “I didn’t know the Colonel well. I did know that he used laudanum to control pain from an old war injury, but . . . no, Colonel Barnes didn’t strike me as the sort of chap to suddenly end it all.”

“Could he have been . . .” Mrs. Bergen took a step forward to theatrically whisper the last word, “. . . *murdered*?”

Conan Doyle saw McCarthy’s eyes narrow in interest.

Hitchman responded, “All I can tell you is that Colonel Reginald Barnes was one of the true faithful, and I’ve no doubt that his spirit lives blissfully in the Summer-Land.”

“Perhaps he’ll contact us tonight,” Mrs. Sidgwick said.

“It’s entirely possible,” Hitchman said. “I’ve had one sitting with Miss DeLisle, and that was enough to convince me to allow her to stay here so I could share her great gifts with Liverpool’s Spiritualists.”

“So she’s not from Liverpool?” asked McCarthy.

“No,” replied Hitchman, “she’s originally from Manchester, although for the last few years she’s been touring the States.”

“Ahh,” Sidgwick mused, “the States . . . that explains why I’ve not encountered her before.”

“Who is her control?” asked Mrs. Bergen.

“The spirit’s name is Annie Morgan. She says she was daughter to the pirate Henry Morgan.”

A door opened, putting an end to further conversation. King reappeared, calling out, “Ladies and gentlemen, it’s time to begin. Please step this way.”

Conan Doyle and Budd stood back to allow the others to precede them. As they waited, Conan Doyle whispered to Budd, “What’s all this about ‘her control’ and some pirate’s daughter?”

“Every medium has a spirit guide who helps them connect with other spirits. Apparently Miss DeLisle’s is Annie Morgan.”

"And you actually believe all this poppycock?" Conan Doyle asked.

Budd shrugged, gave him a half-smile, and said, "Come now, man—the game's afoot."

As Conan Doyle followed the others, he wondered just how far his friend's belief in all this went. He considered himself a man of science and assumed Budd did as well, but now he wondered. Or was this all just a trifle for Budd, an early All-Hallows prank?

Following King, they entered a spacious dining room with a hearth, a table large enough to seat all of them comfortably, and an attractive young woman seated at its head. "This is Miss Daniela DeLisle."

The medium nodded and smiled.

Conan Doyle's breath caught. He had expected someone like Mrs. Sidgwick or Mrs. Bergen, an older woman . . . but Miss DeLisle was young and very pretty, with dark eyes that reminded Conan Doyle of his beloved Elmo, who he'd left in Ireland—Elmo, who he'd nearly asked to be his wife, to come with him on the voyage aboard the *Mayumba*.

Conan Doyle was so immediately taken with Miss DeLisle that he barely noticed when John King took his arm. "Mr. Doyle, perhaps you'd agree to being seated immediately on Miss DeLisle's left . . . ?"

Feeling his face flush, Conan Doyle let King place him in the chair next to Miss DeLisle's. This close to her, Conan Doyle felt her charisma like a rush of heat into a cold room.

"Mr. Conan Doyle," King said, leaning over him, "with your consent, of course, you will act as one of Miss DeLisle's observers, so she asks that you place your hand upon her left arm throughout the proceedings." Conan Doyle let King place his hand on the medium's bare arm, and he felt a redoubling of her erotic force, especially when she turned her kohl-lined eyes upon his.

"May I call you Arthur?" she asked.

Conan Doyle gulped before replying, "Most assuredly, Miss."

Hitchman sat on the other side of Miss DeLisle, and Conan Doyle thought he detected a whiff of jealousy in the other man; the way Hitchman laid his hand atop the medium's, his fingers nearly digging into her flesh, made Conan

Doyle wonder if there were reasons other than Miss DeLisle's mediumistic skills that had convinced Hitchman to house her.

However, it was McCarthy's behavior that most intrigued Conan Doyle: as he waited for the others to take their places, McCarthy stood before the room's one large window, his back to them, his right hand moving. Was he signaling to someone outside? Conan Doyle leaned over to Budd, seated on his other side, and murmured, "What's that chap doing at the window?"

Budd watched for a second, and then whispered back, with melodramatic emphasis on the last word, "Maybe he's a *murderer*!"

All of the guests were now positioned, with McCarthy placed opposite Conan Doyle and the Sidgwicks and Mrs. Bergen filling the rest of the seats. King stood a few feet from the table, waiting.

"Ladies and gentlemen, please join me in prayer . . ." Miss DeLisle closed her eyes and tilted her head down, as did the others—but Conan Doyle kept his eyes open, watching the proceedings.

"Our Father, who watches over the Summer-Land," the medium intoned, "we call upon you tonight with humility and love to allow us to commune with those who have passed beyond the veil . . ."

As the prayer continued, Conan Doyle noticed the aide, King, moving around the room. He drew the curtains tightly over the window, lowered the gas on the wall lamps, and untied black draperies that covered the two doorways at opposite ends of the room. For the first time Conan Doyle realized the hearth in the dining room hadn't been lit, and he shivered slightly in the autumn chill that had crept into this part of the house.

The medium finished the prayer. The sitters joined in with "Amen" and lifted their faces again, which Conan Doyle saw were filled with eagerness.

"Now, please join me in singing 'Lead, Kindly Light' as the spirits begin to gather."

Miss DeLisle's clear soprano sounded above the other, older voices: "Lead, kindly light, amidst the encircling gloom . . ." As they sang, King once again walked the edges of the room, turning the gas down on the lights until only the barest flames still flickered and the room was largely cast into impenetrable gloom. Conan Doyle's eyes tried to adjust, but he could make out only dim shapes. He felt Miss DeLisle's hand twitch beneath his, and he thought he saw her head move side to side.

The sitters finished the hymn. A few seconds of silence followed, broken only by the sound of the medium's heavy breathing. Conan Doyle could feel anticipation building—

The table jumped. Gasps sounded from the sitters, and then Miss DeLisle spoke, or rather, a voice Conan Doyle hadn't heard before issued from the general direction of the medium. It was deeper, huskier than hers. "Good evening. My name is Annie Morgan." Almost immediately, Miss DeLisle's normal speaking voice reasserted itself. "Annie, you came through easily tonight."

The lower voice sounded again. "Those assembled here tonight possess great spiritual energy."

Hitchman abruptly cried out, "My leg! A spirit touched me!"

Laughing, the medium said, "There will be many such wonders tonight."

Conan Doyle started as he felt something brush his ankle. Budd must have felt his friend jerk, because he said, "What just happened?"

"Something touched my leg, too," Conan Doyle said. It had to be the medium, but her hand was still secure beneath Conan Doyle's. Had she used her feet? He supposed it was a possibility, but—

The table leapt up six inches and crashed back down to the floor. It began to bounce, a nervous, spasmodic dance, arrhythmic yet powerful. The sitters gasped, struggling to keep their hands atop the table. Mrs. Bergen wailed in something like ecstasy.

Conan Doyle kept his grip on the medium's hand. How, he wondered, could she be doing this with just her legs? Was it King? Had he somehow crawled under the table without alerting anyone to his presence?

The table's movement stopped. In her normal speaking voice, DeLisle said, "Thank you for that display, Annie. Would it be possible to let those gathered here speak with some of their loved ones who have crossed over?"

The other voice responded, "There are many here, clamoring to come through . . . I can't hear them all clearly . . . there's a man here who's name begins with 'E'—"

Mrs. Bergen interrupted. "Edward! Is it my Edward?"

"He says . . ." DeLisle, or rather Annie Morgan, took a deep breath before answering. "It is your husband, Mrs. Bergen. He wants to tell you that he's happy, although he misses you."

They now heard Mrs. Bergen's sobs. "Edward, I've missed you!"

The medium continued, "He wants you to know that he thinks about your anniversary every . . . is it April fourth?"

"Oh, my darling, as do I," said the elderly widow.

Budd leaned into Conan Doyle and whispered, "How do you explain that?"

Conan Doyle responded, as quietly as he could, "A simple visit to any newspaper archive would have sufficed."

"Mr. Conan Doyle," said the medium, "I detect skepticism."

"I am perfectly ready," he answered, "to be convinced."

"You are about to embark on a journey. You've packed several books for your time at sea, including one by an author who just departed this realm recently . . ."

Conan Doyle froze in shock: there were indeed two books by Thomas Carlyle in his luggage, and Carlyle had just passed away in February.

A man's voice—he thought it was Sidgwick—asked, "Is that right, Mr. Conan Doyle?"

"It is. But I—"

Again, the medium interrupted. "The author in question is here and has asked me to relay a message: he says to tell you that you will find great success with your writing when you base a character on the man who rings."

The message meant nothing to Conan Doyle. "I don't understand—"

Another voice rang out in the darkness, cutting him off; it was McCarthy. "I'd like to know if Colonel Reginald Barnes can come through." Several of the others muttered approval.

There was a pause before the medium said, "Colonel Barnes is here."

"I'd like to ask him about his death."

"He says," DeLisle replied, "that he barely remembers it. He's at peace in the Summer-Land, and not anxious to re-experience that particular event."

"Surely he can—" McCarthy broke off as Mrs. Bergen squealed.

Then Conan Doyle saw what had elicited that reaction: something glowed in the darkness above the table, bobbing to and fro. It took a few seconds to recognize that the greenish glimmers were actually *hands*, two glowing hands floating just over their heads. Conan Doyle felt a stab of fear and wonder, something so primal it made him forget all else. For a few seconds he simply stared, paralyzed, at the impossibility just above him.

The voice of McCarthy, however, brought him back. "Surely," he said, apparently disinterested in the spectacle of the ghostly hands, "the Colonel can tell us why he took his own life."

The medium answered, "He says that was all explained in the note, and he has no reason to address it further."

McCarthy said, "The note, eh?"

Conan Doyle cried out as Miss DeLisle's hand was abruptly pulled from beneath his. He heard chairs drawn back and felt a rush of air. A gaslight was turned up to full, revealing a chaotic scene:

Miss DeLisle was out of her chair and pushing through the heavy black drapes that hung over one of the doorways.

John King stood against a wall, still holding up a telescoping rod from which dangled a pair of gloves dipped in phosphorus oil.

McCarthy's hand was still on the gas he'd just turned up on a wall lamp. "Don't try to run, Miss Marston—I've got men stationed outside all the exits."

Hitchman rose from his chair, staring about in alarm. "You, sir, had best explain yourself! Who is 'Miss Marston'?"

McCarthy motioned at the medium with one hand as he fished in a pocket with the other. "She is," he said, before producing a leather holder, which he flipped open to reveal a badge on one side and a card headed with "Metropolitan Police" on the other. "I'm Inspector Stephen Hobart of Scotland Yard, and Elizabeth Marston, you're under arrest for the murder of Colonel Reginald Barnes."

"I don't know what you're talking about," DeLisle—or Marston—said.

McCarthy grinned. "The *note*, Miss Marston. We haven't made it public knowledge that the Colonel was found with a suicide note, and we know that note was forged. There's no way you could have known about that note, unless either you wrote it, or the spirits told you, and I think we both know how unlikely that second possibility is, don't we?"

King dropped the rod and tried to run for it, but Budd stuck a leg out, tripped him, and was on him instantly, pinning him to the dining room floor. Marston, meanwhile, once again tried to dash through the draperies, but Conan Doyle leapt up, caught her by one slender arm, and held her as she struggled. Two uniformed police officers entered the room then, taking custody of King and Marston. As Conan Doyle released her to the officer, her eyes met his for a moment, and Conan Doyle couldn't stop himself from saying, "I'm sorry."

As she was taken from the room, Miss Marston said to him, "Remember what you heard tonight." That was the last Conan Doyle saw of her.

With the two criminals escorted out, McCarthy turned to the stunned onlookers. "I apologize, ladies and gentlemen, for the deception I engaged in tonight, but it was necessary. You see, I've been following Miss Marston since she fled London after killing Colonel Barnes. We believe that he had caught Miss Marston and her associate—whose real name, by the way, is Charles Cadgett—in imposture, and threatened to expose her. Miss Marston had been working London's Spiritualist circles for some time and had accrued a devoted following of wealthy patrons; exposure would have ruined her. So, after seeing to it that Colonel Barnes ingested more than his usual nightly dose of laudanum, she forged the suicide note and then ran. I heard of the arrival of a new medium 'Miss DeLisle' in Liverpool, but I couldn't be sure it was Miss Marston until I caught her in her own lies."

Hitchman sagged into a chair. "A murderer . . . dear God . . ."

"I'm sorry, Doctor. I know you wanted to believe."

McCarthy bid them all good night and left, anxious to return his two captives to London. Mr. and Mrs. Sidgwick made a quiet exit shortly thereafter; Mrs. Bergen took longer to compose herself before leaving. "You don't suppose," she said to Hitchman before stepping out into the cold night, "that she really *did* bring back Edward, do you?"

Hitchman didn't answer.

Budd and Conan Doyle left last. As they climbed into their carriage, Budd said, "Well, old man, don't tell me *that* wasn't worth two-bob."

Conan Doyle didn't laugh, however. Instead, he asked, "Tell me one thing, George: Do *you* believe?"

"Arthur, my boy, don't forget the words of the Bard: Our dreamt philosophies are really very small."

They rode in silence for a while before Budd said, "I'm sorry I couldn't give you a wee bit of proof tonight, though."

"Oh, but you did."

Budd looked at his friend quizzically. Conan Doyle asked, "Did you tell them anything about me in advance?"

"Only your name."

"Then how could they know I was a writer?"

Budd thought for a moment, said, "Perhaps she'd read something by you, or maybe her associate—King, or whatever his name was—did some research on you."

"Perhaps . . ." Conan Doyle hesitated before adding, "but that other thing she said, about a character based on the man who rings."

"Yes . . . what the devil does that mean?"

Conan Doyle looked at his friend carefully. "You know him, too, George: our old professor from Edinburgh, the one whose powers of deduction always astonished us . . ."

Understanding, and astonishment, spread across Budd's face. "Joseph Bell. *Bell*—the man who rings."

Conan Doyle nodded, thinking again about Bell's astonishing powers of observation and deduction. He rolled the thought around in his head—a character based on Bell might be *very* interesting indeed. He smiled as a picture began to take shape within his mind's eye.

"You know, George," he said, as the night drew on to the next step in his journey, "you might have made a believer of me after all."

# BENCHLEY

## *by Derek Haas*

Gerard James would not be attending his niece's christening at the Southwark Cathedral on Sunday—an event that was to be exhausting but obligatory—because he had been murdered. As it was not uncommon to find a factory hand lying face down in the mud outside the George and Dragon, James's body went unnoticed well past time when assistance might have proved beneficial. He was twenty-three years old, the same number of stab wounds in his side and back.

The body's discoverer, a man named Benchley, sent for a peeler, and an officer named Rice arrived a half hour later, scowling. Rice had enlisted the Thursday before to fight the Russians in the Crimean Peninsula. He did not much like being in the Metropolitan Police. This was his last shift before reporting to Dover.

"Stand clear, stand clear," he ordered in an officious voice he was fond of employing. Rice toed James's body from its back to its side to its front like rolling a felled log.

The crowd of a dozen or so gasped at the dead man's bloodless face and the expression fixed forever upon it. Horror. Fright. Recognition?

Rice's face soured and his mustache, usually horizontal, pulled down into an arch. "Hup. Who are you then?" he asked the man who had sent for him.

"Me, sir?"

"Aye."

"Benchley, sir. I'm a printer's apprentice. That's me shoppe across the street."

Rice sniffed like he smelled something spoiled. The accent pinned Benchley for a Scotsman, and there was little he detested more than a thin Scotsman. "Don't need your life story. How came you upon this body?"

"I just said, me shoppe's across the street."

Rice eyed him, then looked at the crowd to see if they were enjoying or encouraging this witness's insolence. Neither was the answer; the gawkers were too focused on the unfortunate victim's expression. Rice took his hand off the handle of his billy club. He sniffed again, one nostril widening, then the other, a habit he'd had since he was a boy.

"Well. He has passed beyond. Send for a horseman and alert the funeral house—"

"Are you going to ask his name?" Benchley asked.

"His name?"

"Aye."

Rice straightened. A few of the lookers turned their eyes to him and then to this thin printer's apprentice as though they were attending the theater.

"Right, then. What's his name?" Rice asked.

"Gerard James, sir."

A few members of the audience—as that was what they were becoming—stirred at the sound of this name.

Rice stiffened.

Benchley examined him, his expression as blank as a debtor's ledger. "D'ye know the name, officer?"

Rice's nostrils flared again, left, right. "Why should I?"

Benchley shook his head as if he couldn't fathom an answer to that question. Rice was starting not to like the man.

"Right, then. As I said before—"

"How d'ye s'pose he died?"

"S'pose he died?" Rice blurted, his voice pitching upward like a ship rolling in the ocean. "It's obvious, innit? By knife."

"By concealed knife."

"What's that now?" Rice looked at Benchley with increasing annoyance. He glanced at the crowd, hooked a thumb at the wee Scotsman as if to say, "This one—aren't we all nettled by this gaunt fellow with the unflappable air and the lack of respect for authority?" The lookers, however, just stared back at him, dumbly, as though Rice was an actor who had forgotten his lines in a play.

"Concealed knife, I said."

"And how d'ye know concealed knife unless ye did witness the murder, in which case y'should've said so when I arrived?"

Benchley pointed at the cobblestone walkway. "Drop, drop, drop, then nothing," he said in his maddeningly Scottish accent and his maddeningly stoic tone.

Rice saw what he meant, a few drops of blood caught the sunlight, forming a bread-crumb line away from the body before stopping as though the knife wielder had vanished. The arch above Rice's mouth drew even more narrow, his lips disappearing completely inside his frown.

Benchley mimed a villain stabbing a man and then sheathing his knife as he steps away. "The blood on the dagger trapped inside its sheath."

"Is it now?" Rice knew his voice had risen to a tea kettle whistle but he couldn't seem to control it, so flummoxed was he by this printer's apprentice.

The crowd was murmuring now, a few ayes and that's sos, humming like stirred bees. Rice did not like the sound nor the image. He felt suddenly tired and stifled a yawn with the back of his hand.

"Did'ye sleep last night, Officer Rice?"

"Sleep?"

"You've tree branches growing out of your irises, and you just yawned."

"Yawned?" Rice stammered.

"Over a dead man, yes, officer."

Rice felt his hand sliding back to the handle of his knocking stick. He'd like for this crowd to disperse so he could maybe rattle a few teeth in this Benchley fellow's saucepot. Instead, he puffed out his chest, offering, "Matter o'fact, I had news. I'm sent to Dover tomorrow to join my regiment. Didn't sleep a wink." He thought this might garner some sympathy, but Benchley's face remained inscrutable.

"You kept your pants on but changed your boots?"

"What's this now?"

"Well, your boots are clean, not a spot on them, as you'd expect if you cleaned or changed them from yesterday, but the creases in your pants have softened from wearing them an extended time. You changed your boots, but not your pants."

Rice heard the words and knew they were uncannily accurate, but he also didn't hear them, because a ringing in his ears seemed to drown out some of the sound. More Londoners were joining the original crowd of lookers, drawn like flies to rotten meat. "I don't know why—"

"You didn't answer my original question, sir."

"You don't—"

"Do you know the name Gerard James?"

Rice felt his nostrils marching again, left, right, left, right. Why did his face, his voice, always betray him?

Benchley continued. "I see you pass this walk every day, a dozen times. Here, right at the corner, up and down the streets, regular as a clock."

"Well."

"And there are posted bills on each corner with the name Gerard James in 36-point type. I know because I printed them."

"Well."

"And since Gerard James is organizing factory hands to demand safer conditions and higher wages, proclaiming loudly and boldly this controversial position on posted bills up and down the streets you pass every day, it stands to reason you might be familiar with the name?"

"Who are you?" Rice asked in wonder.

"Benchley, sir. I am the printer's apprentice across the street, as I said before."

"He did, he did," one of the lookers agreed.

"A fault in cognition is another sign of a sleepless night."

Rice's head was spinning. Benchley? Benchley? Who was this man who seemed to know so much about him, though they had never met? And why had the mere act of thinking grown so difficult? This was not how things were supposed to go before he left for Dover.

"Right, yes, I know the name," Rice admitted.

"How are your own wages, sir?"

"My own wages?" he asked incredulously. Were there octaves of incredulousness? If so, he was entering a new register.

"A metropolitan police officer with three years of service such as yourself, Officer Rice, will make sixteen pounds per week, or roughly eight-hundred pounds a year."

Rice reddened.

"Yet you moved from a quarter flat above the Haymarket to a capacious room in Albert Gardens, where my runner fetched you just now. Along with your equally new watch chain, I would say you came into a supplemental salary recently."

Rice looked down at the watch chain extending from his buttonhole to his pocket. It was shinier than the watch it held. What had possessed him to purchase it?

"The loops in your watch chain? They are unique, would you agree?"

Rice was still staring at his watch chain. He hadn't really noticed the loops. They looked like every other watch chain loop. The chain was fancy, yes. It had caught his eye, yes. He had purchased it without thinking.

"I'll answer for you. They are unique. The egg-shaped design is crafted in Geneva, Switzerland, by Elias Schweis, and only sold in one shop in London, not in this area but on Lansdown Road on the same block as the supervising office of the Griffiths Textile Company, the same Griffiths Textile Company employing one Gerard James, the dead man lying at your feet!"

Rice's thoughts continued to fly across his mind like larks darting in and out of thorn bushes. He wanted to stop this whore's son from talking but couldn't think of how to achieve the task. Worse, Benchley was no longer speaking to him, but addressing the crowd of lookers, now numbering two dozen, as though he were a crier standing on an apple box.

"Officer Rice was hired by Griffith's Textile to murder Gerard James on the night before he left to fight on the Crimean Peninsula. He stabbed Mr. James with a knife currently sheathed inside his billy club, then walked home where his murderous thoughts kept him from sleep. He waited to be summoned, only changing his boots when he noticed blood on the toes." Benchley pointed at a pool of blood on the cobblestone, and a couple of half-moon impressions there. He turned to Rice, again speaking to him directly. "And now, officer, if you will hand me your billy club, I will prove it."

Rice looked at the crowd, back at Benchley.

"How did you—"

"There is a slight gap between your nightstick's handle and the baton itself."

Rice's face flushed. His mustache leveled again as his brows knitted in a V. He had one move to make, and he had always been a quick man for his size.

He grabbed the handle of his nightstick while his other hand held the baton still and unsheathed the concealed knife, still red with James's blood.

Before he could plunge it into this smug mosquito's chest, however, he felt his nose explode, and he windmilled backward, landing on his backside. The meater had beaten him to the punch, literally, knocking him with a right cross that sent his knife flying and his knees buckling.

The last thought he had as the crowd piled on him and held him down was, "Benchley? Who the devil was this Benchley?"

Benchley walked home to his small flat on Keppel Row. A fire was awake in the fireplace, and his wife, Elcie, was cooking stew in a kettle above it.

"Mrs. Holmes," Benchley said by way of greeting.

"Mr. Holmes," Elcie answered. "Busy day?"

"Interesting one."

His son, Mycroft, raised his hands to him, and Benchley scooped him up. "Were you good for mother, then?"

Mycroft nodded vigorously, and Benchley buttoned his nose with his finger and thumb.

Benchley moved to his wife, kissed her cheek. "And how is he?" Benchley asked, patting her protruding stomach.

"This one? This one's a she," Elcie answered. "A sister for Mycroft."

Benchley deduced from her heart rate when she slept, from her lack of morning sickness, from the way she carried the baby high in her frame, that she was wrong about the baby's sex.

Still, he kept that information to himself.

# THE MURDERER'S PARADOX

## *by David Corbett*

I presume you were expecting Dr. Watson. Sorry to disappoint.

This happens to be one of those tales, however, that the dull-witted doctor would never think to share. It casts far too damning a light on his beloved paragon, Sherlock Holmes.

Indeed, the faithful physician never committed this particular episode to paper at all, but kept it locked away in the darkest corner of his mind, to be guarded jealously by an agonized conscience every day for the rest of his miserable life.

### I. The Chosen Pair

It began, naturally enough, by mere coincidence—to the extent anything in this life can be attributed to chance.

I had decided to investigate the protest outside a lecture hall where a preeminent doctor, Sir Arthur Conan Doyle, intended to defend the representations made in a booklet he'd written: *The War in South Africa: Its Cause and Conduct.*

In that humble little screed, Conan Doyle had sought to counter the arrogance—or apathy—of the British people in making a case to the world in their own defense. Not only, he believed, was the British cause in the Boer conflict entirely just, but its execution by the British military had proven impeccable in every conceivable manner.

Typical pap. The English love to brag about their devotion to justice and fair play, while exhibiting neither, except by force.

Furthermore, as the increasingly volatile protests against his lectures showed, a growing number of his kinsmen proved neither apathetic nor arrogant at all; they simply exhibited that enthusiasm in service of the exact opposite cause he intended to advance.

Many were humble people, from the classes typically dragooned into military service. Others were simply smart enough to see through a lie when it's spat in their face.

Regardless, whatever their reasons for showing up, they spared little effort vehemently opposing the good doctor's slander of the Boer populace as subliterate primitives, his defense of starving women and children to death in concentration camps, and his laughable conviction the war was premised on anything but greed.

My interest in the matter, however, had nothing to do with who owned the truth. Nothing of the sort ever resides in politics, let alone war. Rather, I sought, in the continuing waves of anger against the conflict and its prattling advocates, an opportunity for mischief.

I found what I was looking for in a pair of particularly vocal protestors, one man, one woman, both young, struggling against a pair of bobbies dragging them toward a Black Maria. Several of my confederates, at my signal, fired pistol shots into the air, and in the ensuing chaos—protestors scattering in all directions, the police abandoning their prisoners to locate and subdue the gunmen—I managed to collect my young couple and get them to follow me down an alleyway to my waiting carriage.

## II. Preliminaries

We retired to an apartment I maintain in Portman Square. Once safely inside, I encouraged my new companions to warm themselves by the fire while the housekeeper prepared a light supper and a pot of strong black tea.

Given a moment for more careful inspection, I took note of the young man's ragged black hair, his classic jaw, and an oft-broken nose that amplified the effect of his quarrelsome blue eyes. His clothing was threadbare but neat, with the shoes lacking any semblance of a shine. More revealingly, he seemed too thin, even gaunt, given the breadth of his shoulders; his skin possessed a ghostly pallor, possible sign of internal bleeding; and a slight tremor afflicted his left hand.

As for his companion, she wore a felt jacket, a long black skirt, and a high-collared blouse. Her wavy blonde hair was tucked up beneath a simple cloche hat, which she only removed once sufficiently warmed by the fire. Her strangely delicate features contrasted sharply with her fearsome disposition, just as her constrained manners seemed in perpetual conflict with a kind of coltish energy. At the same time, she exhibited a pronounced solicitude toward the young man, like that of a doting sister, or a hopeless lover.

"You're a gentleman then," the young man said, not kindly, as he inspected the furnishings. He retained a distinct measure of his Irish accent, but the words were vaguely slurred, another symptom of his illness.

"If you mean by 'gentleman' a friend of the crown, you're mistaken. I'm anything but."

"Do well enough off the imperial dugs, though, I'm guessing."

"Not in the manner you suggest, I assure you."

"How then, if you don't mind me asking?"

"I'm a professor."

The young man grinned. "Professing what?"

"Mathematics."

He and the young woman shared a puzzled glance. "That pays?" He eyed my housekeeper as she entered with a tray of sandwiches and the pot of tea. "Pays for the likes of all this?"

I offered an indulgent smile. "I do not pursue my profession for the income. That is supplied from elsewhere. I teach and pursue the science of mathematics because it possesses not only truth but supreme beauty—a beauty beyond the nature of mortal man."

He and the young lady had already dug into the sandwiches, and my housekeeper had no sooner doled out their tea than they shoveled in sugar, poured in milk, and gulped down several mouthfuls. One could only guess at how recently either had enjoyed a decent meal.

In time, the young man said, "So this 'elsewhere,' the place your money comes from, where might that be?"

I waited until both stopped chewing before answering. "I have certain benefactors, men and women who share our view that it is time the British Empire got knocked down a peg or two. More, if it can be done."

It was the young woman's turn, at last, to speak. "Who says that's 'our' view?"

"Please," I replied, "let's not insult each other. The cause of women. The cause of a free Ireland. The cause of the Boers and India, the Mahdists of the Sudan, the—"

"They pay," the young man interrupted, waving his sandwich about. "For all this?"

"Those who find common cause and have the means—they are my benefactors."

The young lady, wiping her fingers on a napkin, let out a mordant sigh. "Please don't consider this ungracious. I very much appreciate what you did—saving us from arrest, bringing us here, offering us your hospitality. But unless I am very much mistaken you want something. And I can't see just yet why we might oblige."

"Of course not," I replied. "We have not yet had time to become fully acquainted. Only then might any of us consider the issue of trust."

"Ah, luv, hear that?" It was the young man. "The gentleman's proposing an 'issue of trust.'"

"That will take time, naturally," I continued. "But for now, please understand, I want nothing *from* you. The issue is quite the other way around—I'm wondering what it is that I might be able to offer *to* you."

"Like there's a difference," the young man said, reaching for another sandwich, "when men of your station want something from ours."

"All right," I replied, "let me extend at least this minor bit of personal biography. In the service of trust."

Their gazes rose to mine, and I held them for a moment before speaking.

"Not so long ago, a Pinkerton agent named Birdy Edwards infiltrated a group of west Pennsylvania miners who hoped to form a union. Of course, these men, virtually all of them Irish, were labeled terrorists, criminals, robbers, and such by the bosses and the law. Birdy Edwards, insinuating his way into the group, succeeded in getting several of the leaders exposed, prosecuted, and hanged."

"I thought this was about you," the young man remarked.

"Patience, please. Not all the union men were brought to heel, meaning the informer Birdy Edwards was a marked man. And so he absconded to England, changed his name and hid, for fear of being tracked down and killed. It took a few years, but that plot indeed progressed, with the help of the Irish Republican Brotherhood. They almost brought the plan to completion, too, but Birdy foiled it by murdering his assassin, trading the dead man's corpse for his own, and thereby faking his own death—at which point a man named Sherlock Holmes entered the picture."

"I've heard of him," the young woman replied. "He's linked somehow to this Conan Doyle."

"So go the rumors. Well, Holmes botched things by being too clever, even by his own standards. His perverse curiosity must always, always be gratified. Birdy Edwards was now exposed. And so Sherlock the All-Wise instructed him to flee the country to ensure his own safety. A farcical suggestion—his flight only exposed him once more. On a steamship heading for Africa, he was supposedly 'lost overboard.'"

The two exchanged glances once again. The young man tried to hide his uneasiness behind another mouthful, while the young lady said, "And how, if I might ask, do you know all this?"

I glanced at the clock. It was time to conclude this first encounter.

"Because I arranged the matter."

Several more meetings followed, a dozen or so, during which the various background details emerged that confirmed my initial impression. I had judged wisely. These two would serve. And serve well.

The young man's name was Flannery MacGreevy, originally from County Clare, one of ten children, only six of them still alive. The young lady was Penelope Collingwood, a refugee from Sussex, or rather from the brutal father who lived there with her servile mother and two siblings.

Flann and Penny to each other, and soon enough to me.

I made sure the housekeeper provided something home-cooked and nourishing for these occasions, a shepherd's pie or the always reliable sandwiches, thick with freshly roasted meat and good Somerset cheddar. I think it was this offer of sustenance, and the appearance of kindness it conveyed, that at last prompted the spilling out of their distinct but intersecting stories.

## III. Flann, in His Own Words

Everything we read in the British press, all that the recruiters told us, followed up by what our officers said once we were there—complete and utter bosh. We came to believe the Boers were savages, worse than the Zulus, and vehemently anti-Catholic. It doesn't take much to get the Irish to fight, especially when the only other way to keep your family from beggary is to emigrate, though it's typically against the English we'd rather strike a blow. But my friends and me, desperate for work, decided to do our duty for the sake of Mother Church if nothing else.

I was assigned to a Maxim gun unit in the 18th Hussars, and shortly learned the officers weren't just liars—they were cowards, reprobates, fools.

The regiment was at Glencoe when the war broke out, and the 18th was sent to assist in the siege of Talana. Once the Boers retreated, we were sent in pursuit.

The weather, Christ—a ceaseless, soaking drizzle, been like that for days when it wasn't raining bishops and blaggards. Drenched to the bone, the lot of us, while the fog crept across the veld and utterly obscured the hilltops.

For some reason, Colonel Moller split up the regiment, sent two squadrons east to cut off the enemy's retreat while the rest of us blundered north. We entered the open plain too soon. Despite the fog, the Boers caught sight of us and in short order descended in droves.

As their numbers kept growing, the colonel ordered us to pull back to a farm compound where he hoped to hide until nightfall, then use the cover of darkness to escape. Like the Boers were that lazy or stupid they wouldn't come for us with everything they had.

Men were falling all around, horses screaming in hope of a rider. It was madness. The Maxim gun got stuck in the muddy bottom of a spruit, and the Boers fell upon us before we could work it free. Every man in the crew ended up wounded or dead—Lieutenant Cape a shot through the throat, me a round to the hip. Thank God the Boers weren't yet using dum-dum rounds like we were, or I would have bled to death right there on the mudbank.

I was taken to a Boer field hospital. There I spent the worst night of my life, listening to the dying scream out to God in their pain and fear, suffocating from the stench of blood and rot and death.

Remember, given all we'd heard, I was certain that the moment they guessed I was Catholic I'd be dragged out, flayed, strung up, a human sacrifice in some heathen ceremony.

But when I emerged from my fever dreams come morning, the first thing I heard was a murmured recitation of the rosary. And when I cracked my eyes open, I saw not a savage or even a priest, but a volunteer in the Irish Transvaal Brigade.

When the lad saw me waking, he broke off his prayers and rolled me a smoke. Told me all about himself, how he came from Kilkenny seven years back to work in the Rand gold mines, and elected to fight alongside the Dutch, if only to get a crack at an Englishman. Some members of the brigade had come only recently from Ireland, others from America, like their leader, a dashing man named John Blake, who reminded the men of Wild Bill Hickock.

Little surprise, it wasn't ten minutes before I asked—barely able to move on that cot, hip aching like fire—if I might join them. A great many of the Irish prisoners, now aware of how much their officers had lied, asked the same question as it turned out, but the Boer commanders refused to allow it. From compassion, not distrust. If we were re-captured, the British would shoot us on the spot as deserters.

So I was handed back to Her Majesty's forces in an exchange of the wounded. The officers loathed the Irish as it was, but those who surrendered? Though not officially a reprimand, I got transferred from the Hussars to the unit guarding the concentration camp in Bloemfontein. It was there I met Penny.

## IV. Penny, in her own words

I was desperate to get away from the brutal nightly rages that my father's Calvinism found so obligatory. No sooner did I learn of a recruitment effort by the Colonial Nursing Association than I leapt at the chance to join.

I was assigned to the Langman Field Hospital at Bloemfontein, the same one at which Conan Doyle volunteered. I even met him once or twice as he made his rounds, treating the soldiers wounded in battle or, as was far more often the case, stricken with enteric fever. Typhus. Nearly twice as many soldiers died from that than died from battle wounds.

By the time Lord Kitchener arrived, the Boers, badly outgunned, had resorted to guerrilla warfare. So the Hero of Omdurman, who let his officers murder the wounded, instituted his infamous scorched earth policy, with its weekly "bag" of killed, captured, and wounded, like it was all good English sport. But not half so jolly as burning farms to the ground, razing crops, slaughtering livestock, driving families by the tens of thousands into the camps.

It was then I was transferred from the military hospital to the "camp of refuge" along the railway track. Let me make this clear—those people were not refugees. They weren't even rightly prisoners of war. They were hostages, pure and simple, meant to force the Boer commandos in the field to surrender for the sake of saving their loved ones from a miserable, senseless death.

Children died by the thousands, withering away into flesh-covered sticks. How many dozens of times did I have to pry the corpse of an infant from his mother's arms?

If your family was suspected of having a man serving in the commandos, you were given half rations, and even full rations were barely enough to keep a rat alive.

Then came typhus and dysentery, because of the lack of latrines and the terrible water so contaminated it ran black. After that, the measles outbreak. That's how the majority of children died. Influenza took most of their parents.

I could barely keep my feet from exhaustion, having to not just care for patients but cook food, clean the rags we used for bandages, all of it. For far too long the camps were administered by soldiers, not medical men, and the welfare of tens of thousands of Boer woman and children rated very low on their list of priorities.

Worst of all, some of the officers snuck into camp at night, sought out the prettier teenage girls, and offered food to the parents in exchange for a romp back at their quarters. Flann saw this, too—didn't you, luv? It's what first brought us together, seeing that, sharing our disgust, our contempt. He was obliged to let the lechers in, salute as they passed, laughing. Do it again as they came back out, the girls squirming in their grip. Don't discount the tales of suicide among those girls. The Afrikaners are a very moral, very chaste people.

Oh, but please do behold the wisdom of Sir Arthur as he thunders away on the impeccable decency of the average British soldier, and the inherently defective nature of the average Boer, who remains by nature ignorant and unclean.

By the time of the truce, I no longer felt like a nurse. I was an accomplice. And the crime was apocalyptic.

Flann turned out to be one of those soldiers stricken with typhus. I visited him in the field hospital, looked after him as best I could. He survived—I won't say "luckily." You can see for yourself, his health is seriously compromised. But he earned his decommission, and thank God for that. I returned home first, promised to wait. And here we are.

## V. Prelude to a Plan

For the next few get-togethers, I guided the two of them back again and again to their wartime experiences, exploring the most horrifying and unforgivable episodes they endured. Gradually but inexorably, the intensity of their hatred hit its trigger point.

For the decisive get-together, I had the housekeeper work up a hearty fish chowder, and a hint of the musty tang of the seaside lingered in the room, mingling with the scent of wood smoke from the fire. As they finished their meals, I went to the cabinet, removed a decanter of brandy, and poured out a respectable portion for each of us.

"What if I told you that three officers very much involved with the atrocities in one of the camps—not Bloemfontein, where you served, but Middelburg, in the Transvaal—could be found every Tuesday evening at the Royal Geographical Society on Savile Row?"

They both glanced up at that and held my gaze as I delivered their brandies.

"During the war, they commandeered food and medical supplies intended for the captured families and sold it at inflated prices to local businesses. Impossible to know how many deaths can be hung directly at their door, but I'd guess it to be in the hundreds."

"Try thousands," Penny remarked. "You say these men are in London. I assume that means they were never caught?"

"Their crime got brushed under the rug, for fear of tarnishing the war effort."

"Imagine that," Flann said.

"Not surprisingly, now that they've hung up their sabers, these three men have turned their military experience to great financial advantage. They're serving as shills for a diamond syndicate in competition with DeBeers. Their job is to drum up investors for a mine outside Pretoria."

The pair of them remained silent for a moment, the crackling of the fire for backdrop. Then Flann said, "Every Tuesday?"

Penny reached out a cautioning hand, as though reading his mind. His health had deteriorated considerably in just the few weeks we'd been meeting.

The typhus had inflicted too much damage, which inclined him to a desperate, fatalistic point of view.

"I wouldn't mind sharing a word or two with men like that. At close quarters, if you catch my meaning."

"I believe I do," I replied.

We talked a while longer, returning again to the subject of the vain, contemptuous, venal British officer class, the sense of entitlement they embrace, the thievery at its core. As Flann wandered this bleak inner landscape—call it the scorched earth of his soul—his intentions grew increasingly bold, committed, and clear, just as Penny's protestations became more forbearing.

By the time they rose to leave, it was almost as though he had conceived the plan himself. And so as the two of them headed down the hallway to the door, I slipped the young man a revolver, the better to carry out the scheme.

That was the last I ever saw of them.

## VI. Enter Sherlock Holmes

From this point forward, I will need to rely on my best judgment of the facts rather than firsthand observation to convey what occurred. Now, of course, as you are accustomed to the accounts of Dr. Watson, I trust you will indulge me as I similarly recount actions I could not possible have witnessed, conversations I could not conceivably have overheard, and thoughts or impressions that arose within the confines of another man's skull. Should your demand for "verisimilitude" remain unappeased, let me merely reply that I have my sources and trust the accuracy of what they reported to me, according to which I now relate what follows.

Begin with a gunshot—four shots, to be precise, three in quick succession, with the fourth and last coming a moment or so later.

This was reported by a certain Abel Severington, a cartographer who heard the shots while doing research in the library of the Royal Geographical Society on Savile Row. The shots seemed to come from the floor above, the location of several private suites.

Mr. Severington rushed up the stairs to see what the matter might be, only to find the door to one of the suites securely locked. No one within responded to his vehement pounding, but he could smell what he believed to be spent gunpowder. He rushed to a phone. The police arrived shortly, broke down the door, and discovered a scene of sordid malevolence.

Four bodies altogether. The first three had been shot in the face, the throat, the breast, the fourth in the temple. Apparently a celebration of some sort had been in progress, for a bottle of champagne sat in a bucket of all-but-melted ice, and three crystal flutes lay scattered across the carpet amidst their spillage.

It was the identities of the dead, however, that called for the highest discretion. Three of the four were well known in the Royal Society—renowned ex-officers of Her Majesty's armed forces, distinguished veterans of the Anglo-Boer Wars, now agents for a fledgling diamond syndicate based in South Africa seeking investors.

The fourth victim, the one with the bullet wound to the temple, appeared to be a waiter of some sort, presumably the deliverer of the champagne.

Given the delicacy of the matter, Inspector MacDonald of Scotland Yard, one of those rumpled, taciturn misanthropes who somehow rise above the level of their talents, summoned Sherlock Holmes to the scene within minutes of the bodies' discovery.

Holmes, with Watson, as always trundling alongside, spent less than a minute reviewing the scene, observing the dead, and inspecting the weapon—a Beaumont-Adams Mark III, once standard issue for the British Army—before standing erect and declaring the matter an obvious case of murder-suicide, with the waiter being the principle culprit.

Inspector MacDonald, to his inestimable credit, responded, "All due respect, sir, but even an investigative mediocrity such as myself can readily surmise that much. The question is, why—and how do we keep it under wraps?"

Holmes replied, "Well, at the risk of once again seeming overly obvious to your exquisitely perceptive mind, Inspector, the first finger of suspicion might be pointed at the chief competitor to the syndicate the three gentlemen represented."

The inspector's eyes narrowed. "DeBeers."

"Precisely."

MacDonald clasped his hands behind his back and rocked slightly back and forth. "You want to accuse the most prominent mining concern in the empire of hiring this . . . waiter . . . whoever he turns out to be, to serve as their assassin?"

"To send some sort of message," Dr. Watson interjected.

Holmes gestured toward the waiter. "You touched on the principle point, Inspector. Until we discover this man's identity, the rest is mere conjecture. Have you had the chance to check his pockets?"

The inspector withdrew from his pocket a small booklet. "This was all we found."

It was a copy of *The War in South Africa: Its Cause and Conduct* by Sir Arthur Conan Doyle. Across its cover, someone had scrawled in red crayon, "Imperialist Propaganda" and "Racist Lies."

Holmes flipped through the pages, looking first for some indication of its owner, and when that proved fruitless searching for anything scrawled in the margins or underlined that might prove revealing. It turned out there was some sort of marking on virtually every page.

"Glanced at it a bit here and there myself before you arrived," MacDonald said. "Seems whoever left those remarks in the margins took special exception to the Zulus being labeled 'bloodthirsty,' and the African bushmen being referred to as 'hideous aborigines' and 'the lowest of the human race.' How fortunate for the Boers they merely come off as disorganized brutes."

"The uninformed," Holmes replied, continuing his brisk scan of the pages, "always take offense easily."

"Puts a slightly different complexion on our range of possibilities, though, doesn't it? Rather than someone purely motivated by financial interests, I mean." The inspector smiled deferentially. "If I might offer my humble, unsolicited opinion."

"The booklet may be entirely irrelevant," Watson offered.

Holmes practically gagged. "Nothing is irrelevant at a murder scene, Watson. Have you learned nothing in our time together?" Turning back to MacDonald, he said, "I will need some time to review this more closely."

"As you wish," McDonald replied. "Interesting choice in reading material, though, wouldn't you say?"

"There are a great many malcontents roaming the streets still complaining about the war, Inspector, even in the wake of victory. And the unhappy are notoriously easy to recruit into criminal acts."

"I meant the item's author. Sir Arthur Conan Doyle. I believe he and you are acquainted?"

"Not in the way rumor suggests."

"Ah."

"Regardless, to give good Dr. Watson his due, that matter, at least, deserves the mantle of irrelevance. Now, let me retire to someplace quiet to look this over."

Holmes vanished for a little less than a quarter hour. When he returned, he was feverishly turning the pages of the booklet and thinking out loud.

"This isn't definitive, of course, but look here. There are two separate handwriting styles here, one distinctly masculine and right-handed, the other unmistakably feminine and left-handed."

Watson's eyebrows shot up. "An accomplice?"

"Did I even say the writing belonged to the killer?"

"No. No, of course not, so sorry."

"And here, amidst perhaps a dozen other markings, notice these three letters: I.R.B."

MacDonald pushed back his hat. "Irish Republican Brotherhood."

"You no doubt have informants in the Fenian community here in London, Inspector."

"Of course. The only thing there's more of than Irish touts is Irish babies."

"How quickly might you find out if any of them have heard of this plot?"

"I'll need a few hours, bare minimum."

"That will have to do. In the meantime, I suggest a sketch artist come in and make a rendering of our killer's face. We'll post a notice in tomorrow's

*Times*, requesting information about this young man, saying he was found deceased without identification. No mention of anything else, certainly none of this." He gestured with vague opprobrium to the room. "We'll ask anyone in the public who recognizes his face to come forward. By noon I think we'll be very far along in identifying our murderer."

Indeed, the following day, someone popped up no more than an hour after the papers hit the streets—a young lady by the name of Penelope Collingwood.

## VII. Penny's Account, Revisited

"His name is Flann MacGreevy," she told the men assembled in MacDonald's office—Holmes, Watson, the inspector himself, and a sergeant named Benton. "We met at the refugee camp in Bloemfontein during the war. He was one of the guards. I was a nurse."

She recounted much of the information I've already provided above, with a few other salacious details underscoring Flann's contempt for the average British officer.

"So you're saying," MacDonald remarked, "that MacGreevy—"

"Would it be too much to ask that you refer to him as Mr. MacGreevy?"

"He bore an extreme contempt for the order of men we found dead with him in that room."

"I tried to be a sounding board, hoping if he just had someone to talk to, his anger would subside. But it was like a fever that refused to break—an apt analogy, I suppose, given how the typhus had come to affect him."

"He suffered neurological debility." This from Holmes.

"Like many who suffer the disease over a long period. Flann tried to hide it, but his episodes of anxious delirium were increasing. He knew he was dying, and felt he'd wasted his life. He wanted to make some great effort to strike back against a world he no longer believed was just or decent or even recognizably human."

MacDonald and Benton and Watson nodded thoughtfully. Holmes held out the Conan Doyle booklet.

"Have you ever seen this?"

She took a moment to inspect the cover. "Of course."

"Was it MacGreevy's?"

"*Mister* MacGreevy."

"Was it his?"

"Yes."

"And the handwriting inside?" He opened the booklet to show her.

"Not all. Some." She didn't so much as glance at the offered page. "We both read the book, read it together aloud some nights, felt the same disgust. Such vulgar, vainglorious stupidity. But I imagine you approve."

"Are any of these comments yours?"

"Am I under suspicion for despising the illustrious Sir Arthur Conan Doyle?"

"Would you care to pick out which ones are whose?"

"Honestly?" She rose from her chair, absently brushing off her skirt, as though the gathering had deposited some kind of residue. "I believe I've provided all the information I can reasonably offer."

"What about this?" Holmes quickly turned to the page with "I.R.B." written on it. "Is that your handwriting, or *Mister* MacGreevy's?"

She regarded the great detective with cold-hearted loathing, but then obliged his question, leaned forward, and studied the note in question. "It isn't mine," she said. "Nor can I say with certainty it's Flann's. I simply don't know."

"But you know what the letters mean, what they refer to."

"Should I?"

MacDonald crossed his arms. "Did Mr. MacGreevy ever show an interest in Irish republicanism?"

"He dreamed of a liberated Ireland, if that's what you mean. As do I, Inspector. As does anyone with a conscience."

"Do you know of any others in that movement with whom he might have shared or expressed such a sentiment?"

"What he *expressed*," she responded, "was his contempt for mendacity, for greed, for indifference to suffering. Now, you know where to find me if there are any further questions. Good day."

She turned to leave, took several steps, then stopped just before reaching the door.

"Just to be clear," she said, glancing over her shoulder. "I feel deeply responsible for what happened. I should have done more. I should have insisted Flann see a doctor, a priest, someone to ease him back from the darkness. He wouldn't listen to me, except to smile and say I have too forgiving a heart. Well, I doubt I'll be forgiving myself anytime soon. I'm a nurse, after all. If only I'd been more decisive, more insistent, those three men might . . ."

The rest of her thought hung there, unexpressed, the same way the tears that welled in her eyes refused to fall. "You'll excuse me," she said at last and hurried out.

She did not walk home alone, except in the strictest sense. One of MacDonald's undercover men shadowed her the entire way. The surveillance remained in place for two full weeks, but except for regularly scheduled, openly held suffrage gatherings, there were no clandestine meetings to report, nor did any suspicious visitors appear at her apartment in Shoreditch. She dutifully attended work six days a week at the Naval Lunatic Asylum—Coleridge's "Hoxton madhouse"—and on Sundays attended services at St. Leonard's.

At the end of the fortnight, MacDonald deemed the matter closed. He apologized to Holmes for bringing him into such a pedestrian and tawdry affair, knowing how much the esteemed detective preferred a case that demanded the whole of his faculties. He considered making Sir Arthur Conan Doyle aware that his booklet had served as something of a suicide note but thought better of it. Nor, to the inspector's great satisfaction, did word of the incident ever reach the papers. The mining concern that had retained the services of the three men, fearing the guilt by association that might accrue to the enterprise if the tawdrier aspects of their military pasts became known, offered a round of very significant payments to every paper in London in the form of overpaid advertisements. And with that, word of the killings simply melted away into the fog of rumor and gossip.

It was then that I decided the moment had come to reassert my influence on matters.

## VIII. Presentation of the Paradox

Recruiting the services of a newsboy, who for five shillings agreed to approach the door of 221B Baker Street, slip an envelope through the mail slot, then dash off without being caught, I managed to deliver to Sherlock Holmes a message reading as follows:

> *The Murderer of Savile murders all those and only those who do not murder themselves. Who murders the murderer?*

Given the ground-floor flat belonged to Mrs. Hudson, I imagine she collected the envelope, noted it was addressed to her eccentric tenant, and climbed the stairs to deliver it, whereupon Holmes ripped it open, read the message inside, smiled insidiously, then handed the single sheet of paper to Watson.

"What's this?"

"Just read it," Holmes replied, still smiling, as though in triumph. "Give me your assessment."

The doctor read the thing over several times. "I can't make anything of it—what is it, some kind of riddle?"

"A paradox, one somewhat in vogue at the moment in certain mathematical circles."

"But what does it mean?"

"It's quite technical in its original form, but has come to be known as Russell's Paradox. It reveals a logical flaw at the heart of Frege's *Basic Laws of Arithmetic* and Cantor's set theory."

"You've lost me, Holmes."

"The common way of wording it is something along these lines: 'The Barber of Seville shaves all those and only those in the town of Seville who do not shave themselves. Who shaves the barber?'"

Watson stood there for a moment, brow furrowed like a spring field in Yorkshire. "Is there some relevance to the fact that 'Seville' and 'Savile' are pronounced quite differently?"

"None whatsoever."

"I thought it might be some kind of pun."

"Do try to think a bit more deeply, my friend."

"Of course." Watson reapplied his mind to the problem. "If the barber shaves himself, then he doesn't shave himself, and vice versa."

"Exactly."

Watson returned his gaze to the message. "So what are they saying here? That the waiter killed all those and only those who did not kill themselves. That's rather obvious, no?"

"Obvious, but incomplete. He kills *only* those who do not kill themselves."

"Meaning he did not kill himself."

"Bravo."

"But if he didn't kill himself that means he did, because he kills all those who didn't . . . it just goes round and round in circles."

"You're missing something."

"Oh, damn it, Holmes, can we stop playing games? Just tell me what you're getting at."

"In the paradox, as originally worded, the individuals being considered are all part of a closed group—the men of Seville."

"Assuming women don't go to the barber to be shaved."

"Let's put that aside for the moment. The paradox falls apart if the group is not self-contained. Allow an outsider into the picture . . ."

"I knew it—an accomplice!"

"Precisely. The person who wrote this message is trying to alert us to the fact that someone else is involved in these murders."

"And who do you suppose that might be?"

"Who do we know of a distinctly mathematical turn of mind who would involve himself in such a ghastly act?"

Watson stood there, blinking. "Moriarty."

Holmes collected the slip of paper and returned it to its envelope.

"Can you see now the relevance of the notation 'I.R.B.' in the booklet found on MacGreevy at the scene? The manhunt for Birdy Edwards was financed by the Fenians, the Irish Republican Brotherhood's American wing, and it was carried out by members of the group here in England, all in conjunction with Moriarty, who provided the coup de grace by having Edwards murdered on his attempted escape to Africa."

"I do see," Watson replied, "I think."

"You mentioned women who might go to the barber to be shaved."

"Ah, well, I was just—"

"I believe Miss Collingwood deserves another visit."

## IX. The Murderer Revealed

That evening, Holmes and Watson stationed themselves outside Penny Collingwood's apartment building, waiting for her to return from work. When she arrived sometime after eight o'clock, they met her at her doorstep.

"My apologies for coming unannounced," Holmes told her, "but there has been a significant development in the Savile Road incident. I was wondering if we might have a word."

She stood there, wavering on her feet. "I am really quite tired."

"It will only take a moment. But there some particulars I need to discuss with you, matters of some importance."

"To whom?" Her eyes were bloodshot from fatigue. "Flann did what he did and now he's dead, what possible benefit to anyone—"

"The pursuit of perfect clarity, the insistence on absolute truth, is to everyone's benefit, Miss Collingwood. Everywhere, and at all times."

"Is it now." She reached out for the iron railing outside the premises for balance. For a moment, it seemed she might faint. "Fine. Come up if you insist."

They climbed the stairs to the topmost landing, six floors up, then turned and walked to a rearmost corner where her apartment lay. Not surprisingly, her lodgings were cramped and spare but immaculate. Nothing lay in open sight for Holmes to discern and analyze with his usual deductive flair.

"As you can see," she told them, "I have but the two chairs. Feel free to take them. I hope it will not appear unseemly if I sit on the bed."

Once everyone had found their proper place, Holmes said, "Does the name Professor James Moriarty hold any significance for you?"

"Should it?"

"He is a criminal mastermind whom I believe exploited your friend, Mr. MacGreevy, and manipulated him into murder."

"And what if he did?"

"Do you have any reason to believe that was the case?"

"To what end, Mr. Holmes? Do perfect clarity and absolute truth have the power to resurrect the dead?"

"No," Holmes retorted, "but they do have the power to guide the living."

"How fortunate for the living." She rose from her bed. "I'm sorry, how discourteous of me, I've not offered you tea."

"That is not at all necessary," Holmes assured her.

"It is for me," she replied, and headed to the doorway to the small kitchenette. As before at MacDonald's office, however, she took only a few steps before stopping.

"You know, Mr. Holmes, many of us who worked as nurses during the war talk about how far one's ideals should really extend. Does a dying man truly deserve all the possible care we can offer? Does a child? And a few of us, those whose hearts were broken by what we were obliged to do, came to the unpleasant realization that the best intentions often cause the greatest harm. Especially if those good intentions are born in ignorance."

"Which is why," Holmes said, "the pursuit of truth is so very important."

"But there's the paradox," she said.

Both Holmes and Watson alerted at the word, like bird dogs.

"What if obsession over the truth is itself a form of ignorance?" She turned back to the doorway. "I'm finding the air a bit close in here. You may open the window if you prefer. I'll likely do the same in the kitchen."

With that she left to put on the kettle. The two men, left alone, heard the soft whoosh of the lighted gas flame, the clatter of cups and saucers, the grumbling moan of the window being pushed open. Several minutes passed. Too many. Holmes and Watson traded glances then rose and entered the kitchen to see what the holdup was, only to discover the young woman had vanished. The only trace of her to be seen were her shoes, arranged neatly beneath the window. At approximately the same moment they made this observation, someone in the alley below cried out in horror.

Peering out the window, they saw in the dimness the figure of Penny Collingwood lying motionless on the pavement, a charwoman crouched beside her, calling for help.

They ran down to the street as fast as they could, but she was already dead. Holmes pulled the charwoman aside and inspected the body. Crushed skull, broken neck—and clutched in one hand, an envelope. When he collected it from her lifeless grip the charwoman objected, "Leave that for the coppers," to which Holmes replied, "I am a detective, woman. And a gentleman."

He did not read the note until he and Watson returned to their lodgings on Baker Street. Watson waited anxiously for some account of what it said. In time, Holmes handed it over.

*Mr. Holmes,*

*If you are reading this, I am dead. And that will likely mean I came to the conclusion that you would not relent in your inquiries until you discovered that it wasn't Flann who perpetrated those killings at the National Geographical Society. It was me.*

*We arrived together, him impersonating the waiter bearing champagne, me an emissary from their syndicate wishing them luck on their venture. We had intended, if caught, to share responsibility for the deed, but once we were in the room alone with those men, my mind changed. I knew Flann didn't have long to live, and I couldn't let his final act be one of murder, even of men so deserving of death. I removed the gun from my handbag where we had concealed it, but refused to hand it over. Instead, I myself fired the fatal shots into each of those men.*

*Flann forced me to leave, so he could take the blame himself, a way to atone and ask God's mercy. My atonement would come by continuing my work, nursing the poor unfortunates confined in the Naval Asylum. I should live, for the sake of them, so they might not drink as deeply from the abyss as he had. I didn't know he would take his own life. I imagine he did so to make sure he would never, ever betray me.*

*And why did we do these things? Because we loved each other. We understood each other's pain, understood it in excruciating, inescapable detail. We shared a vision of Hell, with only our love to quench the flames.*

*But what would you know of that, or care? For you, there is simply the singular, relentless, arrogant satisfaction of being in the right.*

*Doubt me? Ask Birdy Edwards, if you have connections with the beyond.*

*Well then, here it is, the final truth: my confession. There will be some who believe I jumped to my death, but you and I know otherwise, Mr. Holmes. We know precisely why, how, and by whom I was pushed.*

*Given the fabled brilliance of your mind, I no doubt also suppose you have, by now, discerned the involvement of the professor in this affair. Accordingly, let me then end with this:*

*The murderer of Savile murders everyone and anyone who doesn't murder themselves.*

*Who murders the murderer?*

*Sherlock Holmes.*

# A SCANDAL ON THE JERSEY SHORE

## *by Brad Parks*

*"To Sherlock Holmes she is always the woman. I have seldom heard him mention her under any other name. In his eyes she eclipses and predominates the whole of her sex."*

*—Dr. Watson, "A Scandal in Bohemia"*

**SEASIDE HEIGHTS, NEW JERSEY**
**SUMMERTIME, 21ST CENTURY**

I became aware of the scandal shortly after my first Jell-O shot.

To the rest of the patrons at the Beachwalker Bar & Grill—most of whom were substantially more lubricated than I—it was no more consequential than a grain of Atlantic Ocean sand wedged under a tourist's flip-flop.

To me, it might as well have been shining from the top of the Barnegat Lighthouse: a narrow pink smudge on the shoulder of Danny Coniglio's white tank top, near his bulging deltoid muscle.

But not just any pink smudge.

A lipstick smudge.

Danny was my best friend Nicole's boyfriend. And that smudge was definitely *not* her color.

So naturally I rushed over to her and I said, "Nickee."

That's how she spells her name—which is good, because that way no one confuses her with Nikki, Niki, Nickey, Nicky, or Nicki. Or, I guess, Nicci. But Nicci doesn't count, because we don't really hang with her anymore.

Anyhow, I was like, "Nickee."

And she was like, "What?"

And I was like, "Check out Danny's shirt."

And she was like, "He's wearing a shirt?"

(Danny was super into his abs. He seemed to believe everyone else was as well.)

And I was like, "Yeah. Look!"

And she was like, "What are you talking about, Irene?"

Yeah, my name is Irene. More about that later.

Anyway, I directed her attention to the offending lipstick smudge.

"Oh my God, do you think he's cheating?" Nickee asked.

And maybe I should have done the best friend thing and been all, *I don't know, probably not, I'm just being paranoid, blah blah blah.* But it is an old maxim of mine that when you have excluded the impossible, whatever remains, however improbable, must be the truth.

Okay, I didn't make that up. That's Sherlock Holmes.

But I think it sounds banging; and, besides, no one messes with my girl and gets away with it. She's the kind of BFF who holds your hair for you when you throw up and doesn't even make you feel guilty about it the next morning. I'd cross the Garden State Parkway at rush hour for her.

"Not only do I think he's cheating," I said, "I know who he's cheating with and when he cheated."

"What? How?"

"Elementary," said I. "The shade of the lipstick on his tank top is UltraShine, Naked Salmon No. 637. The only establishment on this entire island that sells that particular brand and color is the Rite Aid in Lavalette, which is just down the street from Kohr's Frozen Custard. As everyone knows, Kohr's uses blue cone wrappers. Note the fingers on Danny's right hand, which are stained that very color blue from where the ink of the wrapper rubbed off. This establishes beyond a doubt that Danny has been at Kohr's this evening.

"Additionally, notice the faint bruising on the right side of Danny's neck? I grant you it's difficult to detect under his spray-on tan, but surely you can see it now that I've directed your attention to it. That is not a bruise, my dear; but, rather, a hickey. And a fresh one—no more than two hours old, judging from the irritation of the recently burst capillaries. The fact that the hickey is on the right side suggests the kisser is almost certainly left-handed, while the angle of the mark indicates that it was administered by someone who was standing. Danny is approximately five-eleven. The position of the hickey, precisely one inch below his earlobe, tells me the kisser is between five-foot-five and five-foot-seven.

"Now, you know the efforts I undertake to maintain a certain plumpness to my booty—and my corresponding affinity for Kohr's orange twist. As a regular at Kohr's, I can faithfully report that the only Kohr's employee who is left-handed, the correct height, and hot enough to attract Danny's attention is Phoebe Kalchik—who, it so happens, wears UltraShine Naked Salmon No. 637. Ergo, Danny cheated on you with Phoebe approximately two hours ago."

"Oh my God," Nickee said. "That vassal."

Except she actually used a word that rhymes with vassal.

"The game is afoot," I said.

"I'm totally going to kill him," Nickee huffed.

I followed her as she charged up to Danny. In addition to his tank top, he was wearing jeans, which struck me as way too much clothing for the hot weather. But she immediately cooled him down by throwing her drink in his face.

Then we walked out, and I assisted her in administering Scorned Jersey Girl Justice, which involved keying his car.

After that, we got a pint of ice cream at Wawa and ate it on her bed as she eulogized their relationship. Though, eventually, we agreed that she never really liked him for anything other than his body; and, perhaps, a washboard stomach wasn't a basis for a lasting union.

As I left her late that evening, I would have told you that was the end of the scandal on the Jersey Shore.

But it turned out it was only the start.

Eight hours later, Danny Coniglio was found dead at his beach rental.

And not long after that, Nickee was arrested for the murder.

Now, a bit about my name. Yes, I'm Irene. But I swear I'm not ninety-two years old.

I'm named after my great-great-grandmother, Irene Norton (née Adler), who was born in New Jersey in 1858 and was a famed contralto—the Lizzo of her day. She was also the only woman to best Sherlock Holmes in a battle of wits.

Since then, there's been a lot written and said about her that is not remotely true. Like that she had some kind of fling with Holmes? Or that she was a dominatrix? I swear, you'd think some of this stuff was generated by TMZ, not the BBC.

My mother says it's just because most television writers are horny middle-aged men who are trying to get their rocks off.

Anyhow, my family knows the real story. After she got the best of Holmes, she moved back to Jersey with my great-great-grandfather, a lawyer named Godfrey Norton.

And, yeah, she was a slammin' hottie—"the daintiest thing under a bonnet on this planet," according to Holmes—but she was also empathetic, caring, and supersmart. Like if she had been born in this era, she probably would have invented TikTok.

So, anyhow, that's how I came to be Irene. And I was spending the summer in Seaside Heights, that great cesspool into which all the loungers and idlers of the Empire are irresistibly drained.

(Okay, that's Holmes' BFF, Dr. Watson, not me.)

My plan for the season was to work, tan, hook up, and hang with my girls.

And, apparently, solve a murder. Because no way was Nickee a killer.

It didn't take long to learn about what had happened that next morning, because my phone had gone absolutely nuclear.

I had a network of informants that would rival MI6. Some of my sources were just feeding me gossip, but I got the straight dope from Gina Giancarlo, because her cousin Johnny was best friends with Mikey Mihaly, who worked part-time for the First Aid Squad—and those guys know *everything.*

So this was basically firsthand: Danny did not meet a violent end. He wasn't shot, stabbed, beaten, hanged, or anything else involving obvious trauma. His roommate, Trey Lobach, told cops he had spent the night burying his balls in some skank from Staten Island and was coming back from his walk of shame around 8 A.M., when he found Danny facedown in the kitchen.

It wasn't a drug overdose. Everyone knew the only drugs Danny abused were the horse steroids he was taking in an effort to turn his six-pack of abs into an eight-pack.

It wasn't alcohol either. The only thing Danny had been drinking at the Beachwalker were non-alcoholic Muscle Monsters.

When the cops checked Danny's phone, it appeared he was in the midst of googling "poison control center" as he expired.

The cops had put a rush on the tox screen. And, in the meantime, they were all over Nickee. They based this on two factors: One, there was no sign of forced entry, so Danny must have known his killer; and, two, they believed women were more likely to use poison—and, really, whatever—which to them implicated Danny's nascent ex-girlfriend.

Anyhow, I had heard enough that I thought it was time to set the cops straight. I walked the few blocks to the Seaside Heights Police Department, went up to the front desk, and told the officer I was a witness in the Danny Coniglio case.

Twenty minutes later, I was introducing myself to a Detective Dumont.

"I'm told you have information on the murder of Danny Coniglio?" he said.

"Yeah. Nickee didn't do it."

"I see, and how do you know this?"

"Because I was with her all night."

"If you were with her all night, why weren't you there when we arrested her this morning?"

I rolled my eyes at him. "Look, I left her at midnight, okay? So I am being quite precise. Anytime after that would have been morning. But it doesn't matter, because when I departed she was at home and unquestionably staying there."

"How do you know she didn't go back out?"

"Because she was wearing her BCGs. Birth Control Goggles," I said, and I thought that should have settled matters once and for all, and that the next thing that would happen is they would fetch Nickee from her holding cell and apologize to her before shooing her out the door.

But Detective Dumont was all, "Her . . . what?"

"Nickee's glasses are like a foot and a half thick. She wouldn't let anyone but close friends and family see her wearing them. Believe me, when she takes out her contacts and puts on her BCGs, that means she's in for the night. There's no way she went back out killed Danny Coniglio."

The detective scowled. "I have a bar full of witnesses who saw her throw her drink into Danny's face. Three of them overheard her saying, 'I'm totally going to kill him.'"

"Officer, this is New Jersey. We threaten to kill five people while driving to the grocery store. If we actually went through with it every time we said it, there would be like twelve people left in the whole state."

"Yeah, except Danny Coniglio is now dead. So, tell me, if Nickee didn't kill Danny, who did?"

"Give me your number," I said. "I'll call you when I figure it out."

My first stop was the scene of the crime. Danny's apartment.

It took five minutes of insistent knocking to summon Trey Lobach, Danny's roommate. I knew Trey in passing, in the casual way one knows her girlfriend's boyfriend's roommate.

He looked like, well, like he had spent his evening trying to solve the mystery of what lurks beneath a Staten Island girl's Juicy Couture. He had raccoon eyes and five-alarm bedhead.

Clearly, Danny's death had not disturbed Trey to the extent that he was incapable of depositing some quality drool onto his pillow.

"What do you want?" he grumbled.

"Hey, sorry to bother you. Nickee left a few things in Danny's bedroom and she wanted me to get them."

"Why does she need her stuff when she's going to be serving a life sentence?"

He turned his head, and I was distracted by a flash of refracted light coming from his ear.

"Hey, that's Danny's diamond stud earring, isn't it?" I asked.

"Yeah. What about it?"

"Don't you want to show some respect for the dead before you take his stuff?"

"I didn't take anything," Trey said. "He told me I could have it. Anyhow, get lost. I'm sleeping."

He started closing the door.

"Listen, firetrucker"—another rhyme—"if you close that door, you'll regret it."

That stopped him. "And why is that?"

"Because I know you lied to the police about hooking up with some girl from Staten Island."

In point of fact, I didn't *know* it yet. But I strongly suspected it.

"What are you talking about?" he asked, and I noticed his voice had gone up by a diminished third. I may not have been a world-famous contralto like my namesake, but I still had a good ear for such things.

"Miss Staten Island," I said. "What was her name?"

"Uhh, Judy."

"Oh yeah. You're definitely lying. It is statistically improbable that you hooked up with a girl named Judy from Staten Island. Judy was one of the most popular baby names for girls in the United States from the forties through the sixties, but then it started fading fast in the seventies. By the eighties it had dropped off a cliff. So unless you got cougared by a fifty-year-old, you weren't shagging any Judys last night.

"My guess"—I whipped out my phone, pulled up Facebook, and poked at it as I continued talking—"is that Judy is really your mother's name. It is psychologically *fascinating* that the first fake name that comes to your mind for someone you hooked up with is your mother's. But I'll let you work that out in therapy someday. And, yes, here we are. Judy Lobach. Aww . . . her profile pic is a throwback of you as a five-year-old in footie pajamas. Adorable. Now, what were you *really* doing last night?"

His jaw was somewhere near the floor, which told me he wasn't going to be answering me immediately.

"Never mind," I continued. "I've already figured it out. Really, I'm embarrassed it took me this long. You have a dent in your bedhead from where the headphones matted down your hair. The tips of your thumbs beyond the interphalangeal joint crease are flattened and shiny from overuse. Your index fingers are reflexively curled as if still wrapped around trigger buttons. You weren't exercising your Oedipal complex with 'Judy.' You were playing Fortnite. Now, if you want, I can go to the cops and get them to subpoena Epic Games for their server information, which will establish your account was active all night. Or you can come clean and we'll keep this between us."

He stared at me. "Okay, fine," he huffed. "I was playing Fortnite."

"Why make up the thing about Judy?"

"Because I didn't want the cops to think I was involved in . . . whatever happened to Danny," he said. "Plus, I knew my alibi was going to get out, and it's bad for my reputation if people think I'm some dweeb who stays in his room and plays Fortnite."

"So what really happened?"

"I kept getting sniped by this pack of fourteen-year-olds from Ohio, that's what happened. Then, finally, around eight this morning I gave up and came out to get something to eat. Danny was just lying there in the kitchen. I swear that's all I know."

There were no obvious tells that he was lying. Though, as far as Nickee was concerned, it was a perfectly useless account—one that implicated as much as exculpated her. Trey's ears would have been ringing with the sound of computer-simulated gunfire. The cops would say Nickee could have easily popped in, poisoned Danny, then slipped out without Trey ever being the wiser.

"I might believe you," I said. "But now, if you'll excuse me, I'm going to search Danny's room."

Trey knew better than to even try to stop me as I tentatively entered Danny's inner sanctum.

The blinds were drawn. The air was still. The bed, which was unmade, was in the exact geometric middle of the room, not shoved up against any of the walls. Odd.

One entire corner of the room was filled with a pile of dirty clothes—the sad consequence of a mama's boy spending the summer away from the only person in his life who did his laundry.

I meandered over to the bed, ducked low to look underneath it, and was immediately rewarded with an item of interest that was hiding next to some fist-sized dust bunnies, beneath a stained T-shirt.

It was a small metal case that, upon being opened, contained a row of clear, unmarked plastic bottles. They had been filled with a clear liquid with a greenish tincture. Alongside the bottles was roughly a month supply of hypodermic needles and a plastic bag with some unmarked white capsules.

Clearly, I had found Danny's stash of horse steroids.

I closed the case, shoved it back in with the dust bunnies, then straightened.

The landing pad for everything that wasn't clothing or performance enhancing substances appeared to be the top of his dresser, which was strewn with mail, muscle magazines, nutritional supplements, hair product, and no less than five varieties of Axe body spray.

I walked over and peered into the slop until I spied an old-school spiral-bound appointment book, which I immediately opened. I turned to the current week and looked at what Danny had scheduled for the final days of his life.

A lot of working out, apparently. Each day listed different body parts—"CHEST AND BACK!!!" or "SHOULDERS, BIS, AND TRIS!!!"—along with the sets he planned to do and the person he had spotting him. His workout buddies were a colorful cast of characters whose names (all nicknames, I presume) clearly had stories behind them: "Kraken" was Monday and Thursday, someone named "Van Penorzo" was Tuesday and Friday, "Gunzy" was Wednesday and Saturday.

In the margins there were exhortations that seemed to come out of that place where motivation meets narcissism; things like, "LOVE YOUR LATS!!!" and "DON'T FORGET—THE ABS ARE THE STAIRWAY TO THE PECS!!!" And so on.

Or should I say: AND SO ON!!!

The only entry not related to lifting was from the previous day: "4 P.M. Dr. Afzelius."

Curious to see how typical this week was, I perused the remainder of the book.

From this I confirmed two things: the man had a predilection for punctuation, the exclamation point in particular, and he had been visiting Dr. Afzelius every two weeks, which seemed like an odd pattern of behavior for a healthy, twentysomething-year-old man.

Unless he *wasn't* healthy. Was Danny actually sick? Had he died of natural causes that the cops weren't paying attention to because they had tunnel vision on Nickee?

As I finished thumbing through the book, I discovered another curiosity wedged in the back. It was a thin, yellow piece of carbon paper.

A summons. From two weeks ago. The arrest had been made by an Officer Provenzano of the New Jersey State Police. Danny had been charged with violating N.J.S.A. 2C: 35-10.

I googled it. It was for possession of a controlled dangerous substance, a third-degree felony that could result in three to five years of jail time.

Thus, I went away from Danny's apartment puzzling over at least two curiosities:

Why was someone who didn't do drugs hit with a drug charge?

And why did someone who didn't appear to be sick need to go to the doctor all the time?

In an attempt to answer the second question, I decided to visit Dr. Afzelius.

My phone told me his first name was Bertil, that he was part of a sprawling local medical system, and that his practice was located in nearby Point Pleasant—which made sense. Danny grew up in Point Pleasant.

On the way, I made a detour to my apartment for a change of clothes. Much like my great-great-grandma Irene, I have been known to don the occasional disguise.

In this case, I went for a short pencil skirt, four-inch heels, nerdy glasses, and a blouse with a plunging neckline—because few people get more attention at a male doctor's office than a female pharmaceutical rep who flashes a little cleavage.

I quickly faked a business card on my laptop, stopping on the way to get it printed on heavy paper. Then I entered the building that housed Dr. Afzelius's practice and a dozen others. I lingered just outside the entrance to his waiting room until I saw through the glass door that the doctor was near the front desk.

Popping one extra button on my blouse, I made my move, sidling up to the receptionist and introducing myself, my company, and the hot new must-have drug I was representing. As I slid my card across the counter, I briefly caught the doctor's eye, which was giving me the up and down.

"I'm sorry," the receptionist said, "but Dr. Afzelius is booked solid this afternoon. If you could—"

"Actually, I might have a minute or two right now," he interrupted. "Might as well get it over with."

Smiling coquettishly, I said, "I promise I'll be quick."

I was soon following him into his private office. As he offered me a seat, I studied his personal effects. Diplomas, of course. Boring. A plaque proclaiming a hole in one. So a golfer. Pictures of teenaged kids, but no wife—and no wedding ring. So divorced. Vacation photos of all sorts. So a traveler.

Which struck me as the safest conversation starter, because even I wasn't a good enough actress to feign interest in a man's golfing exploits.

"Oh my God, is that Vienna?" I asked, pointing to one him in front of some castle-looking building.

"Prague," he said. "It's a beautiful city."

"Oh, I've always wanted to go there," I said, then gestured toward a photo of him in a rain forest, hooked to a zip line. "What about that one? Costa Rica?"

"Bolivia, actually. I go every spring, before the summer rush starts here on the shore. For my money, the Andes are far more spectacular than the Alps."

"I'd love to travel more," I said. "If only I had someone to go with. I don't have a boyfriend or anything. And as a woman traveling alone, I just don't know."

I recrossed my legs.

"Yes," he said, tugging at his collar. "Perhaps I can . . . show you more pictures sometime?"

"I'd like that, Dr. Afzelius."

"Please, call me Bert. Here, I'll send you a text. Maybe we can connect when we're both off-duty sometime. What's your number?"

I gave it to him and soon felt the buzzing in my pocket.

"Anyhow, what's this hot new drug?" he asked.

"It's called tanmaxamil. It's an oral tanning aid that's different from everything else on the market. It boosts the body's natural melanin production, giving you darker skin without the harmful effects of sun exposure or the risks associated with dyes."

"Interesting," he said. "How have I not heard of this? Has it passed all the trials?"

"It made it through with flying colors—and, by the way, those colors are bronze, beige, and tawny."

He chuckled at my joke, then asked, "Are there side effects?"

"Some Caucasians report they start dancing better."

"I might like to try tanmaxamil myself first before recommending it to my patients. Do you have any samples with you?"

"Yes," I said, pulling out a pill bottle whose label I had stripped off. "You may notice a slightly minty smell and flavor. We added that because otherwise the drug tastes a little bitter."

And because the bottle was actually filled with Tic Tacs.

"Wonderful," he said.

"We're rolling out the product on a limited basis in this market first, given its affinity for sun worship, and—"

I pretended to stifle a sob.

"I'm sorry, Bert," I said. "I just can't—"

And then I let the waterworks start to flow.

"What's the matter?" he asked.

"I can't stop thinking about . . . about . . . Danny."

"Danny?"

"Danny Coniglio. He . . . he died this morning. Didn't you know?"

"Danny Coniglio from Point Pleasant?"

"Yes," I said, making a show of trying to compose myself. "Didn't the police come talk to you?"

"No. This is the first I'm hearing of this."

It was just as I thought—the cops were so focused on Nickee, they hadn't even bothered looking at other angles.

"I'm so sorry to be the one to tell you," I said. "I'm guessing he was a patient of yours?"

Bert stiffened a little. "You know I can't discuss that. HIPAA rules still apply to the deceased."

Drat.

"Yes, of course, I'm sorry," I said. "It's just . . . the police seem to think my friend Nickee had something to do with Danny's death, that she poisoned him or something. But if Danny actually had a medical condition . . ."

I let the thought dangle. It hung out there, twisting about until it morphed from unanswered suggestion to awkward silence.

"Well, I'm sure the police will get to the bottom of this," Bert said. "Thank you for this sample. Do you have some material you can leave with me? Results of the clinical trials and whatnot?"

"I'll email you some journal articles."

"Thank you," he said, standing up. "I really do have to get back to my patients. But I hope I hear from you sometime. I have some great shots of Isla del Sol you just have to see."

I had no use for my cunning disguise at my next place of call, so I changed into more Jersey Shore-acceptable clothing and was soon joining the line at Kohr's Frozen Custard.

"Hey," the girl at the register said when my turn came up, "orange twist today?"

"Actually, I was looking for Phoebe. Is she here?"

"She's on break. Check the Lava Java."

"Thanks," I said.

Lava Java was, as its name suggested, a place that specialized in servicing caffeine addictions. It was across the street.

I spotted Phoebe sitting by herself underneath a sun umbrella at one of the plastic picnic benches that fronted the establishment. Her Naked Salmon No. 637-painted lips were wrapped around a straw that was plunged deep into an iced coffee. Her face was half-covered in overlarge sunglasses.

"Phoebe?" I said.

She looked up from her phone and immediately went rigid. It was not unheard of on the Jersey Shore for the best friend of a cuckoldress to seek restitution on her friend's behalf—probably in the form of loudly calling the other woman a whore in front of the most people possible. And maybe pulling her hair.

"I swear," she said, holding her hands up. "I had *no* idea Danny and Nickee were still together. He told me they had broken up."

"Relax. I'm just here to talk. Do you mind if I have a seat?"

I waited until she nodded at the bench across from her.

"I've been thinking about him all day, ever since I heard," she said. "I don't know whether to be sad about it or angry with him, so I've sort of been going back and forth. Danny had been working on me pretty hard for a couple weeks. He bought me this necklace and everything."

She held up the pendant, which said "Phoebe" in fancy script. "I had thought we were, y'know, starting something," she continued. "I played hard to get at first, but those abs of his. . . . Anyhow, I was *mortified* when I heard he and Nickee were still together."

"I suppose you know they arrested her."

"Yeah."

"She didn't do it," I said, explaining to her about the BCGs.

Phoebe was soon bobbing her head in total understanding. "So if Nickee didn't kill him, who did?"

"Maybe no one. Did Danny ever mention to you that he was . . . sick in any way?"

I could easily see Danny using an illness to talk Phoebe out of her panties, but she was already shaking her head.

"No. He seemed pretty healthy to me," she said. "*Really* healthy."

"Right. What about his legal troubles? Did you know Danny had recently been arrested?"

"Well, yeah, I sorta couldn't miss the ankle bracelet he had on."

An ankle bracelet. Given to him when he got bonded out. That explained the jeans he was wearing the previous night at Beachwalkers.

"Did he tell you it was for drug possession?" I asked.

"He didn't say what it was. He swore it was no big deal, that it was some kind of misunderstanding that was going to straighten itself out."

"Did you ever see Danny use drugs?"

"Danny?" she asked, aghast. "God no. He treated his body like a temple. The only dangerous substance I ever saw him ingest was an almond creatine shake. Have you ever tried one of those? Nasty."

She shivered, then checked her phone. "I'm sorry, but my break is over," she said. She rattled off her number and added, "I'm off at seven. You can text me if you have any more questions, but I really don't know anything else."

"Thanks," I said.

"Good luck, I guess," she said, then hurried across the street, tossing her spent iced coffee in a garbage can before ducking back into Kohr's.

After watching her go, I went for my phone, which had buzzed three times while we had been talking. The news was coming in from all over: the results of the tox screen had come back.

Danny Coniglio had died of curare poisoning.

And that's when I knew.

My first call was to Detective Dumont. I told him who the killer was, why, and how the murder had happened, and where the detective would be able to arrest the guilty person.

Dumont was circumspect, to say the least; but he at least agreed to perform some due diligence.

Then I texted the killer with instructions:

> *There's something I need to discuss with you. Meet me at the Casino Pier Ferris Wheel in Seaside Heights at 7:30 P.M.*

And don't be late.

---

The boardwalk reeked of the grease of a thousand fried foods. The tourists had been baked in shades ranging from golden brown to lobster red.

The appointed time had arrived. The sun would be setting soon, making this what photographers referred to as "magic hour"—that period when the light changes and you can see things for what they really are.

That's when the killer walked up, and said, "I have to admit, I didn't expect to hear from you."

"Do you want to go on the Ferris Wheel with me?" I asked. "The view is pretty spectacular this time of day."

"I'd love to," the killer said.

With the swipe of a card, I paid the twelve credits needed for two people to take the ride. We were soon alone together in a gondola as it began a slow, steady climb over the thin strip of sand where Danny Coniglio had experienced some of the best parts of his life—and his untimely death.

"So you said there's something you need to discuss with me?" the killer said.

"Yes. Did you know that Danny Coniglio died of curare poisoning."

"Is that so?"

"Yes, Dr. Afzelius, but you knew that already. After all, Danny was not only your patient. He was your customer. The only reason a healthy young man like Danny would need to see a doctor every two weeks was to buy steroids. He received his latest batch when he went to your office at four o'clock yesterday. It had been laced with curare. That's why the bottles I found hidden under his bed had a greenish tint to them."

We were now high in the air, dangling 120 feet above the ocean.

"I have no idea what you're talking about," he said. "I had no reason to kill Danny."

"Oh, but you did. Danny had been arrested for drug possession. That threw me off at first because Danny wasn't known to be a drug user. It took me a while to remember that anabolic steroids are considered a schedule three, controlled, dangerous substance under New Jersey statutes. Danny had gotten jammed up in a steroid sting operation by the New Jersey State Police. One of his frequent lifting buddies, Van Penorzo, was really an undercover state trooper named Provenzano—Van Penorzo being an anagram of Provenzano."

The gondola began its descent. I continued: "Danny was telling people that he wasn't going to jail. How is that possible when he had been arrested and charged with a third-degree felony? Easy. He was about to cut a sweetheart deal to inform on his source—you. I suspect that one of your other customers either tipped you off, or you figured it out on your own when Danny came to your office with an ankle bracelet stuffed under his jeans. Danny's downfall was that he didn't want to cycle off the juice when he was *so close* to getting the eight-pack abs that he yearned for. So he went to your office one last time to get the two-week supply that he thought would put him over the top."

"This is ridiculous," Bert huffed. "I wouldn't know the first thing about how to lay my hands on curare."

"Oh, but you do. Those annual trips to Bolivia? The curare plant is native to the rain forest. Its leaf is found on a woody vine that was actually in the background of that photograph of you on the zip line in your office. Indigenous peoples in South America long ago figured out that they could dip their darts in curare poison and use it to paralyze their prey." (I knew this from reading about it in a story by Dr. Watson.) "When ingested, it's harmless—that's why you can still eat the meat of an animal poisoned by curare, and it's how I knew Danny's drink hadn't been spiked. But when injected in high enough dosage, it's deadly. It causes paralysis that overtakes every muscle in the body, including the diaphragm. Danny had just googled 'poison control center' when he lost the ability to move his fingers. His breathing would have stopped a short time later."

"You can't prove anything," the doctor said.

We were nearing the end of our ride on the Ferris Wheel.

And Dr. Afzelius was nearing the end of his time as a free man.

"I don't need to," I said. "The police are searching your office and residence as we speak. I suspect they'll find all the evidence they need to put you in jail for a long time."

Our gondola came to a stop.

We were greeted by Detective Dumont. He was brandishing a pair of handcuffs, with two uniformed officers at his side.

"Doctor Bertil Afzelius," Dumont said. "You are under arrest for the murder of Daniel Coniglio."

When a doctor goes wrong, he is the first of criminals. He has the nerve. He was the knowledge.

Again, that's not me.

That's Holmes.

*This story is dedicated to the loving memory of Laura Caldwell, a great writer, lawyer, and friend—and a previous contributor to this series.*

# THE ADVENTURE OF THE NORTHRIDGE BILKER

*by James Lincoln Warren*

When I got home, my roommate, Shirley Ho, forensic linguist extraordinaire, was sitting in the living room across the coffee table from a good-looking guy—he had black curly hair and soulful brown eyes. There were some papers lying face down on the table, next to a ballpoint pen.

"Juanita, just in time. We were just about to get started," she said. "This is Roberto Lo Presti. He teaches high school calculus. Roberto, this is my colleague, Juanita Gutierrez. She's a Stanford-educated software engineer and handles all of my computing needs."

"Stanford? I'm jealous," he said. "I got my B.S. and M.A. at Northridge."

"What can I do for you, Roberto?" she said.

"My cousin has gone missing. I'm hoping you can help me find her."

He paused, and then reached into his pants pocket and withdrew three clear plastic dice, one red, one yellow, and one green. He put them on the table.

"But first, tell me what you make of this."

Shirley picked up the red die. Each face had a squiggle on it.

"It has Devanagari numerals engraved on each face instead of dots," she said.

"Devanagari?" I asked.

"The alphabet used in Indian languages. Unusual."

"Look at it closer," he said.

An eyebrow went up.

"It has only three numbers on it—they're each repeated on the side opposite. This one has, if I remember correctly two, nine—and four?" She showed it to me.

The sign looked like this:

४

"You remember correctly. Now look at the numbers on the other two."

"The yellow die has—one, six, and eight. And the green one has three, five, and seven."

"Just before my cousin vanished, she gave them to me, told me they were 'simply divine,' and said I should play with them to see if I noticed anything odd about them."

"They're already odd."

"True, but that isn't what she meant."

"Let me see if I can figure it out."

She gathered all three up and examined them in the palm of her left hand, rolling each one around.

"*Shǒushìlìng,*" Shirley said.

"Excuse me?"

"That's Chinese for the rock-scissors-paper game."

"You figured out how the dice work."

"Yes. The green die will beat the red die five-ninths of the time. The yellow die will beat the green die likewise. And the red die will beat the yellow die—the same way that rock beats scissors, scissors beats paper, and paper beats rock."

I was dazzled. "So . . . what are they for?"

"Cheating," Shirley said. "The cheater challenges the mark to roll against him on a bet, and tells the mark to pick his own die. Then the cheater picks the one die left that's most likely to beat it."

"You're right," Roberto said. "But I think the actual scam these were used for is more complicated than that. Have you ever heard of 'cleromancy'?"

"No," I said at the exact same moment that Shirley said, "Yes."

Shirley turned to me to explain. "It means determining the future through a random process, like casting dice. A good example is drawing yarrow stalks or tossing coins to choose which hexagram to consult in the *Zhōu Yi*—what you would call the I Ching."

She turned to Roberto. "Apparently you regard these as some sort of a clue."

"I think they're used in a fortune-telling scam."

"I'm not a private detective, Mr. Lo Presti. I work with recordings and texts, not with dice. You should consult the police." Shirley suggested.

"I did," he said. "No help there. Because of her job, my cousin, Diana Butler, goes off the grid for weeks at a time. They told me she'd most likely turn up when she was ready."

"Then hire a detective agency."

"I did, but they came up with nothing," he said. "Let me explain. It all started with my late Aunt Luisa's husband, Joseph Butler—Diana's father. He's the one who gave the dice to Diana.

"He was a successful businessman, and pretty well off. He was also a compulsive gambler. Said that gambling made him feel alive.

"Four years ago, when Luisa died in a car collision, Uncle Joe was devastated. Before that, he'd always been a church-going man. But with Luisa gone, Joe stopped going to Mass altogether. His gambling became even more of a problem.

"One night, after too much bourbon, he told us that he'd converted to a new religion, the Cleromantic Council. Said he'd taken an oath to protect its holy secrets. Apparently, the cult worships luck, and that involves praying—through gambling! It's got to be a scam. Crazy, right?

"But the religion didn't help," Roberto continued. "Joe committed suicide three months ago. Shot himself in the head with a revolver. He'd always said he wanted to be buried next to Aunt Lu, but his will directed that he be cremated instead. And that wasn't the only oddity."

"What else?"

"Diana's an only child and expected to inherit everything. But Joe's will left her only one-third of the estate, and the rest to the Council. Diana wasn't going to settle for that. She decided to investigate the cult."

"You said Diana's off the grid for weeks for her job. Is she a detective?"

"An investigative journalist."

"No wonder your PI didn't find anything," Shirley said, "especially if she was protecting her confidential sources, as journalists do."

"The leader of the Council is a woman who calls herself Tyche Clarke."

"Obviously an alias. 'Tyche' was the name of the Greek goddess of luck. And 'Clarke' means 'cleric.' Hence, 'priestess of luck.'" Ms. Clarke hadn't fooled Shirley.

"You see?" said Lo Presto. "That's why I came to you—nobody else caught that. Not me, anyway, nor the police or the agency. And there's one other thing—Diana was convinced Joe didn't kill himself, but was murdered, although the evidence was conclusive that he fired the gun.

"Diana was routinely checking in and emailing me her notes for safe-keeping, so I saved everything on my phone to keep it with me. I got worried when, a couple weeks ago, contact abruptly ceased. The last thing she sent was a picture of a mansion—I have no clue where it is—and I haven't heard from her since.

"That's it," he said. "Will you take my case?"

"Give me what you have," Shirley replied. "But I can't say what I might find, or whether it will be any help."

"There must be something. Anything. I'm at my wit's end."

Shirley nodded.

"Give me all the data you have. I'll wipe it when I'm done. I'll contact you with the results of my analysis after I've finished."

The next morning, Shirley came out of her bedroom late, dressed in her robe and slippers, and made coffee in the French press.

"Roberto gave me a big clue yesterday when he said Diana had called the dice 'divine.' She appears to enjoy messing around with wordplay and double meanings. And as I found out, anagrams. There's one entry in her notes that says, 'they crackle date culler.' The first two words are an anagram of 'Tyche Clarke' and the last two unscramble to 'cult leader.' Once I realized that, her notes became more legible, but they don't provide any insight into her disappearance. They do paint a pretty picture of the operation, though.

"It's a variant of a classic grift. The fortune-teller cons the mark into believing he's suffering from a curse. This can only be lifted by burning a bag containing most of the mark's cash. The bag is burned in front of the mark, who then believes he's been saved—but the fortune-teller has already switched the money in the bag with newspaper. The Council dressed it up with high probabilities of winning a gamble with the dice."

"That's despicable."

"But not very helpful for our purposes. On the other hand, Diana used an unusual word several times in her texts and notes: 'Zelzah.'"

"Somebody's name?" I asked.

"A place," she replied. "That's what made it odd. In the Bible, Saul is told to go there."

"What makes it important??"

"Diana's use of it wasn't Biblical. It comes from her familial register—a 'register' means a particular way of verbally communicating. You use one register when speaking with your colleagues, another register with a cop who pulled you over for speeding, and yet another with your girlfriends when you're out on the town. Formal, informal, cant, professional jargon—those are all registers, and everybody also has a *personal* register, an *idiolect*, unique to themselves.

"Diana signed off her IM chats with Roberto with it, so it was obviously some kind of complimentary closing, like 'roger, out,' or 'later, dude.'

"For comparison, I examined Roberto's sign-off, and it was almost always 'CUSN.' 'SN' is the Morse code abbreviation used in amateur radio for 'soon'—and Roberto told me he's a ham radio operator, so 'SN' is in *his* idiolect. 'CU' is obvious. His closing means, 'see you soon.'

"If Diana was using 'Zelzah' the same way, it's not unlikely she was either echoing his sentiment, or he was echoing hers. There's a distinct possibility that it means the same thing: 'see you soon.'

"Remember when Roberto told us he got his degrees at California State University Northridge? That school is also known by its initials: CSUN."

"I get it. CSUN. CUSN."

"Right. And knowing Diana's love of anagrams, it seemed to me that Zelzah might somehow mean 'CSUN,' and she was making a joke of it. So I looked up the university, but at first I found nothing to support my hypothesis. But then I noticed that there was a web page on the site called 'About Northridge.'

"It provided a history of the neighborhood. Before 1929, that neighborhood wasn't called Northridge at all. It was called, wait for it—"

"Zelzah?"

"Bingo. But that's not all.

"The key was the picture of the mansion that Diana sent to Roberto, taken with her cell phone."

"You found the mansion?"

"The latitude and longitude were recorded in the photo's metadata by her phone's GPS. The building is on a private street in Northridge, in an upscale neighborhood. And it's not a house, it's a home."

"Sorry?"

"A *funeral* home. Or it once was. I think we've found the Cleromantic Council."

Shirley called Roberto. Her phone was still against her ear when she walked into the living room.

"That's an unbelievably bad idea, Roberto," she said. "Hold off. Let me do some more digging. . . . Good. I'll call you."

She terminated the call and stared at her phone. "Idiot."

"What's wrong?"

"I gave Roberto my report, and now he wants to burst into the funeral home and confront whoever's there."

"Well, wouldn't you?"

"No, I wouldn't. The only thing we know about Tyche Clarke is that she's a con artist. We have absolutely no idea how dangerous she is. True, con artists are rarely violent, but we have no probative data, nor do we have any evidence she had anything to do with Diana's disappearance. At best, Roberto's going to get himself arrested. At worst . . ."

She shook her head. "I talked him down, but only after promising him that I would obtain more information."

She speed-dialed her phone and lifted it to her ear.

"Hey, Cody. Video conference tomorrow, ten o'clock. I'm going to borrow Toby if you don't mind, and I can use some help from your best buccaneers. . . . Sure," she said. Pause. "*Hasta mañana*."

"Okay, Shirley," I said. "Who are Cody and Toby? I want to know what's going on."

"You met Cody when we moved in, the teen leader of the Bay City Pirates. Toby isn't a who, it's a what. T-O-B-I, for Transactional Online Bot for Investigation, a software bloodhound optimized for the dark web."

"That could be illegal."

She shrugged. "Not at all. Corporations use bots all the time."

"But the dark web?"

"Where else are you going to look for somebody who apparently doesn't exist on Google? The Publishers Clearing House mail list?"

We'd just finished breakfast when Cody rang the doorbell. Shirley let him in, and he zoomed past her, straight into the lab.

I started to follow, but Shirley held back.

"Coming?" I asked.

"He gets nervous when I watch over his shoulder," she said. "You go ahead."

When I entered the lab, he was plugging a flash drive into Shirley's main computer.

"Mind if I watch?"

"No, I don't mind," he said, grinning with adorable dimples. "You're Juanita Gutierrez. Ho said you went to Stanford. That's so cool!"

"Yeah, I think so, too," I said. "What's that you've plugged into Shirley's machine?"

"Tails," he said. "You know, The Amnesiac Incognito Live System."

Tails is a Linux-based operating system that runs independently of a host computer's own OS. It's very popular among hackers. "Amnesiac" means it leaves no trace of itself behind.

He rebooted Shirley's computer, changed the boot priority to the USB port, and voilà! Up came the Tails interface.

He plugged a second thumb drive into another port.

What came up on the screen was a not-too-bad animation of Johnny Depp as Captain Jack Sparrow mapped to Shirley's webcam—Cap'n Jack on the screen echoed Cody's movements in real life.

He blushed and muttered, "You can't be too careful."

The screen split as Glinda, the Good Witch of the North, joined the conference, further splitting in rapid succession as we were joined by Harry Potter and the Jodie Whittaker version of the Doctor.

"We've got a job," Cody said, and I saw Cap'n Jack mouth the same words on the screen. "There are two parts. I've already been asked to sic Tobi on one of them, so that's up to me.

"That leaves the second part, which is up to you three. Whoever gets the most or best information on, and I quote, 'Cleromantic, Council, Northridge'"—he typed these words in, and they appeared at the bottom of the screen, so his cohorts could see how everything was spelled—"will be handsomely rewarded. The rest of you will get the usual cash. You've got twenty-four hours. Any questions?"

"Aloha."

"On it."

"Roger."

The avatars vanished.

He shut down Tails and rebooted Shirley's machine again, changing the boot priority back to Shirley's hard drive.

As if he'd never been there.

"Give this to Ho," he said, handing me his cell. "It's Tobi."

Kid had skills, I had to admit.

Shirley stuck her head in the door.

"I heard the telltale clatter of skateboard wheels riding off into the distance," she said. She pointed to what was in my hand. "Ah. Cody's most prized possession."

I handed it to her, and she sat down in front of her primary computer.

She lit a stick of rosemary-scented joss and I couldn't help but think that the smoke was bad for her computers, even if it was good for her brain.

When she showed up in the kitchen, she plopped down on her chair and said, "It turned out to be a two-stick problem."

"A two?—oh. You mean you burned two sticks of incense while running Tobi."

"I'm not done running Tobi. Or more accurately, it's not done running us. Get your keys. We ride. Westwood, ho!"

On our way, Shirley explained why we were headed to Westwood.

"The reason that Roberto's detective agency couldn't find out anything about Tyche Clarke is because they couldn't do a deep enough search—and there was a lack of imagination in their search criteria. They accessed local public records and used regular internet search engines. They had nothing the likes of Tobi, which has a relentless search algorithm—even for evidence that isn't available on the internet.

"One of the tasks I gave Tobi was to find and correlate similar aliases to 'Tyche Clarke.' It found three names that almost mean the same thing: a Lakshmi Pujari in London, a Fortuna del Monaco in Rome, and a Felisa Obispo in Madrid. None of them seem to exist except on the internet and in the post offices of each of the three countries. All three were successful high rollers on dark web gambling sites and banked their winnings in the Bahamas."

"Did Tobi find Tyche Clarke on any of those underground gambling sites?"

"No."

"They all had postal addresses?"

"Yes. Which means somebody real was using those names as aliases."

"Somebody who travels, then. If they are all the same person, it's a lot easier to fake your nationality online than it is in person."

"That's why we're going to UCLA," Shirley said. "Because I got another name, but this one didn't fit the pattern. Tobi cited several journal articles by a scholar named Jacqueline Seaworth. I don't have a UCLA library card to look them up, so I'm going to borrow my sister's."

"Your sister?"

"Brooke Ho. She's a professor in the philosophy department. Semiotics. As hard as it may be to believe, she's even smarter than I am."

Professor Ho was older and stouter than Shirley, with nothing of her sister's wired energy, but she complacently accompanied us to the Young Research Library and helped us look up Jacqueline Seaworth's articles.

We learned that Jacqueline Seaworth had doctorates in both mathematics and anthropology from Cambridge. In Italy, she was a Research Fellow at the American Academy. In Spain, she'd been at the Real Academia de Ciencias. But she hadn't published anything new in years.

There could be little doubt that this was Tyche's true identity—but we had no proof. Her trail had gone cold.

The next day, Cody showed up with another thumb drive.

"Hi," he said, standing on the front porch. "Can't stay. But here's the stuff on the Cleromantic Council."

He dropped the stick into Shirley's hand, got his phone back, and rattled off.

"Let's see what we've got," she said, and went back into her lab. This time the incense was basil.

"Success," Shirley announced. "Of a limited sort, though."

"Who won?"

"Won? Oh, the competition. Honorable mentions for Doctor Who and Harry Potter, but first prize goes to Glinda. Not bad for a twelve-year-old girl."

*Twelve?*

"Oh."

"But her information is too technical for me. I need the assistance of somebody who can understand it."

"Why not Cody?"

"Let me rephrase: I need the assistance of *an adult* who can understand it. I don't want to involve the Pirates any further."

"You mean, for example, someone with a Stanford degree in computer science."

"That would be nice. Do we know anybody like that?"

"We might. Let me look at what she found."

"I thought you'd never ask."

Shirley handed over a sheaf of printouts.

It took me hours to unravel what it was—well, not what it was, so much, but how it was done.

When I'd figured it all out, I demanded a goblet of the Sauvignon Blanc that Shirley had stashed in the fridge.

"All right," I said. "Online gambling is illegal in the U.S."

"How very true."

"Some online casinos use cryptocurrency."

"So the gamblers can't be traced. I knew that, too."

"Cryptocurrency is like keeping all your cash in a secret safe, and it's not backed by any government, but by its users.

"Every time you take money out of your secret safe, the transaction is reported to everybody, but the report doesn't say where the money's from or where it's going. You can only transfer money to somebody who has their own secret safe.

"And then, to make sure that nobody can crack the combination of your safe or anyone else's, every time a safe is opened, the combination gets changed when it's closed.

"That's how it works—the transaction isn't secret, but the safe combinations are different for every transaction, protecting your identity.

"But what if the money can be corrupted to secretly report when it is taken out of or put into *your* safe specifically? The corrupters wouldn't need the safe's combination. They'd have the means to match reports of transactions with the identities of safe owners. It's no longer a true cryptocurrency, but something that only *looks* like a cryptocurrency, a *pseudo*-cryptocurrency. That's what's at the heart of the Council's operation. They issue it through their underground online casino. The rest of the scheme is like an M.M.O.R.P.G. That's a—"

"Massive Multi-Player Online Role-Playing Game," Shirley said.

I raised my eyebrows. "You know what an M.M.O.R.P.G. is?"

"Well, gamers have their own lingo. But instead of obliterating ogres to move up to the next level, are you saying that the players gamble instead?"

"Essentially, yes. They still form teams like in a regular multi-player online game, but they pool their wins and losses. But unknown to the players, one member of every team is always going to be a shill for the Council, a bot instead of a human.

"Along the way, you can win scrolls that explain how God controls the outcome of every game, and how to worship him to improve your odds at winning. This always involves a 'sacrificial offering' in the form of a bet. Getting to the highest level of the 'game' will get you an invitation to the Secret Cathedral—which isn't a virtual place at all, but a real one."

"In Northridge?"

"Not only that, its full name is the Secret Cathedral of *Zelzah*."

"Then that must be where we can get the data we need," Shirley said. "I read something about a chat room?"

"The entry portal. It ostensibly exists to share information on underground online gambling, but it's really a recruiting ground for the Cleromantic Council. A bait and switch."

"All right. I can participate, then."

"It's not that easy. First of all, they use the pseudo-cryptocurrency to learn everything there is to know about you. You'd have to have the CIA provide a fake identity for them not to know who you really are. Secondly, it would take months to work yourself up high enough to be invited. Third, we can't afford it."

"You misunderstand. What I want to do is capture what's said there for forensic analysis. I haven't told yet you what Doctor Who and Harry Potter found."

"I assumed it was similar to what Glinda gave you."

"Nope. Those two know they can't compete with Glinda—she's second only to Cody—so they took a different tack.

"They teamed up and used the *normal* web to find the most likely places where the Council might recruit. They joined online gambling addiction twelve-step support groups, then asked the people using them if they knew anything about the Cleromantic Council.

"Because the members of support groups are anonymous, the kids had absolutely zero risk of being discovered for who they really were, and those they chatted with were precisely the sort of people who would be most vulnerable to the Council's pitch.

"It turns out that the Cleromantic Council also recruits more directly. There's an app for that."

Shirley planted herself in her office chair and went online. When I walked in, she was wearing headphones and controlling an on-screen macho elf fighting a dragon in the courtyard of a hulking gray castle.

I tapped her shoulder.

She looked up, glassy-eyed, and said, "Just a minute."

Then she continued playing. For another three hours.

I went back to the living room and watched TV alone. Just when I had decided to go to bed, she came out of the lab, bleary-eyed.

"How did your research go?" I asked, trying to keep my voice neutral.

"It took much less time than I expected," she said. "We were invited to attend services tomorrow morning. Well, later *this* morning."

"We were?"

"Yes. At ten o'clock."

"Are you going?"

She didn't answer right away.

"Maybe we should call it off," she said. "I probably shouldn't have pretended to be you online."

"*What?*"

"You said you'd help."

"I didn't give you permission to steal my identity!"

"Look, you're the one who said we couldn't use a false identity. You fit the profile much better than I do. You've just gone through a debilitating divorce, you're desperately trying to find a job, and you're depressed. You have 'target' written all over you."

What she said was perfectly true.

"Shirley, it's after midnight. Why don't we sleep on it? We're both exhausted."

"Okay," she said. And then she turned around and went back into the lab. Back to her computer.

I woke to the obnoxious burble of the landline.

"Hello?"

"Oh. Juanita. It's Rob Lo Presti. Is Shirley there? I need to talk to her."

I looked at the clock.

"Roberto, it's 6 A.M. She was on the internet until the wee hours. I'm sure she's sleeping."

"It's important. Can you wake her? Please."

I went into Shirley's room and shook her by the shoulder.

"Roberto Lo Presti is on the phone. For you."

I went back to bed.

And minutes later, I had my own shoulder shaken by Shirley.

"Juanita. We've been fired."

"Well, not exactly fired," Shirley said. She showed no sign of having been up all night. "More like dismissed. He's paying us the contracted fee. He said Diana has reappeared, so there's no need to continue the investigation. It's all wrong."

"Well, if she's back, she's back, end of story," I said.

She looked at me as if I were stupid. "Then why did he call at six freakin' A.M.? Couldn't he wait until a more reasonable hour?"

"He probably didn't realize you were up all night massacring orcs."

She frowned.

I tried again. "He's a schoolteacher, Shirley. That early is normal for him."

"Maybe, but he knows it's not normal for me. Another thing. Do you remember what he said when I told him I'd wipe all of his data after I'd finished my analysis?"

"He said he didn't care what you did with it, as long as he found his cousin."

"Well, he says she's back. Then why did he specifically remind me of that clause in our contract? Not only remind me, but insist on it?"

"Maybe he told Diana that he'd shared all her notes with you," I said. "Maybe she's the one who insisted."

"I'd like to hear that from her. Because I don't think she's back at all. I think Roberto was responding to a threat: Destroy the evidence or else."

"Or else what?"

"Let's look at facts. Diana is an investigative reporter, probing a cult. She suspects that cult of causing the death of her uncle and defrauding her of her inheritance. How do you suppose she went about it?"

"She interviewed witnesses," I said.

"That's only preliminary research. To get the real scoop, she'd have to dig much deeper. She'd go undercover. She'd join the cult."

"I don't see how that could work," I said. "They would know who she was."

"You're right. It *didn't* work. They *must* have known who she was, and played along. After reeling her in, they put her on ice to find out what she knew. And what they found, probably from her phone, is everything she sent to Roberto."

I sat up. "Oh, no. So they gave him an ultimatum? Meet their demands, or he'd never see Diana alive again?"

"Exactly. There's something else that's been bothering me, too. When cult members disobey their leaders, what happens to them?"

I knew the answer to that.

"They get punished."

"Correct. But the Council *ostensibly* worships luck, and *ostensibly* lets God decide everything through a game of chance. The dice prove that such games are rigged in the Council's favor. Joe gave those dice to his investigative journalist daughter, which means he had to be punished.

"I started thinking about Joe's death being ruled a suicide, and Diana's conviction that he'd been murdered. Maybe both are true."

"How could they be?"

"Juanita, think of a dangerous game of chance that requires the use of a revolver."

I gasped. "Russian roulette!"

"If Diana is still alive, she's in deadly danger. And now Roberto is, too." She looked grim. "We've got to keep that appointment."

"The police—"

"—would never believe us. This will probably be dangerous. Bring your revolver."

We arrived at the former funeral parlor that morning about 9:45, dressed for church. The double front doors were locked, but buzzed open when we pressed the doorbell.

Inside, the vestibule looked calm and welcoming. Like a funeral parlor.

Hanging over the reception desk was a painting of a beautiful, pale woman wearing angelic white robes.

"That is our founder, Sister Tyche." We looked down. Sitting at the desk was a plump middle-aged brunette woman wearing a conservative pantsuit.

"You must be Juanita Gutierrez," she said, looking at me, kindness exuding from every pore. "I am Sister Felicity."

She looked doubtfully at Shirley.

"This is my friend Shirley," I said. "I felt a little nervous coming here alone."

"You are certainly welcome here, Shirley," Sister Felicity said, "but I'm afraid that the only appointment I have is for Juanita."

"Can't she come with me?" I asked.

"I'm sorry. The invitation was for you alone, Juanita. Before you can attend services, you must be interviewed by one of our deacons. We carefully screen postulants, because the world is not yet ready for the truth—that is reserved for the elect. I'm sure you understand."

"You go ahead, Juanita," Shirley said. "I'll be fine."

"Ah! Here's Deacon Díaz."

He entered through a door on the left. He was tall, broad-shouldered, my age.

"Hi, Juanita. I'm Carlos," he said, smiling. "Don't be frightened. This won't take long, and believe me, you'll feel better after our talk."

Shirley gave me a casual wave, and Carlos led me into a well-appointed office with another desk. He offered me a comfortable-looking leather armchair on one side of the desk, and then sat down behind it, across from me.

"Before we begin, I must insist that what passes between us in this room be held absolutely confidential," he said.

"All right. Yes." I clutched my purse, all too aware that my gun was inside.

He reached into the desk drawer and drew out three dice, identical to the ones Roberto had shown us.

"These are cleromantic dice," he explained. "Do you know what cleromancy is?"

"I looked it up. It's casting lots to determine the will of God."

He beamed from ear to ear. "Excellent! Pick them up and look at them."

"They're very strange. What are these symbols?"

"They are ancient numerals from India," he said. "They have mystic properties."

He reached into the drawer and withdrew a diagram, which he placed in front of me:

१ २ ३ ४ ५ ६ ७ ८ ९
1 2 3 4 5 6 7 8 9

"This should make them easier to read. You probably don't believe, not yet, so I will show you how they work. Each die has three numbers on it, engraved twice on the die on opposite sides.

"We divide the nine numbers into three Sacred Triads: one through three, four through six, and seven through nine. Each die features one number from each Triad.

"This is not a game. It is how God speaks, only most of us don't understand what He's saying. Roll the dice. I will translate."

I obeyed.

"See? You rolled two, six, and three. That's a very good sign."

"What does it mean?" I asked.

"Two and three mean that you are concerned with your relationship with God. We know that's true, or you wouldn't be here now. Two represents division and conflict, but three represents synthesis, coming together. By itself, that would mean transitioning from isolation to community, or the other way around.

"The number that tells us which is six, which represents Creation. In other words, your feelings of abandonment and being disconnected are temporary, that through creating a world with God in it, your life will come together. There is hope."

"That's amazing," I said.

He put his props away and started to probe.

Mostly about my divorce. He was sympathetic and solicitous—and I knew he was doing a cold read—gently exposing my emotional weaknesses to exploit. So I gave him what he was looking for.

I was in the middle of describing my divorce when Sister Felicity opened the door.

"Pardon me, Deacon," she said, "But Sister Tyche is ready to see Juanita. God be praised, she's had a revelation."

I took that to mean the room was wired, and that Sister Tyche was ready to swoop in for the kill.

"Of course, Sister."

I was led to another door by Felicity and Carlos together.

And then they shoved me into the room so hard I fell down. I heard the click of a lock.

"Are you all right?"

Shirley helped me up.

We were in a chapel. There were three coffins aligned in parallel, perpendicular to the altar.

Roberto was sitting on one of the folding chairs filling the room, head down.

"He recognized me when he came in the front," Shirley said. "He didn't mean to give me away, but they knew immediately. We're prisoners. These doors would withstand a tank."

We'd been locked in for an hour before the music speakers started to talk in a woman's voice with a posh English accent.

"Call me Tyche," she said. "I apologize for leaving you incommunicado for so long, but I've been rather occupied, overseeing our exodus. Pity we'll have to say goodbye without meeting face-to-face. You've probably noticed that your mobile phones don't work—I expect you've tried dozens of times to call Emergency Services—but alas, the chapel is a Faraday cage. For the two women's phones, that is. I have Roberto's here in my pocket.

"I can see you clearly via the surveillance cameras, but I can't hear you, so don't bother asking me questions. I require only one signal from you, to be described in due course.

"I expected to address Roberto Lo Presti alone, but let me say that the ladies' presence—I know who you are, Ms. Ho, from Roberto's phone messages to you—was an unexpected stroke of luck."

She laughed. "The whole situation is piquantly ironic. But as we do not have much time, allow me to anticipate one of your questions:

"Are you about to be murdered?

"Well, that depends on you.

"You probably didn't expect to have a chance to survive, but you do. My theological theories have generally been misunderstood. Of course, I intended that they should be, but in their essence, they boil down to one principle: God doesn't care. God is nothing but a field of probabilities that may be twisted into profit. I have therefore decided, for my own amusement, to leave your fate to His discretion.

"You see three coffins near the altar. A cursory examination will show you that they are each fitted with a keyed lock. The same key opens all three. The hinges on the lids have springs that pop open when released.

"One of the coffins contains Diana Butler, very much alive, or was when she was placed there, bound and gagged. If she is rescued within the next three hours, she has an excellent prognosis. But she does not have three hours.

"In lieu of a pillow, her head is resting on a bomb with two fuses. The first fuse will detonate the bomb if one of the wrong coffins is opened. The second fuse is a thirty-minute timer. Diana's survival has a probability of zero if either fuse is triggered. Yours is only slightly higher.

"You might expect that the key is hidden somewhere, and that you must search to find it. But being generous, I will tell you where it is. The only condition for this information is that Roberto must guess which of the coffins contains Diana and indicate it.

"You will then be able to open one coffin. If you have chosen well, it will open, and the bomb will be disarmed. If you have chosen poorly, the bomb will explode, Diana will die, and you three are very likely to be killed or seriously injured.

"You have thirty minutes from—now. Begin."

Roberto couldn't decide.

"Roberto," Shirley said, "It doesn't make any difference. The probabilities are all the same, one-third. The clock is ticking."

"All right!" He went to the center coffin and placed his hand on it.

There was a loud noise as the lid of the coffin on the left suddenly sprung open like the lid of a jack-in-the-box. At first we thought that the bomb had exploded, but no.

We heard cruel laughter over the speakers.

Roberto ran over and looked inside the coffin. It was empty.

"I couldn't resist," Tyche said. "I simply had to see your reaction. As you can see, I disabled the bomb from going off and opened the lid remotely—but now, the fuse is fully functional. On the plus side, you now have only two choices instead of three."

Roberto looked desperate.

"You will find the key under the altar cloth."

Roberto threw the altar covering off and grabbed the key. It looked completely ordinary. It looked completely evil.

"You can change your mind if you like," Tyche said. "At this point, I don't care. With that, let me bid you adieu."

Silence.

He stared at Shirley in horror. Then he rushed toward the center coffin with the key.

But Shirley stepped in in front of him before he got there and struck him hard in his solar plexus.

He collapsed and dropped the key. She scooped it up and went to coffin on the right. He tried to get up and stop her, but it was too late.

She turned the key. The lid opened. The bomb did not explode.

And Diana Butler, all trussed up with duct tape around her limbs and face, stared back at us, tears streaming down her cheeks.

Roberto got the tape off her mouth, and through her weeping, I think she said, "You came! Thank God! You came!"

My revolver was not completely useless, even if I was.

Shirley used it to shoot through the lock of the chapel door. I wouldn't have known how. Then she dialed 911.

She turned to me, glassy-eyed, and said: "I think I'll give a miss to online games tonight. I'm heartily sick of games."

Yay.

We were at home. I had to ask.

"Shirley, how did you know that Diana was in the other coffin?"

"I didn't."

"You mean you *guessed*? But the odds were fifty-fifty. Why did you switch?"

"The Monty Hall Problem."

"I've heard of it, but I don't know what it is."

"Let me walk you through it. What was Roberto's original probability that he'd picked the correct coffin?"

"One in three. That's obvious."

"Probabilities are measured in fractions, Juanita. All the possible probabilities must add up to one. So one in three is a probability of one-third."

"I know. One-third, then."

"Then what was the probability that he'd picked one of the empty coffins instead?"

"Two-thirds. Also obvious."

"Correct. Roberto chose the middle coffin, but he wasn't allowed to open it.

"Now, instead of Tyche, what if Roberto had been allowed to open one of the other coffins without setting off the bomb? What would his probability have been of opening an empty one?"

"Two-thirds?"

"Right. Why?"

"Because—all three of the coffins were still closed, so the chance of any of them holding Diana was still the same as any of the others—a probability of one-third. That means that any one of them being empty had to have a probability of two-thirds."

"Very good. Let's say Roberto coincidentally picked the same empty coffin as Tyche did in the event. At that point, he was free to open one of the other coffins, hoping to pick the right one. How would the probabilities have changed?"

"There were two coffins left. The odds would be fifty-fifty."

"Your answer is correct, but your rationale is incomplete."

"What do you mean?"

"You should have said, 'Of the remaining two coffins, the one he *randomly selected* had a fifty-fifty chance of being empty.'"

"I don't get it."

"Conditional probability. That means that the probability of something changes with new information, which can be calculated. Linguists use it in semantic analysis.

"For example, let's say someone types 'LOL' in a text message. If that person is over thirty, it usually means she's laughing at something witty. But if she's a teen, the probability is that her laughter is derisive—it's the equivalent of rolling her eyes.

"So the probability of what 'LOL' means changes after it's informed by the author's age. It becomes what's called a *posterior* probability.

"Juanita, conditional probability applies to all kind of things besides linguistics. Epidemiology, economics—and gambling."

"I can see that. It's why Roberto's odds improved to fifty-fifty instead of only one in three."

"But that's only true if the empty coffin was opened at random. It wasn't. Tyche *knew* it was empty."

"I'm not following."

"We agreed that the original probability—Roberto choosing the correct coffin at the onset—was one-third. We also agreed that the new information's probability—Roberto opening an empty coffin—was two-thirds. If you divide one-third by two-thirds, the fractions cancel out, and it's the same as dividing one by two. The posterior probability is one half, or as you put it, fifty-fifty.

"Because Tyche knew the coffin was empty before she opened it, *that's new information*, and it changes the posterior probability in a different way. *Her* odds of opening an empty coffin were one hundred percent—a probability of one. That's very different from Roberto's one-third divided by two-thirds. If you divide one-third by *one*, the resulting posterior probability is still only *one-third*. In other words, Roberto's probability of having chosen the correct coffin *didn't change* after Tyche opened the coffin.

"So how was the probability changed for the last coffin?"

I thought about it and didn't like the answer.

"That can't be right. All the probabilities have to add up to one. You say Roberto's chosen coffin still had a probability of one-third. The second coffin had a probability of zero. That means the last coffin had a probability of two-thirds. That doesn't make sense."

"It doesn't seem like it should, but trust me, it does. And that's how I knew which one to open. A third of the time I would have been wrong, and boom. But I'd be right twice as often.

"I remember some fool once saying, 'I never guess: it is an appalling habit, destructive to the logical faculty.' But in life, there is almost never complete certainty. My entire profession depends on assessing probabilities, not sure things."

"Uh . . . I'm having some trouble wrapping my head around all of this. I still don't get it."

She smiled. "Don't feel bad. Even eminent mathematicians have trouble wrapping their heads around it, but there's more than one way to prove that it's true—I can show you the math later."

"Not comforting. One last question: why did you call it the Monty Hall Problem?"

"Because that's its name. Monty Hall gives a game show contestant a choice between three doors. Behind two of them there's a goat. Behind the third is a brand-new car . . ."

# CUMBERBACHELOR

## *by Maria Alexander*

Daphne's wedding was in two weeks, but she might not make it if her older sister, Sam Huber, murdered her now. And she was seriously considering it.

"Where *the hell* is Mom?!?" Daphne poked at her cell phone with growing hysteria. They were at Daphne's favorite French restaurant in Sherman Oaks, a celebrity magnet with glittering hanging lights, mirrored walls, and award-winning pâté, waiting for their mom to show up to discuss the guest reception culinary revolt. Apparently guests were requesting meat at her reception as an alternative to the vegan, gluten-free menu her fiancé had designed as part of an "Earth blessing."

Sam shrugged, slurping her hot French onion soup as she lowered her knees so that they'd stop bumping the table. "I think Mom had one of her fandom meetings." The local *Sherlock* TV fan club met on Saturday afternoons.

"Are you saying that our mother," Daphne lowered her voice, "*is still a CumHard?!?* I thought you'd talked to her about that!"

Sam looked around for a waiter. She was going to need another glass of prosecco to get through this lunch. "Daff, I've talked to her a million times. But she's a grown woman. If she wants to believe that Benedict Cumberbatch isn't really married, that's her prerogative. People believe a lot of nutty things these days." With a sarcastic turn, Sam added, "And, for the record, they prefer to be called 'Cumberbitches.'" Just as Daphne started to protest, Sam continued. "Let it go, okay? It's none of our business. I'm sure she'll be here soon."

Daphne firmly set her cell phone face down on the tabletop. "Fine. I just can't believe they're threatening to bring In-N-Out burgers to my reception! Greasy, charred *cow carcasses*. Unbelievable! What will the Earth think?"

Sam flagged down a waiter, handing him her empty glass of prosecco. That's when she noticed a short, lumpy white guy with a hoodie pulled up over his head hanging around the corner stoplight, peering suspiciously into the restaurant. Just as Sam was going to say something, their mother bustled into the restaurant from the other direction.

Sam immediately noticed something odd about the way she held herself, loosely holding a billowing crimson scarf around her skinny shoulders. Her shapeless light-blue sundress hung on her from teensy strings, revealing a little too much mom-chest for Sam's comfort. Purse strap in hand rather than over her shoulder, she winced with every other step, eyes wild, lips coated with pink lipstick and curled into a maniacal smile.

Klaxons went off in Sam's head.

Oblivious, Daphne popped up from her chair and threw her arms around her mother. "Hellooo, Mother of the Bride!"

"AAAAH!" Her mother yelped and extracted herself. "Careful!" She gave Daphne a peck on the cheek and stepped back. "Hello, Boom-Boom," she said to Sam, and gave her a peck on the cheek, as well.

Sam hated being called "Boom-Boom," but gave up long ago trying to fight her childhood nickname.

Before Daphne could launch into her tirade about "carcasses," Sam interrupted her, pulling out a chair. "What's wrong, Mom? Is it your back again? Here, sit down."

Her mother shook her head. "No, thank you. I'm sorry. I would have called to tell you I can't stay, but I wanted to tell you both the good news."

Sam and Daphne exchanged looks.

Their mother clapped her hands together. "He asked me to marry him! And I said yes!"

"What?" Sam asked, shocked. "Who?"

At that, she threw off the billowing scarf and spun around to reveal an enormous, fresh tattoo of a dazed otter with a broken neck. With dawning horror, Sam realized that it was supposed to be Benedict Cumberbatch's face.

Daphne jerked back, sending Sam's fresh prosecco crashing to the floor.

"We're going to formally announce our engagement at your wedding reception, Daphne. Or rather I'll be announcing it. Ben won't be able to make it because he's on set." Their mother wrinkled her nose and wriggled her fingers at them. "So much to prepare. I'll see you girls later! Bye!"

At that, she tottered off, wincing as she tugged the large scarf thing around her.

Daphne dropped into her chair, staring at her plate, hyperventilating. After a moment, her eyes raised to Sam's face, lower lip trembling. Sam had seen her sister turn every shade of Bridezilla in the last six months, but now her shoulders shook as she broke down in uncontrollable sobs.

Sam embraced Daphne, holding her tight as servers rushed around them, sweeping and cleaning.

Disaster had to be averted. And Sam was the one who had to do it. As always.

Sam couldn't enjoy the bachelorette party that night. Not that she would have, anyway. Her sister had specifically requested a pole-dancing class for her friends—something Sam personally found anathema. (A lover of all things dance, Sam's wife, Bev, would have totally dug it, but she was on business in Osaka, scheduled to return next week.) As soon as she could, Sam faked a shoulder strain and excused herself to watch from the sidelines.

But instead of watching, she grabbed her cell and, squatting against the far wall of the studio, hastily scrolled through her mother's most recent emails. When did she lose it? Could they have seen it coming? Sam could find no indication whatsoever that anything like that bizarre announcement was brewing in her mother's brain. In the few missives she'd sent this last week, she was exceptionally coherent, chewing out Daphne for sending an antivaccination article and explaining to Matt's mother why the vegan gluten-free feast was stirring an outcry from the family diabetics and NASCAR fans.

The lack of emails was worrisome. Usually Sam's mother sprayed emails like a fire hose. News articles. Dog videos. Recipes. Jokes. But now there was almost nothing.

Blond ponytail swinging, Daphne glared at Sam as the instructor barked, "Step—turn—leg—*up*! Spin!" But Sam barely noticed. As she usually did when solving a puzzle, she chewed on her thumbnail, completely consumed. The last time her mother had turned into a total crazy person was when she was dating that character actor two years after their dad's death. No tattoos, but there'd been a new car and sudden change of shoe style that resulted in a twisted ankle. That guy soaked her of cash. She finally got wise and dumped him. Thankfully, he disappeared . . .

"Grip! Leg—up! Sit—on—the—pole! Wow! Don't you feel sexy, ladies? Slay that man or woman in your life!" The perky instructor was at least inclusive.

But Sam suddenly had an idea—a suspicion that made her heart race with panic. Of course, she didn't know for certain, but her mother could be in grave danger.

"Boom . . . BOOM! Boom . . . BOOM!"

Daphne had stopped pole dancing and was chanting at her older sister. Soon, everyone was doing it until Sam looked daggers at Daphne, reluctantly stored her cell, and rejoined the class.

While Sam gripped the pole, the suspicion gripped her far more fiercely.

After the class, the group had dinner and embarked on a bar crawl. As maid of honor, Sam had recommended they go to a drag show in West Hollywood and then a male strip club, but Daphne felt that was somehow too demeaning. The first bar stop seemed to be the last as the women put down a startling amount of alcohol before re-entering the limo. Swaying drunkenly, Daphne stood up in the limo's open sunroof, screaming as she held a banner that read ONE PENIS FOREVER!

The limo crawled to a complete halt on Hollywood Boulevard in its usual epic traffic jam. Everyone started doing tequila shots, but Sam stuck to bottled water, determined to stay awake so that she could follow up on her hunch.

"Whasss wrong with you?" Daphne blurted drunkenly into Sam's ear. "Why youse not drinks?"

"Settle down, Daff. I'll tell you later."

Daphne's best friend, Janill, leaned forward, eyes gleaming from the *reposado*. "Sam! Why do they call you 'Boom-Boom'?"

Sam sighed.

Daphne broke in. "'Cause in third grade, she punched out a boy who grabbed her ass."

"Daaaamn!" Janill broke out into peals of laughter. "Your sister's badass!"

Daphne growled, her lips snarling like a dog's as she addressed her friends. "No, my sister's jealous 'cause she didn't get a party!"

Ouch, that stung. "Daff, you're being hurtful. Stop it."

Daphne flung herself back in the limo seat. "You ruin everything."

Sam hated how her sister acted when she drank. No way was she going to put up with the abuse, even now. She opened the window between them and the driver. "Can you unlock the doors, please?"

The other bachelorettes booed and cried as Daphne waved her hand at him. "Noooo! Don't do it!"

Louder. "Driver, I'm going to be sick."

Those must have been the magic words. The limo locks snapped open. Daphne slumped backward in her seat, booze-soaked and sulking.

Sam jumped out into the gridlocked traffic and slammed the door shut. Daphne rolled down the window, waving an unsteady hand. "Come back, Boom-Boom! Please!"

The tawdry stripper shops and cheap pizza-by-the-slice places were crowded with tourists, street performers, homeless people, and hawkers. For all the people around her, she felt incredibly lonely. Long-buried pain around her elopement with Beverly lurched up. They should have had a wedding anyway. They had plenty of friends in their chosen family to support them.

Past the El Capitan, Sam turned to walk to the nearest corner so she could call a rideshare when the dumpy white man in the hoodie stuck his head out from one of the shops. He caught sight of her, eyes bulging.

Sam immediately recognized him. "Hey! You!"

He bolted, plowing through a clot of club-goers in tight shiny dresses and spiky heels. Sam darted around the scattered women, expertly threading the narrow space between pedestrians in the only place in Los Angeles that had them. Unlike the other bachelorettes, she was wearing premium casual-wear sneaks that gave her great traction on the Walk of Fame.

At the light, the man fled into a swarm of people crossing the street, disappearing into the massive outdoor mall at Hollywood and Highland. Sam gave chase, skirting the crosswalk to bypass the crowd while the music from the Hard Rock Cafe blared over car horns and the competing music of street drummers. As she focused on tracking the disappearing man, a break-dancer spun out in front of her. Sam halted abruptly, narrowly avoiding a collision. When she looked up, there was no sign of the man.

He was gone.

He'd definitely been following them. Either he knew their itinerary beforehand somehow, or he was following Daphne's obsessive Instagram posts. With a deep shudder, Sam pulled out her phone and hailed a rideshare.

As she rode home, she read through her mother's emails again, especially those sent over the last couple of weeks. Now that she could sort through the wedding email drama, Sam confirmed the suspicious lack of missives from her mother. While she hadn't checked out completely, as evidenced by her bawling out Daphne over vaccines, something was definitely afoot.

The driver dropped off Sam at her townhouse in Glendale. Tucked away in a cul-de-sac, far from the glare of downtown Los Angeles, the compact 1976 complex of ten units housed mostly people who worked in Burbank or Pasadena but who couldn't afford to rent in either place. Like Sam and Bev. Bev worked in North Hollywood at Universal Studios corporate, while Sam worked in Pasadena at a tiny tech start-up doing what she loved best: analytics. Numbers and data fascinated her. She really liked the challenge of mining data for clues as to how people behaved. People themselves, however, she wasn't as good with.

Sam slammed the front door shut behind her and leaned against it in the darkness. Shapes lingered in the shadows of the wonderful life she and Bev had built over the last four years. They hadn't had a wedding precisely because it brought out the worst in people. And since half of Bev's family didn't believe people like them had a right to get married in the first place, it made sense to skip it. Or so they'd convinced themselves.

Did it hurt to make that decision? Yeah. And Daphne knew it. And worse, Daphne knew that, as a straight person, she'd never have to deal with this painful family issue. Sam loved her sister, but this wedding business had fucked her up, big time. Why should she help her after that horrible scene? Of course, Daphne had been so drunk off her ass that she might not even remember what happened by tomorrow . . .

Sam commanded the smart-light to turn on, and then flopped down on the comfy living room corner couch with her laptop. Fuck Daphne and her douchebag fiancé with his pretentious food-free bullshit diet he was inflicting on everyone. This was about Mom and her safety. That came before everything. And now Sam was certain something was deeply wrong.

She started by combing through her mother's social media accounts. As Sam wasn't a big social media user, she hadn't really been paying attention to what her mother was posting. In the deluge of "Can I get an amen?" and "I bet you won't share this!" memes—not to mention the *Sherlock* photos—Sam was shocked to discover that her mother had changed her relationship status two months ago on one account to "It's Complicated." Her friends had commented: "So are my taxes" and "Haha, who's the lucky-ish guy?"

This was exactly what Sam was afraid of.

There was no clue as to who this "guy" might be. Obviously no one took her post seriously. They probably assumed she was referring to the Cumbercrush. But Sam knew her mother didn't make jokes of that nature.

Whoever had proposed to her, it obviously wasn't Benedict Cumberbatch himself. Sam knew how gullible her mother could be, and that her heart had been super-vulnerable since their father died. He had been her world for a quarter of a century. Since then, her mother's man-picker had not just been busted but also junked for parts. Last time, the guy conned her out of money. This time . . . who knows?

If Sam wanted to save her sister's wedding and her mother's life, she had two options. She could ask her mother what was going on, and at best probably get some cuckoo-banana-pants answer. Or she could hack into her mother's email.

Which was a potential felony. Because this wasn't Sam's first rodeo hacking into people's emails—and getting caught.

Sam went to the kitchen and poured herself two fingers of whiskey. Swirling the amber liquid in the glass, she glanced at the clock. It was only 12:30 A.M. With a determination she knew she'd regret, she threw back the whiskey in one gulp and returned to her laptop with both the glass and bottle.

Her mother's online accounts had been compromised enough that the first thing Sam tried was simply putting the email address in a search engine to see if a hacker had listed her email address with the password in some forum. She was right! A password showed up. Sam eagerly tried using it to log into her mother's account, but it failed. Apparently, her mother had finally listened and changed it at some point.

*Shit. Figures.*

Next, she searched online using her Tor browser for packs of leaked emails and passwords on hacker forums. She nearly went blind scrolling through their puerile social commentary, and it was for naught.

Next, she tried simply guessing passwords. She'd hoped that some sentimental combination of names and numbers—like her dad's name (Arthur) and Daphne's birthday (050596)—would work, but every combo turned up as cold as Sherlock's tit.

Buzzed and exhausted, Sam took one last desperate stab at solving the puzzle, and sent her mother an email.

Mums,

Send me your Yahoo password, will ya? Some security alert is coming across our tech boards and I want to update your settings.

It'll only take a second. You'll need to change your password again later.

Love, Booms

She'd told her mother a gazillion times not to ever give anyone her password, not even her. But it was worth a shot.

With that, Sam kicked off her sneaks, collapsed on the couch, and fell asleep.

Sam awoke, arms flailing. Where was she? What was that horrible rattling noise? Earthquake?

Earthquake!

Nope. Phone. Vibrating and blasting a Shakira song on the coffee table.

With a crick in her neck and her head full of lead, Sam swatted at the noisy thing on the table, swiping it from the surface.

Bev! Calling from Japan! *Fuck!*

"Hi," Sam croaked into the phone.

"You sound like shit," Bev said, laughing. "Must've had a blast last night, huh?"

"Sort of," was all Sam could say, her tongue sticking to the inside of her cheek. She reached over to her laptop and flipped it open. "Daffy got wasted and turned into Voldemort Barbie."

"Oh, no! But we kind of predicted that would happen, right?" Bev must have been standing on a veranda, as traffic noises sounded like they were floating up from the street.

Just as Sam was about to ask how things were going, a notification from her mother's email zipped across her laptop screen. Sam clicked on the notification and the email opened.

With the password.

Love you, Booms! Thank you!

Mums

P.S. Don't read my emails!

No. She did *not* just give Sam her password, did she? Dammit! Sam was simultaneously aggravated and deeply relieved that her mother had gone against Sam's years of cybersecurity admonitions.

"Honey, you okay? I should let you go back to sleep," Bev said.

"Yeah," Sam croaked again. She couldn't tell Bev what was happening. It would still be illegal to read her mother's emails, even if her mother gave her the password, and she didn't want Bev involved. She had to stay innocent of the whole thing. "It's a wedding crisis. I gotta go."

"Oh, okay." Bev sounded disappointed. "Miss you, honey."

"I love you," Sam said, tearing up.

"I love you, too. Can't wait to see you in two days!"

"Same."

They hung up, Sam's heart in her throat.

As long as Sam's mother never found out she'd read her emails, no one would ever know. Right? But that knowledge somehow didn't soften the moral blow of what Sam had to do. It was bad enough she'd just lied to her mother, too.

After brewing a pot of coffee, Sam returned to the couch with a big mug that read Gray Hat (felt appropriate) and immediately signed into her mother's account.

Oh. God.

To: Amelia Huber (shrlcklvr629@yahoo.com)

From: Ben Cumberbatch (realbenedictcumberbatch4492068@gmail.com)

Dear Mealsy,

I just love that naughty photo you sent me. I should turn you over my knee, you bad girl! Bad Mealsy! Such a minx. Next week when we meet at last, maybe you can recreate that photo for me somewhere . . . comfortable?

Xxxxxx,

Benny

From: Amelia Huber (shrlcklvr629@yahoo.com)

To: Ben Cumberbatch (realbenedictcumberbatch4492068@gmail.com)

Dear Benny,

Oh, yes! Yes! Yes! I'll recreate the photo while you wear the meerschaum? And then we'll take the magnifying glass and—

Sam slammed the laptop shut as she simultaneously spewed her coffee. Oh, God! It was her own fault. She should have known she'd find stuff like this.

But, *wow.* Of all the things she wished she could unsee.

Okay. Regroup. Now that she'd confirmed her mother was actually corresponding with someone and at least having some kind of online relationship, she needed to know this guy's identity more than ever. Whatever he wanted from her mom, Sam was going to stop him. Cleaning up the coffee spew with a handful of tissues, Sam dug back into the emails, this time looking for email addresses. The guy had two different ones that he used with Sam's mother. Sam took screenshots of both and logged out.

Then, using a people search website, she entered both email addresses and whipped out her credit card to pay the hefty report fees.

Bingo. The email addresses both belonged to a fellow named Bob Binkenheimer of Hollywood. Sam mapped the address in her phone, along with his latest phone number.

These sites sometimes had unreliable data. But if this data was accurate, then Mr. Binkenheimer was about to get a visitor. Or three.

Hair slicked back, wearing her Ray-Ban Aviators and a sharp dark suit, Sam rang the bell by the splintered, dingy door on the first floor of the two-story apartment complex on Formosa Avenue. To her left was Ella Vader, a hulking yet fabulous drag queen wearing a black cape and helmet, and to the right was a beefy leather daddy named Beast. They stood a little to the sides and out of sight from the fisheye lens of the peephole.

A squeaky male voice answered on the other side of the door. "Who's there?"

"Mr. Binkenheimer?"

"Yes?"

"Can I speak with you? I'm afraid I have some bad news."

Silence.

"It's about Amelia Huber."

The door cracked open, letting the heavy scent of onions and paprika escape the apartment. A short, froggy man wearing a hastily applied blond toupee and a wife beater squinted at Sam. It definitely looked like the man she'd chased. "Well, what is it?"

"The bad news is," Sam said, tearing off her sunglasses, "*she's my mother.*"

Beast shot out a muscular hand to stop the door from slamming in their faces, using the toe of his motorcycle boot as a stopper for good measure.

Bob whined against the other side. "I'm going to call the cops!"

"If you don't break off this fake engagement with my mother and stop contacting her, Ella Vader and Beast are going to be visiting your door every goddamned day."

"Bobby!" Ella called out, hands on hips. "You said you liked it when I used the strap-on on you! Bobby, don't you love me anymore?" She pushed up on her silicone breasts for emphasis while puckering her lips.

Sam scowled. "You stop this Cumberbatch charade right now, Binkenheimer. You hear me? Stop the stalking! And BREAK. IT. OFF."

His head turned away from the trio, the little man nodded furiously, his flushed jowls shaking. He looked as though he was about to drop through the floor from embarrassment at that very moment.

Beast removed his foot and the door shut.

Ella and Beast walked away, but Sam stayed in case the man was looking at them through the peephole. She pointed two fingers at her own eyes, then at his, then back to her own. *I see you.* She then replaced the Aviators and left.

Although Sam remained wary that Bob Binkenheimer might still be stalking them, watching the social media profiles he'd created with those email addresses for signs of life, the days leading up to the wedding passed quietly. Bev came home, full of stories about Osaka, the food, and the amazing people she'd met. They had mad sex until late at night, talking and eating matcha Kit Kats with white wine.

Sam's mother was extra quiet. Sam called whenever she could to check on her. She complained that the tattoo was interfering with her sleep and kept their calls brief, claiming to be busy with wedding preparations. Which was probably true and hopefully not regarding her own. Sam detected sadness in her mother's voice that almost broke her heart.

Almost.

Meanwhile, right after the bachelorette party, Daphne left several sobbing voice mails on Sam's phone, begging her to forgive her for being "such a bitch." Sam let her stew for a couple of days before calling her back and accepting her apology. She didn't tell Daphne what she'd found, only that she'd handled the problem. Daphne was relieved but too wedding-focused to ask what had happened.

And then the big day came at a swanky hotel in Malibu near the beach. Daphne and Matt (who wore an artfully tied man bun) exchanged vows beneath the outdoor wedding arch hung with sealed red liquid bird feeders being dive bombed by annoyed hummingbirds. One bird kept viciously banging the glass with its beak behind Daphne's head until the feeder finally hit her. Sam couldn't resist stealing glances at Bev, who was trying not to laugh as the angry birds stole the show. Bev was so incredibly beautiful in her light-blue dress with matching pillbox hat and pumps. Her glittering gray eyes found Sam's and she grinned. Wearing her purple tux to match the bridesmaid's dresses, Sam sniffled, swelling with pride, happiness, and hilarity for her ridiculous younger sister. Their mother sat stiffly in the front row, tears pouring down her face. Beside her was their dad's brother, a blubbering yet beaming Uncle Gary, crushing her mom's hand like a beer can. She didn't seem to mind.

The weather behaved perfectly, even if the birds, understandably, didn't.

After the groom kissed the bride—"only with her full consent, as always and from this day forward" the priestess intoned gravely—a great applause went up and everyone trailed the newlyweds from the gardens to the nearby reception hall.

Bev hooked her arm in Sam's and started laughing hysterically. "Oh my God," she choked. "Why the nonfunctioning hummingbird feeders?"

Sam shook her head. "The venue told them they couldn't have red fluids under the arch."

"So they decided to torture the birds with fake ones?"

"Yeah." Sam pulled Bev closer. "Not sure how it all fits in with the planetary blessing, but please don't try to make sense of it."

Bev laughed. "Oh, I won't. But I can't wait to see what's next!"

Before Sam could respond, she spotted a man in a server's uniform peering out the side entrance to the hall. Something about the way he slouched triggered a sting of adrenaline.

Sam released Bev and, well, didn't exactly run but definitely walked faster after the guy as he disappeared into the hall. Sam didn't want to alarm the guests when she could deal with this on her own. Maybe with Uncle Gary's help.

The reception hall entrance was a mess of swaying purple and white garlands hanging from the ceiling. It looked like a serial killer had murdered a couple hundred hula dancers and strung up their leis as trophies. Sam whacked the garlands out of the way to see where the server had gone. Guests were making their way through to their assigned tables according to the name map. The DJ was playing a soft New Age love song, motioning for Sam to take the mike. If the man was indeed Binkenheimer, he seemed to have slipped out of the hall and back into the kitchen. However, a quick look inside revealed nothing but a crew of harried caterers preparing the new mélange of entrées guests had demanded.

Her paranoia was getting the best of her.

Sam returned to the hall and took the mike to start the celebration. Everyone was seated. Matt and Daphne sat at the head table with the bridesmaids and groomsmen. Meanwhile, Bev sat at the table with Uncle Gary, Matt's parents, and Sam's mother, who looked far more subdued than one would expect at her daughter's wedding. Well, Sam didn't feel too bad about that. There was no telling what additional damage Binkenheimer would have done to everyone's life had Sam not intervened. Her mother would get over it, and Daphne's special day would be untarnished.

The servers streamed out of the kitchen with bottles of champagne and wine, circling each table as Sam began to speak.

"Hi, everyone! I'm Sam, Daphne's sister. Thank you all for coming to celebrate this incredibly special day with us. We're honored to have each and every one of you here. Thank you, Oracle Jessyca, for officiating that moving ceremony."

A round of applause.

"And thank you to the Starshine Quartet for the beautiful ceremonial music."

Another round of applause.

"And can I hear it loudest of all for the newlyweds, Mr. Matt Gatlick and Mizz Daphne—"

Sam's train of thought instantly derailed at the sight of what was definitely Binkenheimer dressed as a server wearing a fake mustache, whispering in her mother's ear.

Sam's mother twisted around in her seat and stared at the man coldly for a beat. Uncle Gary noticed and put his hand on her shoulder. She shrugged him off, turning her full attention to Binkenheimer.

"Excuse me." Sam let the mike drop to her side. She pointed at Uncle Gary and Matt's father—a sickly artistic type who would have probably died of consumption in the old days. "Get this guy out of here," Sam ordered. "He's a stalker, not a server."

"Oh, yeah?" Binkenheimer whined in his high-pitched voice. "Well, maybe *you* should leave for interfering in my romance with your mother!"

"I've never seen this man in my life!" Sam's mother spouted indignantly.

Binkenheimer blinked at her sadly. "It's me, Mealsy. Benny. I swear I was going to tell you someday."

At this, Sam's mother stood, drew back her fist, and punched Binkenheimer in the face. Guests screamed and gasped as Binkenheimer spun like a cartoon character and crashed to the floor.

To Sam's surprise, Daphne didn't make a sound. Instead, she guzzled her glass of champagne and slammed back Janill's glass of champagne, too, motioning to the server for more.

Sam's mother stared at Sam in a way Sam hadn't seen since that time in high school when she and her first girlfriend accidentally set the car on fire. "We'll talk about this later," was all she said. She then sat down to sip her champagne as Uncle Gary and the others dragged a dazed and bleeding Binkenheimer out of the reception hall.

The reception party went late, with Sam getting plenty of impatient, irate looks from both Bev and her mother for entirely different reasons. Sam eventually found her mother at the party's end crying on a stone bench in the middle of one of the hotel gardens.

Sam sat down by her mother awkwardly and handed her a fresh pack of ice from the hotel kitchen to put on her knuckles. The sweet scents of jasmine and roses mingled with the salty ocean breeze, the roar of the Pacific louder now that the dance music had stopped. Even in the summer, the ocean wind chilled Sam to the bone.

But despite her thin frame, her mother didn't seem affected, dabbing a wad of tissues at her nose, her handbag sitting by her side. She reluctantly snatched the icepack and put it on her swollen knuckles. "You betrayed me."

"Mom—"

"I told you not to read my emails!"

"You were about to humiliate yourself and Daphne—which . . . still happened somehow . . . but . . ."

"You had no right to interfere! I'm an adult and your mother, and I demand the dignity to live my own life, especially since I'm the one who gave you yours!"

That did it. "Okay, you know what? You gave me mine, yes, but I just gave you yours *back*. I'm sorry for betraying your confidence, but you've been filling up the hole that Dad left in your life with imaginary men ever since he died. Shit, Mom! That guy you punched was a catfisher and creepy stalker who'd been following us all for God knows how long. There's no telling what he wanted ultimately. You think I was going to have that on my conscience? Look, you can get all the crazy tattoos you want. I don't care. But when you get involved with sketchy people that take advantage of you . . ." Sam let her head drop into her hands. What was she even trying to do here? She wasn't really sorry for anything except her dad dying of cancer, and that wasn't even her fault.

Sam's mother blew her nose and said nothing.

Sam stood. "I gotta go. Bev's waiting for me up in the room. I'm sorry if I hurt you."

"Boom-Boom, wait."

Sam's mother got up, lashes glistening with tears as she looked up at her older daughter. "With the exception of the car fire . . ."

"The car fire?"

". . . and the boy you punched in school . . ."

Sam smiled wryly. "Wonder where I got that from."

Her mother smiled back, another tear spilling down her cheek. "You've been an absolute joy to raise, Samantha, and I love you. I'm *proud* of you." Her voice wavered. "I just hope you can someday be proud of me."

Sam threw her arms around her mother, who hugged her back. "You're the greatest mom ever. How could I not be?"

As they hugged, Sam was facing the valet circle. At that moment, a limousine sailed in, and a crowd of paparazzi swarmed out of the bushes, cameras whirring, clicking, and flashing. From the limo emerged a tall, very famous English actor with unusual good looks. Beside him was his raven-haired wife, the brilliant, avant-garde theatrical director. Assistants and hotel staff ushered the two inside rapidly before the paparazzi could get off more than a few shots.

"Who was that?" Sam's mother asked, turning around to look at the commotion. The couple was gone.

Sam shook her head. "No one we'd know," she replied. And they walked together, arm in arm, back to the reception hall.

# A CASE OF MISTAKEN IDENTITY

## *by Chelsea Quinn Yarbro*

"Oh, Watson, Watson, you see but you don't observe, you hear but you do not listen," Holmes complained to me as we began our tea. "The jewel was never *in* the box! That's what you should understand." He smoothed back his thinning hair to keep it from falling across his forehead; he leaned back in his armchair, satisfied for the moment. "You are not unintelligent. I urge you to devote more time to deduction."

Relieved that Holmes was in a talkative frame of mind, I took a more comfortable position in my chair, removed my notebook from my inside breast pocket, opened it, readied my pen, and asked, "How would you like me to accomplish that?"

Holmes poured out a cup of tea from the generous pot that squatted on the tray, surrounded by plates and bowls of scones, Devonshire cream, tea cakes, Cheshire cheese, Stilton cheese, strawberry compote, a plate of short sausages, a jug of milk, a bowl of sugar, and squares of dry toast—a more lavish display than usual. "Consider the case I have just concluded. When Crossley first showed us the diamond in the box, he was about to purloin the stone, but he had not counted on the arrival of Sir Reginald, and that threw him into confusion. So he resorted to trickery." He paused to spoon compote onto a scone and sat back.

"Then how the devil did he manage to do that?" I prompted, hoping that Holmes would not take forever to respond.

"He palmed it, as the pick-pockets and stage magicians would say, and when he tried to retrieve it later, not long after making a mendacious report to the police, I was able to inform Lestrade of what was afoot." He chuckled and bit into his compoted scone.

"All right, Holmes, I'll allow that all this is possible, but what did Crossley intend to do with the diamond? He surely didn't plan to try to sell it on the Continent, did he? He would have to go a long way if he wanted to find a buyer for it, and even then, he would expose himself to—"

Holmes, having swallowed the bite of scone and washed it down with a sip of tea, interrupted me. "It was his intention to throw suspicion on the housekeeper, Missus Hull, and bolt for the Cunard docks once the police had taken Hull into custody." He sipped at his tea again, then set the cup in the saucer and reached for another scone. "I don't know that I shall want anything more tonight. This is more than adequate."

I added some milk to my tea and settled down to listen to more. "Are you certain about this, Holmes?" This was an irresistible provocation to him, as I knew it would be.

"Of course I am, my dear fellow," he said, self-satisfied as a cat. "I noticed at once that he was trying to distract us with his explication of the history of the box and how it came to be in his possession. His boast that it had been brought out of China two centuries ago—preposterous." He fiddled with the belt on his dressing gown, frowning a bit. "I haven't yet deduced how Crossley got the diamond out of the jeweler's safe: that place is as tight as the door of the Treasury, and it is guarded twenty-four hours a day."

This was a change of subject—one I should have expected. "But do you have a notion as to how he might have done it?" I wanted to keep him on track. "It seems to me to require a great deal of planning, and perhaps some assistants to accomplish it."

"Very apt, Watson." Holmes approved, quirking a smile. "It has already occurred to me that he might have had an accomplice or two," Holmes said, somewhat more slowly than before. "But I have yet to discern anyone of Crossley's circle who would do anything so reckless."

"Why would they not help him, considering what the rewards would be?"

"A percentage of the money from the sale of the diamond would seem tempting enough. But that might account for a lack of ebullience at the thought of making off with a twenty-carat, pink-gold, pillow-cut diamond. The penalty for such a brazen act would be discouraging, even for such desperate men as Crossley's set." He looked toward the window, frowning as a news helicopter flew by it. "What kind of machine is that? And what, by the Lord Harry, keeps it up in the air?"

I scowled, wishing the hospital had been advised to discourage such distractions from visiting this side of the hospital. "You were talking about Crossley's associates? And why they would not assist him in that daring theft. I'm afraid that I fail to understand how you've arrived at that conclusion."

Holmes nodded, his face a little blank; the helicopter had unnerved him. "They might have guessed that he would betray them, or would be out of England by the time the theft was discovered, leaving anyone helping him behind without their share of the rewards, as well as half the police in all the British Empire looking for them." He had a second bite of his scone and stared contemplatively at the far wall.

I took another few sips of tea while trying to judge how much I could do to urge him to continue his tale; he was not indicating whether he was about to nod off or that his medication was now fully active. I decided not to push my luck, for his transference was only just begun. "Holmes," I said as if I had suddenly made a connection in my ruminations. "Is it possible that Crossley was working for someone?"

"Do you mean that he was hired to take the diamond?" Holmes blinked, then roused himself. "That has occurred to me, but who is so powerful and wealthy as to command someone like Crossley?"

"There are a number of wealthy men on the Continent who might be willing to pay handsomely for the diamond," I pointed out.

"There are, and those in the Americas as well, not to overlook China and the Raj."

"Are you leaving out England in your list of the locations of wealthy men in your search for likely multimillionaires who might want to have the Lollard Diamond?"

"No, I am not," Holmes said with as much force as he could muster. "I am not so blindly patriotic that I would believe that it would be impossible that a British millionaire would be incapable of setting such a theft in motion." He yawned suddenly and almost overset his teacup, which he had balanced on the narrow arm of his chair. He put his scone on the tray and caught the cup just before it fell. "Dear me, Watson, I seem to be exhausted—my brain must have scattered from—" He yawned hugely, then gave me a look, abashed by his sudden lethargy. He used the serviette to wipe his lips.

"If you'd like that, Holmes," I said, preparing to close my notebook.

"I think I would," he said, drinking the last of the tea in his cup. "It has been a most tiring day, but we have made progress." He stood up, a little unsteadily, tightened the sash of his dressing gown around his waist, and tottered off toward his bedroom, muttering as he went, "I'll see you tomorrow, Watson."

I watched him go, knowing that he would be out for at least eight hours, and would be groggy for two more after that—plenty of time for me to pass on my report to the review committee of the board of directors of the hospital. I took my cell phone from my inner breast pocket and rang up the guard on duty. "I'm coming out," I said, and started toward the door into the corridor; I heard the lock snick open as I reached it.

"So how's he doing today, Doctor Koch?" asked the guard, a square-built fellow of middle age with a face that resembled a basset hound. His uniform was neat and his hair was freshly cut; his name was T. Prezielski, according to his badge.

"Well enough, all things considered," I said, and watched him secure the lock on the door before I turned away and headed for the double-doors at the east end of the corridor. I could feel Prezielski's eyes on my back—no doubt he had wanted to hear about the patient who thought he was Sherlock Holmes, and who was occasionally consulted by police and other investigative officers because of his uncanny talent in solving complex crimes, but also had the unfortunate habit of going into psychotic rages without warning. The patient I called Holmes had been accused of murdering and mutilating more than ten women eight years ago. Once he had been apprehended, he was sent here, where he was assigned to me, which was largely due to my skill at role-playing therapy; I excel at the complex protocol. Working with Holmes was a feather in my cap, as the saying goes, and it validated my regard for using role-playing therapy on such a difficult case as this one.

Three of the board's review members were waiting for me in one of the smaller meeting rooms, two floors beneath Holmes's three-room private apartment. Doctor Amandas, the youngest of the three, opened the door for me since I was not permitted to carry keys when having a session with Holmes.

"Doctor Koch," she greeted me with a weary smile. "Would you like anything? Coffee? Tea? They're on the credenza."

"No, thank you, Doctor Amandas," I said, making my way to the oval table where Doctor Munn and Director Ferrar were waiting to question me.

Director Ferrar was clearly in no mood to indulge in collegial small talk; she had pulled her hair back into a bun and was wearing her most imposing business suit with the buttons on the jacket closed all the way up to her throat. She had her laptop open and she fiddled with the pendant around her neck; her deep-set eyes were on me with laser-like intensity by which she hoped to intimidate me.

"That would depend on what you mean by improvement, Director," I replied, as calm as the proverbial cucumber. "His delusions are continuing; the medications Mister Godwin has been given of late appear to keep him under control."

"But?" she asked.

"But progress in these cases can be a mercurial thing. If the new drugs continue to work without problems, then I think that we have genuine advancement in Holmes's treatment. If not, we'll have to develop another regimen." I saw doubt in her continence.

Doctor Amandas sat down at the table, leaving an empty chair between us. "How is he coming along in the Lollard Diamond theft?"

"That is hard to tell," I said. I brought out my notebook and opened it to the pages I had written in the last hour. "He still refuses to recognize anything invented after the Victorian era. He's not handling the twentieth, let alone the twenty-first, century very well. There are many things he will not discuss, not if they happened after about nineteen fourteen. If you had not agreed to give him the appropriate settings in which to do his consulting, I fear we would not be doing as well as we are now. His determination to relate to the Victorian settings of Doyle's work can be inconvenient, of course, and he is indeed more willing to take on the Lollard Diamond case, as a kind of reinforcement of the identity he has assumed. To compel him to reject his Sherlock Holmes identity might draw him into catatonia or another nonresponsive state, which would make him far more dangerous if he should encounter a trigger that would send him off into one of his demented rages."

"Aren't you overreacting, Doctor Koch?" Director Ferrar made this question a deliberate challenge.

"No, I don't believe I am. He's much safer as Sherlock Holmes than he is as Hannes Godwin, and I would strenuously oppose any attempt on changing his sense of identity, at least for now."

"Are you satisfied that transference will occur?" asked Doctor Amandas.

"It is my expectation. He almost accepts me as Watson, so I am working to provide him with as many opportunities as possible for him to venture to evaluate the nature of the criminals who might have eluded police attention beyond the—"

Director Ferrar interjected. "We're familiar with the theories of your protocols. And I agree that Godwin has been most helpful to the police, but I cannot feel sanguine about the length of time he is taking to come up with a solution in this case. When do you think you will have an answer for the police?"

Goaded beyond my patience, I did not wait for her to finish he complaint. "I beseech you to do all that you can to support his delusion, at least until we have a better idea on how the drugs are working." I met Director Ferrar's steady gaze with an equally steady one of own. "I am not saying that you haven't done a good job, furnishing his quarters with as much Victorian detail, based on Doyle's writing. However, you ought to do something about the windows. When that news helicopter flew over, it upset him. If you hadn't put his medications in the strawberry compote, he might have been in a bad way by now."

Doctor Munn folded his hands and leaned forward, brow furrowed and bushy eyebrows concealing his eyes.

"Are you still convinced that accommodating his fantasies about Sherlock Holmes is working to keep him from acting out more of his violent . . . tendencies?" Director Ferrar gave me another hard look.

"These things take time, particularly in obdurate cases like this one. Holmes was eight when his father committed suicide, and his ability to deal with either the death or the abandonment is minimal. I am not yet able to discover if there were other contributory incidents that would account for his rages, other than the strange encounter with his mother's nurse when he was eleven, since he will only discuss these things in the persona of Sherlock Holmes assessing the elements of a case." I consulted my notes from earlier sessions.

"Do you still oppose the confrontation with the police psychiatrists?" Doctor Munn inquired, his head lowered and his shaggy brows obscuring his eyes.

"I most emphatically object to having Doctor Kestrel examine Holmes at this time." I placed my hands flat on the table. "You see, Holmes is at a hazardous stage in his therapy, and I don't want to do anything that might disturb the very delicate—"

"And how long will that last?" Director Ferrar demanded.

"As long as it does." I began to wonder why she was so eager to get Holmes out of the hospital; was she afraid of adverse publicity? I asked myself.

Doctor Munn sighed ponderously. "The thing is, Koch, the courts are eager to bring him to trial, and that cannot happen until he is . . . himself again. He cannot be tried as Sherlock Holmes, can he?" His rumbling chuckle revealed his own uncertainties about Godwin.

"Impossible!" I cleared my throat and began again. "The man has no recognition that it was he who committed those ghastly murders, and he is in no fit state to learn of it now, in public."

"Are you sure?" Doctor Munn was once again looking directly at me.

"Yes, I am. Not quite one hundred percent—no one could make such a guarantee in cases like this—and we could be set back in our therapy; role-playing is not to be rushed."

"Why do you protect him?" Doctor Amandas asked, her curiosity making her assertive.

"Because I want to understand how such aberrations come to be and how they might be identified earlier in life so that those unfortunate beings who suffer from them, as well as society itself, could be spared the anguish of their actions. If there is an alternative, viable treatment that could stop the rages from developing we could all be spared—" I put my hand to my eyes—a nice touch, I thought. "It has promise, role-playing therapy does, and I feel that this could be a breakthrough for using it with patients like Holmes."

Director Ferrar shook her head. "If that's what you truly want to do, perhaps we ought to put more of the staff at your disposal then, so that we needn't rely entirely on your observations in the case. Or are you having doubts about the success of your therapy?"

I would not be goaded into an ill-considered remark. "How many qualified men do you have on staff with experience in role-playing therapy?" I inquired.

"You're the only one, and you know it," snapped Director Ferrar. "There is Liz Dole, but she's still untested. Perhaps you could provide her some tutelage? Since you're so experienced. Let her get her feet wet with Godwin."

I seized the moment. "It would be irresponsible folly to put a woman in with Holmes, considering what he did to his victims, all of whom were women."

Doctor Amandas abruptly asked me, "Why is it that you make a point of calling him Holmes?"

I turned to her. "I do it so I won't slip and call him Godwin, which would damage the connection that exists between us." I let this sink in, then went on, "We have determined that there is a genetic predisposition to his . . . disease, yet we don't yet know how that interacts with Holmes's other . . . abreactions As he becomes accustomed to his medications, he should have a steadier frame of mind."

"True enough," said Doctor Munn, then asked in a sharper tone, "Is his condition so rare that we need to monitor everything about him?"

"I believe so," I said as firmly as I could. "I surmise, as I have told you before, that I believe varying degrees of this syndrome Holmes has are far more ubiquitous in the general population than is currently recognized. I hope that by demonstrating this, we can offer some relief to those less severely affected by—"

"Are you actually calling it a syndrome?" Director Ferrar interrupted me as she got up and went toward the credenza.

"Yes. Why not?" I responded, watching her pour herself a cup of coffee.

"I thought you said when you first started working with him that you had *surmised* that it was an extreme variant on the post-traumatic stress disorder scale, and should be so described," said Doctor Munn, sitting up more straightly.

"You're right, I did see his condition in that light, when I first began working with Holmes," I admitted, noting the trace of sarcasm in Munn's remark. "And, yes, I have changed my mind. In the months I have been treating him, I've come to realize that his syndrome is so layered, so intense, that it goes beyond the usual states of PTSD, and has become a more"—I broke off to smile at what I was about to say—"complex, if you'll excuse the pun, illness."

"For what reason?" Director Ferrar demanded.

"You would have to see him during one of our sessions. If you can find some way to secrete one of those small, collar-stud cameras in his rooms, and use it for observation purposes, then you might have a better notion of what is going on. You would have to get his conservator's permission." I waited for one of them to speak; when they didn't, I continued in a more conciliatory manner, "I'd think the hospital's legal staff might better advise you on this than I."

Doctor Munn pushed himself to his feet, stopping Director Ferrar from resuming her objections. "You've given us a great deal to think about, Doctor Koch. For now, we'd like you to maintain your daily sessions with Mister Godw—Holmes, and to prepare your notes for our review."

I was not pleased with the sound of this, but I nodded crisply as if I was in accord with him. "That I will," I said, and nodded to the women before gathering up my notebook, returning it to my breast pocket, and starting toward the door; all the while, I was making mental notes to myself as to how to speed up Holmes's decline without it being obvious as to what I was doing.

Director Ferrar's acidic voice reached me as I stepped out into the corridor. "Thank you, Doctor Koch."

I heard feminine laughter as I closed the door.

The following day. I was handed an envelope with an impressive seal on it; this turned out to be a request from the district court, announcing that I make myself available the following morning to explain the level of improvement in Godwin so that the court could schedule a hearing to determine if he was competent to stand trial. "Utter nonsense," I whispered to myself as I hastened down the corridor to Holmes's rooms.

"If you ask me, Doctor, you're playing with fire; he's howling mad and always will be," Prezielski declared as he unlocked Holmes's door with more care than was often the case; I asked him why.

"He had a bad night. Yelling and wrawling and banging on the walls, banging on them with his fists"—he lifted a clenched fist to illustrate—"and God knows what else; the clock on the mantel was in pieces this morning. Towers has already removed what's left of it," he told me, shaking his head in a mix of disbelief and worry. "We've all turned in our reports of the incident. He might be a bit groggy this morning."

I tried to look worried. "Can you tell me anything more about it?" I asked, almost holding my breath as I waited for his answer.

Prezielski coughed. "He kept swearing at that Moriarty fellow, the way he did when he first got here. He knows more hard language than anyone I've ever heard, and that includes the master sergeant in the Quartermaster Corps."

I decided that could be useful to my plan, and I ended my inquiries by asking, "How long was he out?"

"Six hours or so, maybe a little more. He hasn't been up for long this morning, and he was surly when they brought him his breakfast about half an hour ago." He shrugged.

I thought of another question. "Has he eaten?"

"Towers brought out three empty plates on the tray, along with one teacup. He said Holmes had a refill of it." Prezielski smirked unhappily.

"How long ago was that?" I consulted my watch for accentuation.

"About half an hour," said Prezielski

"Was his medication in the food?" I asked with more than a little alarm.

"In the tea. Towers warned me not to drink or eat any of the leftovers. Not that I'd have a lick of anything he touches." Prezielski made a grimace of distaste. "The kitchen thinks that the tea may be safer than oatmeal."

"Best to make sure he drinks it all and provide him with refills as often as he wants them," I said, thinking out loud. "Keep close watch on him," I added with more authority than before.

Prezielski was piqued by my stricture. "I know he's dangerous—none better," he huffed, pulling a lugubrious face to express his disapproval. "Give me a ring when you want out."

I realized that I should accommodate the man's offended sensibility, so I said, "I take comfort in knowing that you are diligent in your duty, Prezielski." As an afterthought, "Is the folder in the usual place?"

"Yessir, Doctor. In the lockbox in the pharmacy. The night staff have copies of it, too. Just in case, you know. This fellow is worse than a tiger." He patted the lock as he might a treasured pet. "Best be wary while you're in there."

"Good advice," I said, anticipating what I had planned to do today.

Prezielski gave me a single nod as he held the door open enough for me to slip through the doorway. "I'll be here," he said, as a kind of gentle reminder of what I might have to face.

I stood near the door to listen to the snap of the lock, then went over to the chair I usually occupied for our sessions. I could hear water running in the bathroom, and so I called out, "You in the bath, Holmes?"

His voice echoed as he answered, but did not sound as if his morning drugs had taken effect yet. "That I am. I've been thinking about the Lollard Diamond case and have hit upon a new theory of what we're dealing with."

"Did"—I stopped myself; I had almost said *the orderly,* an inexcusable lapse on my part—"Towers shave you? He often does, as I recall." Of course, no one here would trust Holmes with a razor, so the orderly shaved him before helping Holmes into the tub.

"That he did, but he still didn't let me sharpen the cuthroat, though I've asked him often and often to let me do it." I decided to warn Towers about this, later.

"Did you sleep well?" I asked in my Watson voice.

"Not at first, but later I was out like stone," he said, hesitantly, but continued more robustly. "I believe I had a number of bad dreams—not that I can call any of them to mind now. You know how that goes, after your days in India." He moved about in the tub, the water sloshing around him. "Have you eaten yet, Doctor?"

"I had something to eat on my way here," I answered, doing my best to seem preoccupied.

"Good, I went through all of what was brought up to me. Towers says it makes things easier on Missus Hudson to have him deal with the chores. I think it's more because she would not like to see me in the altogether." His laugh sounded a little reckless.

"Missus Hudson isn't getting any younger," I remarked.

"Neither are we, Watson," said Holmes. In the next instant I could hear him climbing out of the bath. "I'll be in there in half a tick," he informed me, and I pictured him pilling on his dressing gown and donning his slippers before toweling his damp hair.

"So true," I mumbled, and took my notebook out, and reached for my pen just as Holmes made his way into the sitting room, comb in hand.

I noticed that his eyes were sunken and his face was looking a little bruised—we would have to cut back on his medications for a day or two, which was the last thing I wanted to happen. It would mean a delay in the transference still longer than I had planned for. I cursed myself silently but did all I could to retain my demeanor. "What have you thought about the Lollard Diamond case?"

Holmes sought out his favorite chair and dropped into it as if he had been out and on the case for hours. "I have been thinking that perhaps we have the shoe on the wrong foot in not supposing this to be a robbery at all."

"How do you mean?" I asked sharply, my pen poised. "What on earth could it be, if not—"

"I mean that this robbery, outrageous as it was, might not have been done for simple greed." He folded his hands and leaned forward. "It seems to me that Crossley might have been greedy for his own sake"

This drew my attention. "Do you mean what I must suppose you do?"

"I mean that instead of having accomplices, he might be one himself, caught up in the toils of a more brilliant criminal than Crossley has any hope of being. All for the sake of the diamond,"

I was able to take on a scandalized manner. "Surely you don't believe it's Moriarty?" I asked just as Holmes cried out the name. "But how could he?"

"For the bravura accomplishment; it would be the sort of theft he would rejoice in pulling off. At the end of it, Crossley could flee, for all Moriarty would care—his men would attend to Crossley later." He shook his head. "Would you like a cup of tea?" He pointed to the pot and a pair of cups sitting on the table.

"Thanks, Holmes, but I'll wait, if you don't mind," I responded, adding, "I'm not too fond of the Assam Missus Hudson is serving these days."

"What's wrong with it?" Holmes demanded, some of his bonhomie fading.

"It reminds me too much of my time in India," I told him.

"Then you won't mind if I pour myself another cup, even if it was meant for you?"

"Go ahead," I said, and watched him get out of his chair and go to fill the larger of the remaining cups. "I don't mind a little bitterness," he added.

I studied my few notes on the page. "How have you been sleeping, Holmes?" I inquired.

"Out like a light most nights. I had a little trouble last night, but it was soon over. Nothing to be troubled by." He returned to his chair and sat down, once more balancing the cup on the arm of his chair. "The more I reflect on the possibility that it was Moriarty, the more likely it seems."

"Why is that?" It was the question he wanted to hear.

"It's the sort of grand crime that always attracts him. You said yourself that when he stole that hoard of gold from those South American desperados, that he would not be content with such a brazen act if he did not get the credit for it. Do you remember when that was, Watson?"

I did, and very well; it was before the police had brought Godwin to heel, but I did not want to remind Holmes of it. "Two years or so ago?"

"More like three," said Holmes, the smugness back in his voice.

"I should write about it for *The Strand*," I said.

"Time and enough for that. Once the police have Crossley in their lock-up, we'll find out more regarding Moriarty's exploits and no doubt will be in a position to help the police recover all of Moriarty's loot."

I watched him take a deep sip of tea, then said, "I'll be speaking to the police later today," I began. "Would you mind if I mentioned this to them?"

"Not at all. But warn them that the man's a dangerous fellow. Once they have him in hand, keep him under close guard at all time, in manacles if possible." He took another sip of tea, relishing it as if it were fifteen-year-old Napoleon brandy. "It's amazing how intoxicating tea can feel."

"That it is," I agreed, thinking that his medications were hitting more rapidly than usual. I watched him drink his tea, feeling satisfied that he would soon be drowsy; I began my notes for the day in order to seem as ordinary as I could.

Then, "Is my violin still in the repair shop?" he asked out of nowhere.

It startled me to hear this, since Holmes had been emphatic in his open dislike for the instrument. "Yes. Very difficult to mend, violins are," I said.

"I do miss it," he said, his eyes fixed on the place where the empty case had been put out for him.

"We'll see what can be arranged, Holmes," I said, wanting him to keep to this current subject rather than wander off to others. "I'll let you know when I have some news on the subject."

"That would be most welcome. It seems an age since I could play Paganini," said Holmes. "In your notes, do you have any new accounts on Moriarty's recent activities?"

"I'll have to consult them," I said, buying some time.

"Whatever you like." He coughed twice. "Strange," he mumbled, and got up from his chair, tipping the empty cup onto the carpet. "Tell Towers about this, won't you?"

"If you like, Holmes, as soon as I see him, I shall. For now, be careful not to step on it."

"Certainly. When can you bring me a summary of your notes on Moriarty? I know they are not in that notebook you carry with you—there isn't room enough in it for everything we've discussed."

"Right you are, Holmes," I declared. "If you like, I can go now and return in an hour or so."

Holmes took a few seconds to consider this offer. "That would be most helpful, Watson. I shall be dressed properly when you return." With that, he turned away as if I had already left.

"I'll look forward to it." I returned my notebook and pen to my inside breast pocket and went to the door, signaling Prezielski and hoping that I would not have to wait for the door to open. I was feeling increasingly perplexed as I ran through a brief mental summary of this brief session. I left the room as soon as the door was open.

"Quick session?" Prezielski was trying to hide his alarm.

"He wants to see my notes on Moriarty," I said as I moved out of the way so that Prezielski could lock the door again. "I'll be back in an hour or so.

If he's not asleep, I'll resume what we were talking about, but otherwise, I'll postpone the session until late afternoon."

Prezielski nodded dourly. "He's up to something—I can feel it in my bones. You watch yourself, Doc."

"That I will," I said, and thought about the letter keeping company with my notebook. "Let me know if he falls asleep. You can text me."

"If that's what you want," said Prezielski.

"It is, for now," I told him, and started down the corridor in the direction of my office, my thoughts already churning on the next step in my contrivance.

After I read the letter from an Agent Miriam Croymantle, I entered the number on her letterhead into my cell phone and listened to her phone ring three times before she answered. "Agent Croymantle? This is Doctor Koch. You sent a request that we should meet and discuss the case of Hannes Godwin?"

"Thank you for getting back to me so quickly," she said.

"You say in the letter that the courts want an evaluation of his condition for the purpose of bringing him to trial," I said.

"Yes, Doctor. We have new charges pending against Godwin, and without a full psychiatric evaluation, we cannot proceed in his case."

"You might find that impossible to do; his immersion in the character he—"

"You mean he continues to think he's Sherlock Holmes?" she interrupted.

"Yes. For the present, it is the only way he can be kept stable and nonviolent." I decided not to mention Holmes's episode of the night before—after all, I had not witnessed it.

"Is that what you're seeking to achieve with your therapy?" Her question surprised me more than her first had, and I hesitated to answer quickly. "Isn't that the transference you've been talking about with Director Ferrar?"

"Yes, and yes," I said. "If he can be convinced that I am Watson and he is Holmes, I can better address the terrible crimes that Godwin has committed. He will have to distance himself from the murders in order to comprehend the full scope of those actions. When he can be confident of the identity he has chosen, I'll have the opportunity to delve into his actual history. Once he is firmly in his alter ego, then we can begin to deprogram him."

Agent Croymantle did not speak again for almost five seconds; then she said, "I've been told you don't know how long this will take."

"I don't. There's no way to tell. He may do it suddenly or ooze into it over months."

"Any guess when that could be?" Her impatience was audible.

"I would guess the soonest we can hope for that transference is two to four months from now, but it could be longer." I tapped my finger on the desk where I sat. "I understand that you want him before a judge to decide if he will end up in a jail cell or here for the rest of his life. I've been increasing his medication in the hope of hurrying his transference, but that's a risky way to go at it, and I can't see the benefit in more aggressive measures." I had been speaking rapidly, but now I took a deep breath and added, "Holmes's condition is extreme, and for everyone's sake, I don't want to push my luck."

Again Agent Croymantle went silent for a breath or two. "Very well," she said at last. "I'll give you ten days, and then I'd like to have a sit-down with you so that I can decide how we are to handle his case. By the way, is there any luck about the Lollard Diamond theft? Does your . . . Holmes have any thoughts about it?"

"Nothing that would help you directly, but he is currently of the opinion that Crossley was hired by a master criminal who has been playing Crossley for a fool."

"That could be useful," she said rather slowly. "It's not a line of investigation we've been following." She said nothing for a handful of seconds, then went on. "I hope you make progress as quickly as you can."

"For the most part he takes me as Watson, but once in a while, there is doubt in his acceptance, and that could turn out badly."

"But you think that could happen, and that will enable you and your support crew to ease him back into coming to terms with what he has done?"

"That is what we all want to happen," I assured her evasively. "As Holmes, he can disassociate himself from the lawbreaking."

"And you say that his deductions as Holmes are useful?" She was losing patience with my explanations.

"I can't offer any advice on the worth of Holmes's theories," I said. "Perhaps in a day or two—"

"Or longer," she filled in for me.

"Yes, or longer." I glanced at my watch.

She took a deep breath. "I have an appointment with the supervisor in this case tomorrow morning. What would you like me to tell him?"

I took a moment to gather my thoughts. "I'd like him to know that I am making advances, that Holmes is going toward full transference but hasn't got there yet. When that happens, I'll notify you, and you can inform the supervisor."

"Will it be safe to bring him out to the courthouse when that happens, or should we arrange to come there?"

I shook my head—not that she could see it. "For a first examination, I think it would be best done here. Taking Holmes out in public could get dangerous. That's one of the reasons I don't advise you to arrange to observe him in person yet." It was a prudent answer, and one that would protect both Agent Croymantle, the hospital, and me.

"Very good," she said. "We'll call it a day for now, but I expect to be kept up to date daily. You have my e-mail. By 6 P.M. every day, I'm sure you can do that."

I knew it was an order. "Yes, although it may be nothing more than a few lines."

Agent Croymantle was about to hang up, but something occurred to her. "Does he actually believe that you're Doctor Watson?"

"I hope so," I answered with more honesty than I intended.

"Good luck, Doctor," she said as she hung up.

I hung up, then sat, staring out at the private gardens at the back of the hospital where a number of patients were strolling in the care of their orderlies, and I wondered if we would ever reach a point when Holmes could join them. Having no answer to that conundrum, I got up and went to the break room for a cup of coffee.

Prezielski was not on duty the following morning; in his place was a bean-pole of a man, about thirty or thirty-five, with a badge that named him D. Ivanov—obviously another security man hired from among the increasing immigrant traffic from Poland and points east. When he spoke, it was with a strong New Jersey accent. "I was told you'd be along, Doctor," he said as a kind of introduction.

I responded. "Has Towers left yet?"

"I don't know. Prezielski's gone off to the medical side—pains in his chest." Ivanov shrugged. "Towers might have come before Prezielski left." He looked up at the ceiling. "Nothing in the notes, one way or another."

"Towers should have been here half an hour ago," I said.

"He might have been, and he might have left. Prezielski probably wouldn't have made a note of it, either way, considering his condition," said Ivanov in a lackadaisical manner that made me want to report him for insolence.

"What does the kitchen have to say?" I asked, controlling my temper.

"Haven't asked them yet," he replied, increasing my urge to lambaste him.

I stifled my annoyance enough to request him to open the door to let me in. "I have a session with him this morning," I told him, to emphasize my mission.

Ivanov cocked his head to one side. "It's your funeral," he said with great indifference, and did as I asked.

The sitting room was neat enough; no sign of upset or distress about it. There was the sound of water running in the bathroom, which I assumed was Holmes or Towers filling the tub. I walked over to my preferred chair. "Holmes!" I called out. "I'm a little late. Are you bathing?"

Holmes answered promptly. "Not yet."

"You've had your breakfast?"

"Yes, I've eaten." He laughed at that.

I shifted my position in the chair. "Is Towers still with you?"

"In a manner of speaking, he is," said Holmes.

I had an uneasy moment, hearing this. "He's here or he's not," I said, trying to keep the edginess from my voice. "Where is he?"

"In my bathroom. There are chores to do," Holmes said, and I heard him splash into the tub.

"Is it his day to change your bedding?" I had not memorized the schedule and realized now that I should have.

"You could call it that," Holmes said, and began to sing, in a cracking voice, *I Am the Very Model of the Modern Major General* as rapidly as possible. The delivery was a little haphazard but his diction was impeccable.

I was becoming alarmed. This was not like Holmes at all. "Are you feeling well?" I spoke loudly in order to be heard.

He broke into his rendition of Gilbert and Sullivan long enough to say, "Fit as a fiddle, old man," and then resumed the catalogue of the accomplishments of the character.

This was becoming unnerving; I told myself to gather my wits and find out as quickly as possible what was going on with Holmes. "Would you ask Towers to come into the sitting room for me?"

"Why? Do you need shaving, too?" Holmes laughed again and resumed singing.

"Just do it, please," I said, running out of patience.

"He's busy now," said Holmes. He resumed his impromptu recital.

I had to content myself with that, but that did not give me any sense of certainty. I kept listening to Holmes singing merrily. When he had finished that song, he changed the operetta to *Trial by Jury.* His voice was getting stronger, and I wondered what Towers must make of it. Had Holmes had any tea yet? I listened, hoping to hear what Towers was doing, but the splashing and sloshing from the bath drowned out any of the noise Towers might be making. "How was breakfast?"

"The same as every morning, Doctor. Boring."

I found this more disquieting; I got up from the chair and began to pace the sitting room, trying to clear my mind from the host of anxieties that were taking hold of me. "How long are you going to be in the tub, Holmes?"

"Not much longer." He resumed singing. I listened, still dissatisfied with his strange state of mind. "I cannot thank you enough for all you've done for me," he went on with great enthusiasm. "I did not see the point of it all at first, but I understand now." There was a loud slosh as he emerged from the bath.

"And what is it you understand, Holmes?" I asked.

"For one thing, why you have been keeping me captive," he said baldly. "It troubled me that you went to such pains to make me believe I was still in my flat in Baker Street, when I clearly wasn't."

A jolt of alarm went through me. "Why do you say that?"

"It was apparent to me that you were drugging my food. After all my uses of cocaine and other hallucinogens, I can recognize their effects. Towers made his presence seem sensible, but it didn't take me long to ascertain that I was locked in and Towers was one of my guards."

I heard him moving about in the bathroom. Looking for his slippers, I decided. "This is all quite far-fetched, Holmes," I said with a forced chuckle.

"I wanted to believe that, too, but how could I?" He pulled the plug on the drain. "You may explain the reason why you've done this," he said with calm purpose.

"You've been helping the police and other law agencies," I reminded him as I gave the mantel a swift glance to where the clock had stood.

"Very clever of you, Doctor, although you always were clever, weren't you?" There was a nasty edge in his words now. I heard the bathroom door open, and in spite of myself I looked around.

Holmes was not in his dressing gown; he had a towel tied around his waist, and the towel was speckled and splashed with red, as was his face and the whole of his upper body.

I took a step back and had to resist the urge to vomit. "What have you done?" It had been my intention to yell, but the only sound I could summon up was a little wail.

"You are clever," Holmes said as he started toward me, the cutthroat razor in his rising left hand. "Doctor—or should I say Professor?"

Just before he reached me, I realized that Holmes's transference was complete, but not as I had intended. It wasn't Watson he believed me to be.

I did what I could to block his attack. The razor was so sharp that I barely felt it as it touched my throat. The last thing I heard was, "Have at you,

Moriarty!" before my legs went out from under me, and I saw a swath of blood spreading down the front of my jacket. I tried to laugh, but could not take in enough air to breathe. All my planning for nothing. My lips moved but no sound came out, so that I only heard it in my dimming thoughts: "Moriarty."

# ABOUT THE CONTRIBUTORS

**Maria Alexander** is a multiple award-winning author of adult and teen fiction. Her short stories have appeared in acclaimed publications and anthologies since 1999. She also writes under the name Quentin Banks. When she was in her early teens, she watched part of a Sherlock Holmes movie starring Basil Rathbone and couldn't see what the fuss was about on either account. It wasn't until more than thirty years later, at her first crime fiction convention, that she purchased a set of longer Holmes stories and fell truly, madly, deeply. Her favorite Sherlock Holmes short story is "The Engineer's Thumb," despite its distinct lack of drag queens. www.mariaalexander.net

*New York Times* bestselling author **Robin Burcell** co-wrote five books in the Fargo series with Clive Cussler and eleven novels on her own. Her first foray into the world of Sherlock Holmes was in elementary school, finding a copy of *The Hound of the Baskervilles* on her grandparents' bookshelf and reading that instead of doing her math homework. It explains not only her love of reading but also her less-than-stellar math grades that year. www.robinburcell.com

**David Corbett** is the award-winning author of six novels, including 2018's *The Long-Lost Love Letters of Doc Holliday*, the story collection *Thirteen Confessions*, and the writing guides *The Art of Character* and *The Compass of Character*. He was largely unacquainted with the Holmes canon before marrying his wife, Mette, who put a quick end to that nonsense. www.davidcorbett.com

In 2020, **Martin Edwards** was awarded the CWA Diamond Dagger, the highest honor in UK crime writing. He is the author of nineteen novels, most recently *Mortmain Hall* and *Gallows Court*, and many short stories. His enthusiasm for Sherlock was sparked by the Basil Rathbone films and has never waned; his traditional Sherlockian pastiches are collected in *The New Mysteries of Sherlock Holmes*. He has received the Edgar, Agatha, H.R.F. Keating, and Poirot Awards; two Macavity Awards; the CWA Margery Allingham Short Story Prize; the CWA Short Story Dagger; and the CWA Dagger in the Library. He is consultant to the British Library's Crime Classics series, a former chair of the Crime Writers' Association, and current president of the Detection Club. www.martinedwardsbooks.com

As a child, **Tess Gerritsen** was an avid fan of all things Sherlockian, and for her twelfth birthday, she asked for a magnifying glass so she could follow in Holmes's footsteps. She is now the internationally bestselling author of twenty-eight suspense novels, including the Rizzoli & Isles series on which the television show *Rizzoli & Isles* is based. Gerritsen's mystery fiction has been nominated for an Edgar and a Macavity award and she won the RITA Award (for Best Romantic Suspense Novel) in 2002. www.tessgerritsen.com

Cocreator of the hit show *Chicago Fire*, **Derek Haas** is the author of six novels, five about a contract killer named Columbus. He is the executive producer of *Chicago P.D.* and *Chicago Med*. He is the cowriter of five films, including

*3:10 to Yuma* and *Wanted*. He has been to Baker Street though never to the moors near Devonshire. www.derekhaas.com

**Joe Hill** is the author of the story collection *Full Throttle* and coauthor—with artist Gabriel Rodriguez—of a series of very successful graphic novels, Locke & Key, now a popular Netflix series. His work in comics, short stories, and novels has garnered many awards and nominations, including the Eisner, Bram Stoker, Locus, British Fantasy, and World Fantasy Awards. His history with Sherlock Holmes is remarked upon in the introduction to his contribution to this collection. www.joehillfiction.com

**Naomi Hirahara** is an Edgar Award-winning author of two mystery series set in California and one in Hawaii. Her Mas Arai series, featuring a Hiroshima survivor and gardener who solves crimes, has been released in Japan, France, and South Korea. Her historic standalone based in 1944 Chicago, *Clark and Division*, will be published in 2021 by Soho Crime. Her favorite film featuring a Sherlock Holmes character is *Mr. Holmes*, which includes a scene in Hiroshima.

**Joe R. Lansdale** says, "I have been writing and selling for forty-seven years and have been full-time for nearly forty years. I have written more than fifty novels and hundreds of stories and articles, screenplays, and comic scripts. I grew up with many authors, and Doyle was one of my favorites. At one point I was into all things Sherlockian. I read Doyle's work and pastiches, watched as many movies with Holmes in them as I could find, watched the TV series with Jeremy Brett—which is still my all-time favorite representation of Holmes—and even read comics about Holmes and Watson. I had always wanted to write either a Holmes story, or something close to it, and then it hit me. My daughter [Kasey Lansdale] and I had written several stories about Dana Roberts and her companion Jana Davis. Unconsciously, I think we had modeled them, to some extent, on Holmes and Watson. Unlike Doyle's characters, ours dealt with the supernormal; the evil behind dimensional veils. It was only logical that we would write another tale about those characters specifically for this volume." Joe received the Bram Stoker Lifetime Achievement Award of the Horror Writers Association in 2011. www.joerlansdale.com

**Kasey Lansdale** is the author of several short stories and novellas from HarperCollins, Titan Books, and others. She is the editor of assorted anthology collections, and her collaboration, *The Companion*, was adapted for the 2019 television remake of Shudder TV's *Creepshow*. Lansdale is also the voice for various works, from Stan Lee's *Reflections* to George R. R. Martin's *Aces Abroad*. Her newest collaboration with her father Joe Lansdale is the collection *Terror is Our Business*, featuring stories about Dana Roberts and her assistant Jana. "It was because of the two characters in the new collection that my father and I were drawn to the idea of doing a story for this anthology. Much like Sherlock and Watson, our characters Dana and Jana work best when they are together. Toss in the fact that Doyle is a long-held favorite in the Lansdale household, and here we are."

**Lisa Morton** is a screenwriter, author of nonfiction books, and award-winning prose writer whose work was described by the American Library Association's *Readers' Advisory Guide to Horror* as "consistently dark, unsettling, and frightening." She is the author of four novels and one hundred and fifty short stories, a six-time winner of the Bram Stoker Award, and a world-class Halloween expert. Her most recent books are the collection *Night Terrors and Other Stories* and *Calling the Spirits: A History of Seances* (in which Sir Arthur Conan Doyle visits many séances). www.lisamorton.com

International bestselling author **Brad Parks** is the only writer to have won the Shamus, Nero, and Lefty Awards, three of crime fiction's most prestigious prizes. He once serenaded Sherlock Holmes at Bouchercon. www.bradparksbooks.com

**Kwei Quartey** is a crime fiction writer and retired physician. Now based in Pasadena, California, he was born in Ghana, West Africa, to a Ghanaian father and Black American mother, both of whom lectured at the University of Ghana. Quartey's Detective Inspector Darko Dawson and Emma Djan Investigation series are set in Ghana. Sir Arthur Conan Doyle's famous creation, Sherlock Holmes, was Quartey's most important childhood inspiration to write mysteries, and that remains the case to this day. www.kweiquartey.com

**Martin Simmonds** is a comic artist and cocreator of *Dying is Easy* (with Joe Hill) for IDW, *Punks Not Dead* (with David Barnett) for Black Crown, *Friendo* (with Alex Paknadel) for Vault Comics, and the upcoming Image series The Department of Truth (with James Tynion IV). He is also a contributing artist to Marvel's *The Immortal Hulk* by Al Ewing and Joe Bennett and series cover artist for Marvel's *Quicksilver: No Surrender* and *Jessica Jones*. www.simmonds-illustration.com

In the third grade, **James Lincoln Warren** was mesmerized by Basil Rathbone's depiction of Sherlock Holmes and quickly adopted Holmes as a hero, alongside Superman and Robin Hood. He didn't actually start to read Conan Doyle, though, until the fifth grade, beginning with *The Hound of the Baskervilles*, which he still regards as the greatest mystery novel of all time. Warren is a frequent contributor to *Ellery Queen's Mystery Magazine* and *Alfred Hitchcock's Mystery Magazine* and has received numerous awards and nominations for his short stories. He served as chapter president of the SoCal Chapter of the Mystery Writers of America. www.swordquill.com

Best known for her Saint-Germain historical horror novels, in her fifty-two-year career, **Chelsea Quinn Yarbro** has published more than one hundred books and one hundred and thirty works of short fiction in a wide variety of genres; among these are eight Holmesian-related novels, six in collaboration with Bill Fawcett, and two novelized from Holmesian plays she wrote for Holmes Hounds, a Holmesian group centered in Jackson, California. Yarbro received the Bram Stoker Lifetime Achievement Award of the Horror Writers Association in 2009 and the World Fantasy Award for Lifetime Achievement in 2014. www.chelseaquinnyarbro.net

Anthony and Macavity award-winning author **James W. Ziskin**, Jim to his friends, worked in New York as a photo-news producer and writer, and then as director of NYU Casa Italiana. He spent fifteen years in the Hollywood postproduction industry, running large international operations in the subtitling and visual effects fields. His international experience includes two years working and studying in France, extensive time in Italy, and more than three years in India. He speaks Italian and French. Jim's fascination with Sherlock Holmes has its origins in the great detective's extraordinary ability to reconstruct complex series of events from footprints and scuff marks on the ground. www.jameswziskin.com

# ACKNOWLEDGMENTS

This book started in another lifetime, back when people got together at things called "conventions." We prowled the halls of Bouchercon 2019, pouncing on unsuspecting friends and asking them to join our league of Friends of Sherlock Holmes. Once we had the core, we brainstormed and zeroed in on people who had escaped us earlier. We're thrilled that these willing victims agreed, so that you now hold in your hands the fruit of their labors and ours. Anthologies take a village to nurture, and we're happy to be back with the Pegasus Books crowd, including the publisher Claiborne Hancock, book designer Maria Fernandez, and associate editor Victoria Wenzel. Many thanks as always to Don Maass, who agented the book, and to Jonathan Kirsch, whose peerless legal skills in the publishing field—and courage in combating the Conan Doyle Estate Limited—endear him to us.

To the now more than 60 contributors in our previous anthologies, thank you for stepping into this sandbox and playing with us! To our Sherlockian friends, far too many to name, we hope you enjoy reading these books as much as we do putting them together!

Finally, to *the* women, the two who always stand by us: Zoë Quinton and Sharon Klinger. Without their enthusiasm, patience, proofreading, and love, these books would never happen.

Laurie & Les